PROVIDENCE NOIR

EDITED BY ANN HOOD

ALSO IN THE AKASHIC NOIR SERIES

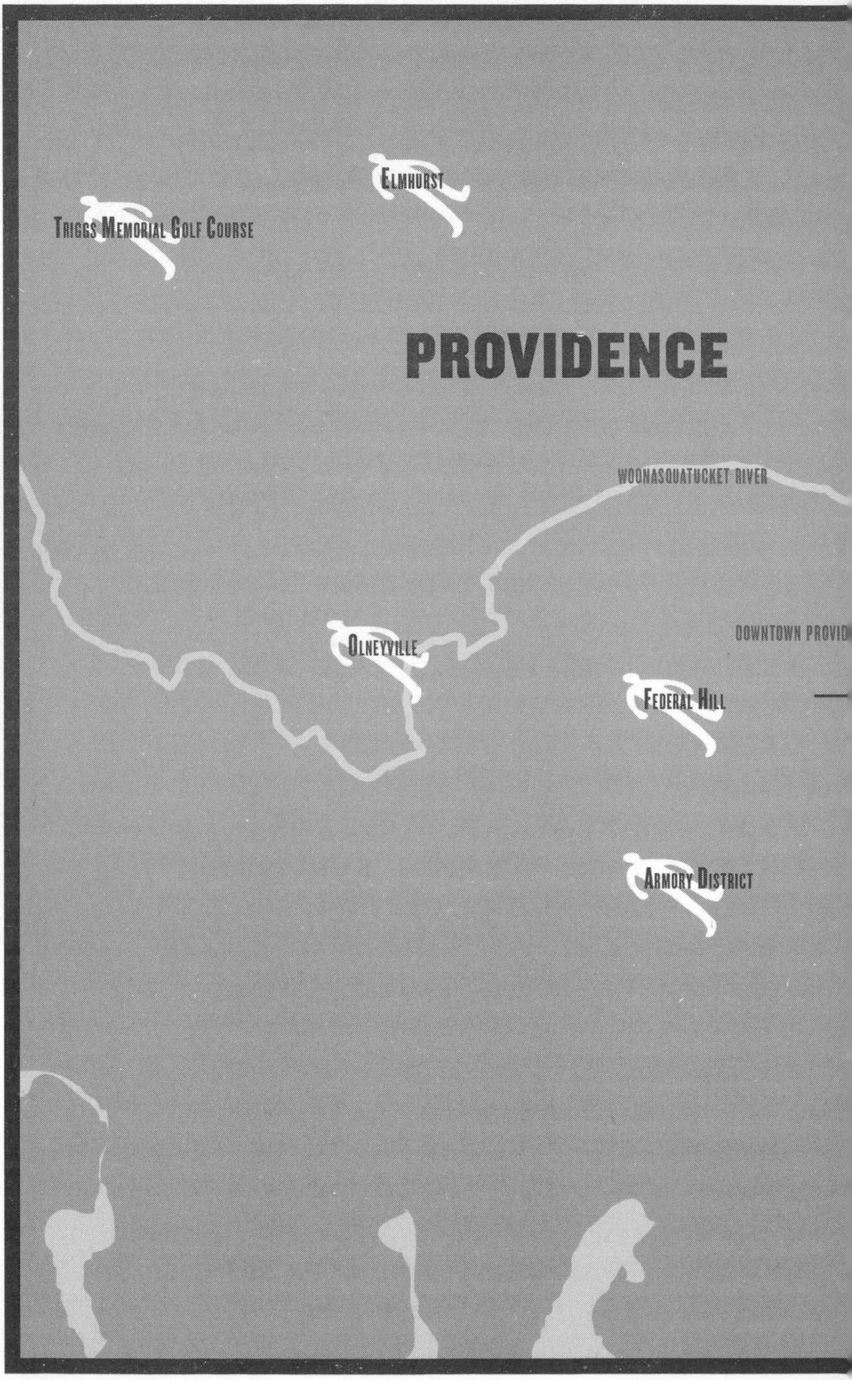

Elmhurst
Triggs Memorial Golf Course
PROVIDENCE
WOONASQUATUCKET RIVER
Olneyville
DOWNTOWN PROVID
Federal Hill
Armory District

BUTLER HOSPITAL

SEEKONK RIVER

MOUNT HOPE

RHODE ISLAND STATE HOUSE

COLLEGE HILL

PROVIDENCE STATION

BROWN UNIVERSITY

WRISTON QUADRANGLE

TRINITY REPERTORY COMPANY

DOWNTOWN

ARNOLD STREET

FOX POINT

WATERFIRE

MILE END COVE

GREEN JACKET SHOAL

UPPER SOUTH PROVIDENCE

PROVIDENCE HARBOR

Table of Contents

PART III: GOD'S MERCIFUL PROVIDENCE

INTRODUCTION

L ike so many things, it started with Sunday Afternoon at the Movies. It started with Barbara Stanwyck appearing at the top of a staircase wrapped in a towel and Fred Mac-Murray (Steve Douglas of *My Three Sons*!) making wisecracks and double entendres. It started with *Double Indemnity*. My grandmother Mama Rose in her faded pink chair, muttering in broken English. Me on the floor in front of the Zenith, munching scorched Jiffy Pop, transfixed.

"How could I know," MacMurray as Walter Neff asks, "that murder sometimes smells like honeysuckle?" This is poetry, I thought. This is sex and mystery and murder. This, I later learned, is noir.

I was a kid who saved her allowance to buy Nancy Drew books, one a week. I read them in order, from *The Secret of the Old Clock* to *The Mystery of the 99 Steps*, lining them up on a shelf in my room. Their bright yellow bindings perfectly matched the yellow and white gingham bedspread and curtains. Everything about Nancy, Bess, and George was bright: their smiles, Nancy's blue Roadster and her boyfriend Ned Nickerson. Even though the covers were meant to look spooky, Nancy always appeared with cherry-red lips and a blond flip hairdo, cast in a beam of light.

Noir was everything Nancy Drew wasn't. From the moment Walter Neff arrived sweaty and wounded at his insurance office, I knew I had stepped into someplace new, someplace dark. I didn't know then that *Double Indemnity* and *The Postman Always*

Rings Twice, and all the other movies I watched on those long-ago Sunday afternoons with Mama Rose, had sprung from books. That, I learned later. And once I did, I devoured them. As an international flight attendant for TWA, I stuffed James Cain, Dashiell Hammett, and Raymond Chandler paperbacks into my fat crew bag, reading them on the jump seat at thirty-five thousand feet over the Atlantic as the passengers slept. This was the world of dames and hard-boiled men, of shadowy cities, of booze and cigarettes.

"Noir is about sex and money and sometimes about revenge," Otto Penzler, the owner of the Mysterious Bookshop in Manhattan, told the *New Yorker* in 2010. In noir, he said, there are no heroes and no happy endings.

As often happens with literature, it finds you when you need it most. Those Sunday-afternoon movies helped move me from childhood to adolescence, away from Nancy Drew's sunny life; they offered a glimpse of what was out there in the big world beyond my little town of West Warwick in the littlest state. The novels landed in my uniformed lap as my world began to unravel.

My brother Skip, my only sibling, died suddenly in 1982. His body was found facedown in a few inches of water in his bathtub in Pittsburgh. The screen in the window had a bullet hole in it. Safe deposit box keys were missing. There were drugs and footprints, a scorned fiancée, and an ex-wife. There had been arguments with both of them, and threats made. There was one witness: Skip's Irish setter, Rogan. After a six-month investigation, the police determined his death was accidental, even though they could never connect the dots of the bullet hole or the missing keys or any of the other suspicious events and characters.

Refusing to accept the police report's findings, my mother began going to psychics to solve the crime. Each one told her the same thing: he had been murdered by a dark-haired man in an army-green T-shirt. But who was this mysterious man? She stayed up nights trying to figure it out, to make sense of a thing that was senseless.

Me? I read noir fiction, fiction full of villains, not heroes. Fatalistic and desperate, the characters appealed to me and my broken, confused heart. Months passed, 1982 became 1983, and then one day I looked up and it was the twenty-first century. Whatever happened the night my brother died remains a mystery. But my love of noir continued to grow as I discovered Patricia Highsmith and new noir writers like Dennis Lehane.

So when Johnny Temple, Akashic Books' publisher, invited me to edit an anthology of original short stories called *Providence Noir* as part of the Akashic Noir Series, I couldn't say yes fast enough. Not only did my love and admiration of noir fiction make his invitation so appealing, but the opportunity to highlight my hometown of Providence, Rhode Island—a noir setting if ever there was one—added to my delight and eagerness.

Providence was founded in 1636 by a rogue named Roger Williams. He escaped here when Massachusetts was ready to deport him back to England. In the almost four hundred years since, we've become infamous for all sorts of crimes and misdemeanors, including serving as home base for the Patriarca crime family for decades. My very own Uncle Eddie—I can hear Mama Rose screaming at me: "He wasn't a blood relative, he was related through marriage!"—was gunned down in the Silver Lake section of town in 1964, just a year after he drove me in his white Cadillac convertible in a parade as the newly crowned Little Miss Natick. The writer Geoffrey Wolff told me that once he went to a barber in Princeton, New Jersey, and the barber asked him where he was from. "Providence," Wolff told him. The barber put down his scissors, raised his hands in the air, and said, "Providence? Don't shoot!"

I've asked fourteen of my favorite writers to contribute short stories to *Providence Noir.* We have stories to make you shiver, stories to make you think, stories that will show you my beautiful, noirish city in a way it's never been highlighted before.

Elizabeth Strout, whose book *Olive Kitteridge* won the Pulitzer Prize for Fiction in 2009, takes us to Providence's esteemed theater company, Trinity Rep. Providence native, novelist, and short story writer Hester Kaplan, winner of the 1999 Flannery O'Connor Award for Short Fiction, sets her story at our local mental hospital, Butler. Alabama native Taylor Polites writes about his own neighborhood, the Armory District, so named for the hulking 1903 armory that makes up one of its borders. Novelist Amity Gaige graduated from Brown University and returns to College Hill for her story. John Searles, who is not only a best-selling novelist but also the book critic for NBC's *Today* show, drops his story on Arnold Street. LaShonda Barnett sets "Waltz Me Once Again" in the Mount Hope section and features Providence's vibrant Cape Verdean population.

Olneyville is the setting for Robert Leuci's eponymous story. Leuci is a former New York City police detective known for exposing corruption in the department; the book and movie *Prince of the City* are partially based on his career. Former Providence resident, essayist, and author Marie Myung-Ok Lee places her story in and around Brown University where she used to teach. I go back in time, to the downtown Providence I knew when I was a kid and people arranged to meet under the Shepard clock. Since 1994, sculptor Barnaby Evans has been igniting Providence's rivers with one hundred bonfires. That's where Pablo Rodriguez, a popular radio host on Latin Public Radio and an OB-GYN, tells his murderous tale.

New York Times best-selling novelist Luanne Rice has previously used Newport, Rhode Island as a setting. But here she writes about Fox Point and its Portuguese heritage. Edgar Award–winning crime novelist Bruce DeSilva has set three novels in Providence, and his short story takes place in the Federal

Hill area. Dawn Raffel is a novelist, memoirist, and short story writer, as well as a graduate of Brown University. Her story takes place in the city's train station. Thomas Cobb's 1987 novel *Crazy Heart* was adapted into the Oscar Award–winning film of the same name. His story is set on the Triggs Memorial Golf Course. And the anthology closes with a story set in the Elmhurst section, written by director, screenwriter, producer, and novelist Peter Farrelly.

What a lineup of writers to illuminate Providence's noir side! The city's landmarks, streets, parks, and neighborhoods come alive in their storytelling.

Edgar Allan Poe, who wrote one of my favorite noir short stories, "The Tell-Tale Heart," lived here ever so briefly. Back in 1848, he became enamored with a Providence woman, poet Sarah Helen Whitman. Poe said that he fell in love with her at first sight when they met in her rose garden behind her house on Benefit Street. A condition of their courtship was that Poe stop drinking. When someone handed Whitman a note telling her that Poe had broken that promise, she immediately ended the romance. Poe left Providence, and died a year later. He had written "The Tell-Tale Heart" five years earlier, but its opening lines seem appropriate for introducing the stories I've gathered for *Providence Noir*: "Hearken! and observe how healthily—how calmly I can tell you the whole story."

Hearken, indeed.

Ann Hood
Providence, RI
February 2015

PART I

DOWN CITY

GOLD LEAF

BY LUANNE RICE

Fox Point

The women of Fox Point wore black because someone was always dying. The men fished on boats out of New Bedford and got lost at sea, but this summer the fishing was bad and the men stayed home. I watched them out my studio window, saw how they crammed into the narrow strip of shade cast by the candy-colored houses, pitching pennies and telling stories while the silent women swept their cigarette butts from the gum-spotted sidewalk.

It was hot. I worked in shorts and my bra, making portraits with the bodies of angels and the heads of local politicians. I received good commissions but it didn't matter because my boyfriend was a lobbyist. He paid my rent.

My studio was the third floor of a blue three-family house on the corner of Ann and Arnold streets. I'd lived here ten years, since my junior year at RISD. The air was a toxic stew of gesso, oil paint, and the adhesive I used to apply gold leaf. I gave the politicians halos. They paid extra for that.

The windows were open for a cross breeze. It came off Providence Harbor filled with exhaust from tankers and traffic on I-195. People drove that highway to the Cape, where Lenny and his wife had a beach cottage. Just thinking about that, him being there in the salt air with her while I roasted on Ann Street, depressed me and got the swarm working. I called it "the swarm" because it felt just like bees buzzing in my head, stinging me from the inside, and it started up every time I thought of Lenny and his wife.

I went to the window to cool my sweaty body, and maybe I didn't mind the men looking up at me. They got an eyeful whenever possible. To them I was exotic. For one thing, I wasn't from the Azores. I wasn't married. They saw my lover come and go and it drove them a little crazy. The women in black hated me. I didn't care. I just wanted the feeling in my head to stop, and the admiration of men helped. I'd been raised Catholic, more Madonna than whore, but all Catholic girls know you can't be one without the other.

It wasn't this clear-cut, but: Lenny was with his wife, so I would get what I could from these husbands closer at hand. You don't want to be set up in life as always competing, but that's what can happen if you grow up with a beautiful mother who sees you as the enemy. She tried to close her eyes to what my father did, and I can't really blame her. Jealousy is a vicious master.

I stood at my window and smiled at the husbands, one in particular.

His name was Dominguez. Every time I glanced out he was watching me; as my grandmother would say, he had a bump on me. He'd helped me out every chance he got, like when he saw me dragging my garbage to the curb, or when I had a big grocery order to carry upstairs, or last winter, when my VW had gotten stuck in the snow and he'd attached chains to his Ford 250 to pull me out of the drift.

He and his wife, who was spending July in bed with a difficult pregnancy, lived with his mother, kitty-corner across Arnold Street. It was neighborhood knowledge that two of his four brothers were in prison for beating a man to death. The guy had come from Fall River to steal TVs from Fox Point families whose men were fishing at sea, but he picked the wrong house. Two brothers were home, and when they caught the intruder they killed him with baseball bats.

Dominguez stared up at me, but that day I didn't smile back

at him. I can't say the plan hadn't begun, but I am sure of this: it wasn't yet conscious. The swarm first came when I was a little girl, seven, and I'd hear my parents in the next room, grunting in the dark, and my own jealousy would attack me, *sting-sting-sting*, until I was swollen from venom and tears. I'd have done anything to make those bees stop.

Down the street the bells of Holy Rosary tolled. It was late morning, not on the hour, so it had to be a funeral. I wished it were Lenny's wife's. If she were dead, I wouldn't have to feel jealous anymore. Lenny would be mine alone. He wouldn't just pay my rent, he'd love me day in and day out. That kind of love was all I'd ever wanted.

All week the temperature rose. Starting around eleven o'clock each morning the men would go in and out of Dominguez's mother's garage, getting beers. Their voices grew louder as the beer went down and they threw the pennies harder, betting on whose would land closest to the sidewalk crack. I heard the coins jingle through the racket in my head. Dominguez focused on my window with that black-eyed laser-beam look he had.

Around noon on Thursday Lenny called from the Cape.

"What are you doing, babe?" he asked.

"Working, love," I said. "What are you doing?"

"About to head out on the boat. I miss you so much."

"On the boat with who?" Oh, I was leaking poison, burning inside from all the bites and stings, and I could barely hear my own voice over the sound of wings humming louder and louder.

"Don't get like that."

"Why are you even calling me?"

"Look, I was going to say, drive out here. I can't take being away from you."

I didn't reply.

"You can stay on the boat, she won't know. I'll meet you there tonight. I can't be without you."

"But you *are* without me. You're there with her, and I'm here."

"You know it's not like that with her and me. I'm only staying for the kids. You're the one, you know that."

"I wish I were recording you." It was my voice, but the words came from someone else. "I'd play it back to her."

"Ha," he said, one swift bark, then silence.

He was waiting for me to take it back. I held my breath; I knew I should say I was sorry, I didn't mean it, I'd never do that, but the relief that poured through me made the pain stop, just for that moment.

"If you ever did—" he started to say. I clung to the receiver. We'd been seeing each other for two years and at first it was okay, but the longer we went on the more I began to feel like a human hive full of venomous insects. She must have walked into the room at that moment, because he hung up. I felt I might die every time he chose her over me.

I'd met Lenny when he asked me to paint his portrait—I'd done many of his friends and clients. He sat for me, and I felt loneliness pouring off him—it's like that with some married men I've painted. They are so unhappy living without real connection. Their wives tend their marriages as if the husbands were plants; they weed, water, and prune fresh growth, and anything new or challenging gets lopped off.

I wouldn't do that. I know what men want. It's my special gift, one I'd always had. It couldn't be celebrated in school, I never won a blue ribbon or high honors for it, but I got my rewards in other ways. A secret glance means everything. The way they can't stop looking at me, and me knowing they think about me when I'm not there. The way my father petted me like a cat and called me his sweetheart, his *real* sweetheart.

I paced my studio. Sweat ran between my shoulder blades and I felt torturous hunger. I was a bottomless pit. I put on a sundress and went downstairs. *Clink, clink,* I heard the pennies still hitting the pavement.

Dominguez watched me open my car door. I did not look at him because I wanted to drive him crazy; and what I was doing—it wasn't in the front of my mind, but somewhere near the base of my brain, in that stew of feelings and instincts, not thoughts, nothing as clear as that—was setting the bait. His mother and her sister stood off to the side in their Cape Verde black, whispering and leaning on their brooms, and their hissing voices sounded like the drone in my head.

I drove a few blocks down Wickenden Street to Adler's Hardware and picked up two gallons of C2 Eggshell acrylic, drop cloths, and a few brushes and wood scrapers—heavy items that would encourage help in carrying them. By the time I got home most of the men would have gone inside for lunch and siesta.

And they had. I took my time lugging my bags out of the car. I didn't have to wait long.

"Hey."

I turned, and there was Dominguez. He gestured at the paint cans. I handed them to him, just like that. The feeling of power made my heart race. I still had it; this was how Lenny had responded to me, how they all did, no words necessary, just the language of desire. I had thrown a glance his way, and here he was. I unlocked the door and he followed me up three flights.

Inside my studio he placed both gallons on the counter. He regarded my canvases-in-progress: Salvatore Delano as Michael the Archangel, Jackie Donnelly as Gabriel, Lenny—my third painting of him—as Raphael, and the extended Guidone family in a large tableau inspired by Botticelli's *Assumption of the Virgin*, showing hierarchies and orders of angels, massive amounts of gilt glowing around their heads in the afternoon light.

"You did these?" Dominguez asked.

"Yes."

"Who are those men?"

"Just jerks."

"Huh. That looks like real gold," he said, pointing at Lenny's halo.

"It is." I use thousands of 23-karat sheets, as fine and fragile as moth wings, mail-ordered from the same Florence studio that had supplied Fra Angelico in the fourteenth century.

I went to my easel, replaced a canvas-in-progress with a blank one. Dominguez watched me study him. I grabbed a brush soaking in linseed oil, wiped it off, and swished it through a glob of olive-tinted flesh tone I'd mixed on the palette that morning. Never glancing away I outlined his head, neck, and shoulders. The steady humming filled my head. I was so tired of it, I wanted it to go away, I'd do anything for it to stop.

"What are you doing?" he asked.

"Painting you. Is that okay?"

He didn't say a word but his lips twitched. Men love to have their portraits done. Twenty minutes later I had a pretty good start. His features were bold, easy to capture. Because of the way he watched over me, I saw him as a first-sphere angel who guards the tree of life.

"You're strong," I said.

"Yeah."

"Are you as good with a baseball bat as your brothers?" My mouth was dry, I was full of histamines, crusty infected sores in my brain, on the inside of my skin, all those bites.

"What the fuck?" He started to move away, but I gestured for him to stay where he was. I kept working. Now his broad forehead was a knot, his thoughts visible to me. I stroked paint on canvas, and even through the noise in my head I could read his mind. Here's what he was thinking: his brothers were in the ACI because they'd bashed a guy's head in, and why was the neighbor lady bringing up blunt instruments?

His gaze flicked at my west-facing windows. "You should pull your shades."

"I need light for my work."

"I don't like the other men looking up at you," he said. Oh God, I got that. He was possessive. Oh yes, I could work with that. His eyes were on me now, his lashes long and thick as a child's. I laid down my paintbrush.

"I don't want them," I said.

The tension in his face relaxed. *Let me take your pain away.* I knew how to do it, the skill came to me as easily as my next breath.

He yanked the cord, lowering the green paper shade. We stood a foot apart in the hot, darkened room. He wore a stained white T-shirt that smelled of sweat and smoke. He kissed me hard, drew blood from my lip. He licked it.

We pulled off each other's clothes, knelt on the floor by my easel. His rough fingers felt so different from Lenny's smooth office hands. He entered me and his chest hit against mine over and over, *slap slap.* I heard waves hitting the boat's hull, banging against it as it slipped offshore; Lenny and his wife in the cockpit, my jealousy stinging and killing me from the inside, *slap slap.*

Dominguez came fast. Soon he sat up. Afternoon light blazed through the cracks between the shade and window frame, illuminating his body, and I saw flecks of gold leaf, dropped from my subjects' halos and wings, caught among the whorls of his black chest hair. The sight made my eyes sting. I know what is holy. I know that love is a sacrament, and I felt it for Lenny. I was going to kill someone, but for love, for the only reason that mattered.

"You going to keep painting me?" he asked.

"Maybe," I said. "You want me to?"

He gave a shy smile. "Yeah."

"There might be something I want you to do for me in return."

"Like what?"

"Don't you know?" I whispered. I stared into his eyes, willing him to figure it out. I had mentioned the baseball bat. He was going to break into Lenny's house, pretend to steal TVs, murder his wife. Lenny would be back at work and the kids would heading to summer camp next week, after they returned from the Cape.

"Hurt someone," he said.

"Yeah." I was chilled by how easily he said it.

"Hurt them bad?"

"Yeah."

"For you," he said.

"Yes, for me." I trailed my fingers through his chest hair. My fingertips twinkled with gold, and I wrote my name on his skin but I felt a little sick.

"You won't look at the other men?"

"Out there?" I gestured toward the window.

"Any other men."

"I won't look at them," I said.

He nodded, pulled my face to his, and kissed me so hard I bit my own lip. The pain shocked me. When he left I ate a pint of ice cream and made myself puke. Bulimia is a pretty word, sounds so much nicer than what it is. I'd been doing it for so many years I didn't even think about it, just did it. In that instant the swarm stopped. Everything was quiet, peaceful inside, just the drip of slow poison, the leaky faucet of jealousy that never really went away.

The days passed. As I worked on Dominguez's portrait, a form emerged: not a guardian angel at all but Lucifer, holding a gilded baseball bat dripping blood. The image gave me nightmares; my own work scared me as it never had before. I always painted what

I wanted to see in someone, not what was really there. Do you think all those politicians deserved halos? But with Dominguez I couldn't disguise anything. For the first time in maybe forever, or at least since childhood, I was painting what was true, not what was wanted.

I avoided Dominguez. The more I painted him, the more I began to blame him for my own thoughts of murder. If not for what I knew about him and his brothers, I would never have thought of killing Lenny's wife. That wasn't me. I'm not a killer, I know what is holy, love is a sacrament that shouldn't end in death.

In the middle of the third night, I got out of bed. I have been known to scrap paintings but I always reuse the canvases. I don't have money to burn, I just gesso them over and start fresh. But I wanted this one gone. I removed the canvas from the wood stretchers, cut the painting into tiny shreds until the scissors hurt my hands, and placed the pieces in the garbage. I prayed for help, *Dear Jesus and Mary, dear angels and saints, help me, I'm your daughter, I'm good not bad.*

The next night, when the men were home at dinner, I took a walk. A group stood outside the Holy Rosary Church hall, alcoholics waiting for their meeting. On Wickenden Street people spilled from bars and restaurants onto the sidewalk. This was the new Fox Point. Back when I'd first moved here, RISD students and faculty were the exception. Now we were taking over, replacing the Portuguese families who had immigrated during the 1800s to fish and work in the factories. I wished developers would knock down the house across the street, send Dominguez and his family packing so I wouldn't have to think about him ever again.

At Amelia's Café, I ordered an espresso. Thunderheads formed over the hurricane barrier. I wished for rain, respite from the heat. Since that hour with Dominguez, slowly, a little more every day, the buzzing had increased. Imagining Lenny's wife's murder had soothed my jealousy for a time, but now I felt the insects inside again. My hands shook. I had gold leaf under my fingernails. I tried to dig it out, but the disturbance just made it sparkle more.

I pictured Lenny and his wife on the Cape. He would be thinking of me and she'd be doing a crossword puzzle that kept her in her own world while he longed and longed for me. Jealousy was back, eating me alive. I had to get rid of it, had to dispel the swarm. Thunder rumbled, and I jumped.

Bulimia is like an internal storm cell: build-up, violent release, and then sudden peace. It gets rid of whatever you've swallowed. At treatment they called it "the daddy disease"—girls who don't get enough love from their fathers, or too much of the wrong kind, like me, the bad touching, become bulimic. Treatment gave me tools to fight the impulse, but what's an impulse but a bunch of nerve endings firing in the brain? What I had was bees.

Oh, I wanted to claw them out of my body. At the India Street market I grabbed the most fattening food I could find—Portuguese sweet bread, chunky peanut butter, Marshmallow Fluff, potato chips, Frosted Flakes.

Hurrying home, my arms ached from the heavy bags. A grape arbor covered a neighbor's driveway. Purple finches had nested in the lush green vines. I slowed to listen. It was dark, but I heard their wings rustle.

The innocence of nesting birds made my throat ache. I could drive away from Fox Point and never return. I would head west, back to the factory town in Connecticut where I'd grown up, erase Lenny and the affair. The only problem about going home was that my father would be there.

"Baby," Lenny said, stepping out of the shadows as I approached my house.

"Len," I said, shocked to see him.

"I had to be with you." Beaming, he held out his arms and I walked toward them. Medium height, thick around the middle, and balding, he looked just like what he was: a middle-aged mid-level power broker. But I saw past that: being an artist's subject can feel like being loved, and although more than one has thought he was in love with me, the only one I have ever loved back was Lenny. He took care of me in small ways and large ways; he paid my rent, and didn't that count for a lot?

Rain poured down, soaking us. Lenny pulled me behind the back steps, out of the neighbors' sight. The plastic handles of the grocery bags dug into my hands, but I dropped them when he pushed me against the side of the house.

My arms went around him; I felt his heart beating against mine through our wet clothes. His hands moved up, over my breasts, up to my throat. I felt his fingers tighten around my neck. I opened my eyes and saw his red face, eyes full of sorrow and drive.

"You were going to tell her," he said, strangling me.

No, I wanted to say. *I would never do that. I'm good, I'm a good person.*

The thud of Lenny's head exploding sounded like a pumpkin being smashed, and the red spray felt hot on my face. I gasped for breath as his hands slid from my neck and he crumpled to my feet. My savior and his baseball bat stood haloed by yellow streetlight.

Oh, Dominguez, oh Lucifer. My painting, destroyed by my own hands, had come to life.

I watched Dominguez drag Lenny by the feet into the weeds alongside my house, behind the garbage cans where I had thrown the cut-up pieces of his portrait. Lenny's blood smeared behind him, a slick and viscous trail washed into nothing by the downpour. Dominguez cleaned his bat on Lenny's shirttail, propped it against the steps.

He kissed me. I smelled copper and cigarettes. I tried to steady myself against the back steps, but he grabbed my hand and molecules of gold transferred to his fingers.

"I don't like you looking at other men," he said. "I told you."

"I know." My voice came out in a croak.

"Is he the one you wanted me to hurt?"

"It doesn't matter anymore," I said.

"You're right. It doesn't. Have you finished my painting yet? Let's go up, I want to see it."

Once again the swarm was gone; for the second and last time, Dominguez had chased it away. I led him up the stairs and felt his hot breath on the back of my neck, and knew what would happen to me when he saw it wasn't there.

THE PIG

BY JOHN SEARLES

Arnold Street

F
ort Lauderdale from October to March, Providence from April to September—that had been Charlie and Joy Webster's plan for retirement. And for the first five years, that plan had worked out just fine. As soon as the air began to cool and the leaves began to turn, the couple closed up their clapboard house on Arnold Street, loaded suitcases into the trunk of their Oldsmobile, and headed south for the Sunshine State. But this year—their sixth since she'd stepped down from her job as a high school art teacher, and he had retired from his work as a high school security guard—Charlie Webster drove home alone to Providence. Beside him in the passenger seat, strapped in by the seat belt, there was only a bright pink, pig-shaped, ceramic cookie jar—a cookie jar he was using as an urn.

Since Charlie was not yet ready to face questions and condolences from neighbors and what few friends they had left in the city, he slipped the car into the garage at the back of the house, then slipped into the back door as well. Normally, Joy called ahead and arranged for a former student they knew and trusted from their days working together at Central High School to come by and use the hidden key to prep the place for their arrival. But since Charlie had neglected to do so, he was left to go down to the basement with a flashlight—flipping fuses, cranking on the water, and sizing up the withered remains of so many unlucky mice that had been snapped in the traps while they were gone. Soon, the house rumbled to life. Baseboards and pipes knocked away, though things remained shadowy inside since Charlie kept the curtains drawn and lights low.

As for that cookie jar, its detachable head had been crafted with an impossibly large snout, flared nostrils, a toothy smile, and googly black eyes. Those eyes stared right back at Charlie as he carried The Pig from room to room. When he sat at the kitchen table eating whatever microwavable meals he excavated from the freezer, The Pig watched him. And when he settled into bed at night, The Pig rested on Joy's pillow, watching his fitful tossing and turning all night long too. But there was more: somewhere back on the highway, deep in the Carolinas, Charlie had begun talking to The Pig. And now that he was home, he kept up the habit, jabbering away to that watchful face as though talking to his wife. The man's rambling sentiments could be boiled down to the lyrics of those country songs he liked to listen to on the long drives north and south: *You were always on my mind . . . I'm so lonesome I could cry . . . I fell into a burning ring of fire . . . I went down, down, down as the flames went higher . . .*

On and on, those strange and sentimental one-sided conversations went, punctuated by bouts of his mournful weeping and long moments of his doing nothing but sitting in Joy's art room at the back of the house, staring blankly at her flattened tubes of paint and dry brushes, trying to put the pieces together of how it had all come to such an unexpected end. Things might have gone on this way forever, but on the third day after Charlie Webster's return, he discovered that there was not much more than ice cubes left in the freezer and canned lemon curd and dried beans in the pantry. For that matter, the toilet paper and paper towel stock was dwindling fast and, without his wife around to keep things tidy the way she liked to do, the place was already a mess.

Not far away on Waterman Street, there was a Whole Foods where Joy had always shopped, but Charlie didn't dare go there because of his growing fear of familiar faces popping up and all the questions and condolences that were sure to follow. In the short while since he had returned home, people had come knocking on the front door—sometimes this was followed by the sound of heavy footsteps walking to the rear of the house and more knocking on the back door. That knocking, those footsteps, the accompanying deep voices in clipped conversation—all of it had caused Charlie to clutch The Pig tight and carry it with him to the narrow bathroom beneath the stairs, where he waited, his heart thrumming like the engine of the Oldsmobile, until whoever they were had gone. The last time it happened, he snuck to the backyard afterward and removed the key hidden beneath a patio flagstone, to prevent anyone who might find it from coming inside.

And so, the lack of basic sundries and his dread of Whole Foods led him to hunt down Joy's old address book from the desk in her art room. In it, he found the number of a woman they used to know who wiped cafeteria tables and mopped floors over at Central High, but who had also cleaned their house a few times when Joy threw out her back. Tünde—that was the woman's name, though a pack of those miserable, wise-ass, shit-for-brains students he was once paid to keep in line had taunted her with the nickname the "Hungarian Barbarian." That name for her, like so many of the names they came up with for the faculty, including the name they came up with for Charlie, had a cruel but uncanny accuracy about it. In Tünde's case, those brats had nailed it with the combo of her ethnicity and great height and broad shoulders, which, despite her pretty face, left her looking like some rough-and-tumble female wrestler.

When he picked up the phone to call Tünde, the line was dead. Had Joy arranged for the service to be shut off while they were away too? He could not recall, since he had left so many of those details to her, particularly after he'd begun having what she referred to as his "little mental slips" a few years before. Charlie might have used his cell, but in yet another "little mental slip," it had been mistakenly left behind in the bathroom of a Florida gas station in the earliest hours of the trip home. It was just as well since he hated the way that thing kept buzzing in his pocket. Without a landline or a cell, his only option was to wait until dark, pull on a hooded sweatshirt, and walk the neighborhood with his head down until finding a pay phone—yes, an actual pay phone—that stood like a mirage in front of the Shell station on Wickenden Street. As he fished change from his pockets, Charlie stared at the page torn from Joy's old address book. His wife, forever doodling, had drawn a thunderbolt over Tünde's name and a squiggly line through her number, though thankfully it was still possible to decipher.

"*Halo.*"

When she answered in her thick accent, that lone word filled Charlie's head with so many memories from his days back at that horrible school. He remembered watching the woman, examining the unusual beauty of her high cheekbones and long blond hair yanked back and twisted tight into a braid, as she silently mopped the filth from that cafeteria. All the while, those kids in their concert T-shirts and ripped jeans taunted her, shouting in the voice of a ringside announcer, "In this corner, we have the Hungarian Barbarian! Standing at a hulking six-foot-one and built like a brick shit-house, the other ladies in the ring better get ready for an ass-whooping like they've never seen!" Tünde always ignored their mocking in such a weird and trancelike way it was as though she did not hear them. That is, until a day came when some creep of a student added something new to the routine: launching a plastic cup in her direction. The cup missed, but a metal fork quickly followed and would have hit her squarely in the face if Tünde hadn't batted it away with the fastest of reflexes. Charlie assumed she would simply go back to mopping the way she always did, but this time Tünde exploded into a burst of broken English, waving her mop in the air like a weapon. Moments like that, it was all Charlie could do not to march down the long hall to Joy's classroom—so serene and colorful it was as though she taught at a different school altogether—and tell her it was time to begin their dream life as retired snowbirds sooner rather than later. Instead, he'd stuck to the plan and dutifully escorted the offending little bastard to the principal's office. And when he walked back to the cafeteria to check on Tünde, he found the woman mopping the floor in that same trancelike state, as though nothing bad had happened at all.

"Tünde?" he said now. Other than The Pig, it was the first Charlie had spoken to anyone or any*thing* in days. As a result, his voice had a foggy, disconnected quality, one he tried to remedy when he said, "This is Charlie Webster. We used to work together at Central High School here in Providence."

Thus began their conversation. At first, Charlie sensed that the woman felt wary of him phoning out of the blue after so many years and at such a late hour. But he pressed on, asking how she had been and listening to an answer he did not fully grasp on account of her muddled English. At last, Charlie circled around to the point of his call: "I was wondering if you would come by, hopefully even tomorrow if you're free, and clean the house and do some grocery shopping for me?"

"I have more jobs tomorrow already in the line," she said in her odd way of phrasing things. "But I need money always. I come only early if good by you?"

Early was just fine for Charlie Webster, and he asked her to go around to the kitchen door, where he would be waiting at the appointed time. He figured that call would be the most eventful thing to happen all evening, but after he hung up the phone and walked back to the house on Arnold Street, he found this note on the door:

Mr. Webster,

If by any chance you made it back from Florida and are here in town and you get this, please call the number below. It is urgent!
Todd

Safely inside once more, Charlie checked to be certain all the doors were locked, then carried the note along with The Pig up to bed. He was no longer used to chilly nights, but since he had come home to Providence earlier than he had in years, he was faced with a long and windy March evening ahead. While he rubbed his arms beneath the pile of sheets and quilts to get warm, Charlie began speaking to Joy as was his way now. He told her about calling Tünde and the things she said when he asked how she had been doing, the specifics of which he found hard to follow but had something to do with a legal matter and her plan to move away from Providence once she saved enough money. He told her about the note from Todd, though given the muddled and weary state of his mind, Charlie could not, no matter how hard he tried, recall anyone in their lives with such a name. And then he told her how hungry he felt, how cold, how terribly he missed her, and how deeply sorry he was for so many things, but in particular, the thing that had happened during their very last fight. And as he stared into the googly eyes of The Pig, saying all that to his wife and more, at long last Charlie Webster drifted off to sleep.

"Your head. What has happened to it?"

Those were the first words Tünde spoke when she stepped through the back door into the kitchen and removed her scarf and wool coat. Standing before him in the gentle early-morning light, no longer wearing a bland beige cafeteria uniform, but dressed in a thick dark sweater, old jeans, and mannish boots, she looked beautiful in her own peculiar way. Her hair was still yanked back in a single braid, and she wore no makeup from what he could tell. He examined those dramatic cheekbones, the wide flat expanse of forehead, and her deep brown inset eyes. *In this corner, we have the Hungarian Barbarian!* those kids shouted in his memory as he studied her. As if to erase the words, Charlie said, "You look different than I remember. Very nice, I mean."

"Yes, well. I was fired from cafeteria. So no more eating that shit food for me. I dropped pounds as result. Now back to your head. What has happened to it?"

Charlie reached up and touched the wound that had been there since leaving Florida. It was on its way to healing, or mostly so, except for the bruising and scabbing. "Bumped it" was the only explanation he gave.

They were standing at opposite sides of the kitchen table, littered with the remains of his microwaved meals. Crumpled aluminum foil. Cardboard trays from frozen dinners with hardened rings of sauce clumped to the sides. An empty box of fish sticks and another box of breaded cod fillets. Charlie watched her sizing up all of it, probably calculating how long it would take to clean, until her gaze came to rest on his pill container parked by The Pig among the mess. The days of the week were marked in giant letters on that container—M, T, W, T, F, S, S—and at the start of each week, Joy used to count out his various pills and fill the compartments for him so there would be no mistakes. Charlie explained this ritual to Tünde, letting her know that, without Joy to keep things on track, he had not been taking his medication the way he was supposed to. As a result, his mind and memory were hazy at best, so he hoped she would understand and give him whatever help he needed.

At this information, Tünde fell quiet. Charlie watched as she picked up the two fish boxes and squashed them in her large hands in preparation for the trash. The Pig watched as well. At last she spoke again, asking, "And where is your wife?"

A big part of Charlie had counted on her broken English and what he had always sensed as her pure lack of interest in others to keep this conversation at bay, but here it was anyway. He did not want to tell her the truth about their sudden surge of fighting after so many years of marriage in their final months in Florida. He did not want to tell her about his screaming and breaking things and about Joy's weeping out on their tiny third-floor terrace. He did not want to tell her about any of it, because it was all too unbearable to speak of ever again. And so, his only answer was to point to The Pig, who smiled at her with a mouthful of crooked teeth.

"I am not understanding," Tünde said, grabbing more garbage from the table and compacting it in her arms before cramming.it into the trash can beneath the sink.

"The Pig is an urn," he said in a voice full of shame. "A temporary one. I have to get something proper, and I will. But for now I put the container with her ashes in there."

Tünde ceased with her garbage crunching and stood upright to look at him. "Mrs. Webster is no longer living?"

Charlie glanced down at the cracked tiles of the kitchen floor, nodding his head, afraid tears would come the way they so often did now.

"When?" she asked. "How?"

He took a breath, lifted his head. "This winter. We were at our apartment in Fort Lauderdale. She fell."

"Fell how? Down some stairs, you mean?"

"I don't . . . I can't . . . It was just one of those freak accidents. That's all."

"I see." Tünde released a deep sigh then offered up her condolences, though in truth, it just seemed like words she was tossing out, because she moved on to cleaning again and moved quickly on to another topic as well. "You must be rich to have place there and here. I did not know security guard make so much. Art teacher either."

"I'd hardly call us rich. Joy's parents left her this house a long time ago. Since we never had kids, we were able to save and buy that apartment in Florida for retirement."

"Sounds rich to me."

By then, Tünde had found a sponge and was wiping the scum of his leftovers from the table with such force that it rocked back and forth. The Pig shook back and forth too, and Charlie listened with a shiver to the rattle of remains inside. Finally, when Tünde paused a moment, she looked up and said, "I tell you again: I am sorry about your wife. She liked me. Then she didn't like me. So no loss for me. But I am still sorry for you."

"What do you mean?" he asked, picking up The Pig because he had grown worried about it falling and crashing to the floor, about Joy's ashes and tiny chips and slivers of bones spraying everywhere in that once-happy kitchen.

"That lady—your wife—she fired me from this place. Told me she did not want me cleaning here no more. That is why I felt the surprise of your call. But I need money to leave Providence so I come back."

Charlie said nothing, remembering that thunderbolt and that squiggly line. He had never known Joy's doodles to have any particular code of meaning, but for the first time, he began to wonder.

"Now," Tünde said, "table is all clean. I help with pills, yes?"

"Okay," he told her.

For the next few minutes, he watched as she studied the prescription containers on the counter, reading labels and instructions. At last, she popped open the days of the week and dumped the various medications inside. "Here," she said. "I am no nurse so you should make certain with your doctor. But for time being,

I think this is the way it is meant for you. Today is Tuesday, so start. Get water and take pills."

Even if he was not so good at remembering the specifics of his various medications, Charlie knew that taking them on an empty stomach would only make him nauseous. That led him to show Tünde the grocery list he had written out for her trip to Whole Foods. She examined it, then took what he offered from his wallet before pulling on her heavy wool coat and scarf and heading out the door.

The instant she was gone, that old house on Arnold Street became unbearably quiet once more, and the quiet brought back all the loneliness and remorse Charlie had been suffering from since leaving Florida. He carried The Pig to Joy's art room and sat at her desk, gazing around and thinking of the life they lived as snowbirds, migrating south each year to avoid the unpleasant weather. In the beginning, that life had seemed the greatest of ideas—the ocean! the pool! the sunshine! the lack of respon-sibilities and fixed schedules!—but it was those last two that became something of a problem for Charlie. While Joy took to their new situation with unbridled enthusiasm, signing up for book clubs and foreign film nights and sculpture classes and lec-tures, Charlie didn't do much more than walk along the nearby golf course every morning and afternoon, collecting stray golf balls and stopping on occasion to stare up at the vast blue sky, so different than the wintery gray ones that hung over Providence that time of year.

He had never been much of a joiner, but Joy nudged until at last he met up with a group of other retired men to actually *play* golf on the nearby course. Those old farts in their sherbet-colored shirts, plaid pants, and enormous sunglasses talked almost ex-clusively of their various ailments, their kids and grandkids, and the big jobs they used to have, all of which left Charlie out of the discussion. His body was in relatively good shape, thanks to a lifetime of regular push-ups and sit-ups, and Joy diligently keeping them on a healthy diet. As for children and grandchildren, back in the days before fertility was such an exact science, he and Joy had been unable to conceive, though for no clear reason as far as the specialists could tell. And when it came to career, working as a security guard was meant to be a temporary job on his way to learning some trade or perhaps going to the police academy and becoming a real officer. But then he met Joy one morning when she needed help carrying art supplies from the trunk of her car to that peaceful classroom of hers. Once they began dating, he liked the comfort of working in a place where the person he loved most in the world was right down the hall. And so, in this way, the years had passed giving him great success and comfort in his romantic relationship, though not much to speak of in the way of a family or career. Still, because he knew it made his wife happy to see him doing something, Charlie kept riding around that course on a golf cart with those men, swinging clubs and taking mulligans and sipping their bitter-tasting cocktails a few times a week. After all, wasn't that the snowbird life they had planned and dreamed of for years, and wasn't it better than his former one spent patrolling those insufferable derelicts at Central High?

But as soon as he'd gotten used to his new routine it changed again. One winter's day, a few years before, Charlie and the other retirees had just finished eighteen holes and were returning to the clubhouse when he asked why they were calling it a day when they had yet to start playing. Those men in their clown clothes and wrinkled faces had stared at him with such an odd look of concern it sent a chill right through his body. And after a few more incidents like that, Joy took him to a doctor who gave the diagnosis they both feared. That's when the ritual of the pill container began. And that's when Charlie went back to just walking along the golf course at the start and end of each day, collecting stray balls in so many bright happy colors. There were orange ones. There were red ones. There were blue and green and yellow and even the standard, old-fashioned white golf balls too.

"What are you doing here in dark?"

Charlie looked up to see Tünde standing before him in her wool coat and scarf. She must have already deposited the groceries in the kitchen, because those big hands of hers were empty. Looking at those hands, he recalled the way she had so expertly used them to bat away that metal fork and shake that mop at those crummy kids. The memory led him to think of how often he used to long for genuine authority at that school, the sort he might have been granted if only he had gotten his act together and become a police officer back in those days. God only knew how many times he'd fantasized about whipping out a Taser or handcuffs or simply grabbing them by their concert T-shirts and shoving their pathetic faces against a locker to teach them a lesson once and for all. Instead, he was left to swallow the fury he felt watching their obnoxious behavior, since his only authorization was to escort any bad seeds to the principal's office, which he did time after time, though no meaningful punishment was ever exacted there as far as he was concerned.

"I'm just sitting here thinking," he told Tünde, looking away from her hands and up at her unusual face, where those deep inset eyes watched him with fresh curiosity.

"Maybe you don't need light to do thinking. But you need light to do seeing when you are done and want to walk around. Otherwise, head gets bumped all over again."

With that, Tünde moved to the curtains and pulled them open. She was about to tug the lip of the window shade and send it flying upward too, but Charlie stopped her. "Let's just turn on a lamp, if you don't mind."

"But sun is shining outside."

"I know. But all that sunshine reminds me of Florida." He paused before attempting to explain something he had only ever explained to The Pig: "What I mean to say is that there was always too much light down there. All that blue sky—so blank and open and empty above. It started to feel that way in my mind too. Does that make sense? Like that vast blue emptiness seeped into my brain somehow. The only thing of substance were those clouds. But try holding onto a cloud and see where that gets you."

When he was done, Tünde stared at him, keeping her face still, much like The Pig's when Charlie had said the same thing. At last she closed the curtains, then walked to a lamp in the corner and snapped it on. "Who knows of you being here besides me?"

"Nobody."

"No family? No friends?"

"My brother is in Detroit, so no family here in Providence. And most of our friends retired and moved away or died. I'm starting to think the people in that last category were the luckiest. Because you know what's worse than dying? *Waiting* to die."

She considered that a moment before saying, "If your mind works so funny now, the way you say, how is it you drive home many miles from Florida?"

Not easily, he thought, remembering the robotic voice of the GPS and so many road signs and rest areas where he stopped to ask the same question again and again: "Am I still on I-95 North?" He kept checking the entire way, because he knew if a "little mental slip" led him to turn off the interstate by mistake, it might be difficult to find his way back even with that machine barking orders from the dashboard.

"It's one highway and one direction. More or less. So I managed. But it took me longer than it used to. And I slept in my car to keep from getting distracted."

"Ask me, it is lucky you did not kill someone or kill yourself in wreck. I suggest no more driving for you."

These words put him in mind of the final conversation on that little third-floor terrace where he and Joy ate dinner most evenings when they were in Florida. She had just poured herself a glass of wine, just scooped a heaping portion of salad onto each of their plates to accompany the broiled fish she had made, then she smiled at Charlie in the flickering candlelight. She had been wearing her hair shorter since they'd begun spending winters in Florida, and she let more of the gray come through too, which had a way of making her appear elegant in her older years. That terrace of theirs overlooked a garden full of bougainvillea and jacaranda and palm trees, but it overlooked a small slip of the apartment complex's parking lot as well. Down below, a truck was making an after-hours delivery. The driver blasted rap music and created quite a clatter as he slammed his door and rolled up the big one in the back before hauling out his dolly full of boxes. Charlie waited for some hiccup in the commotion before finally speaking the words he had been planning to tell his wife all day: "I don't want this life anymore."

Joy put down her wineglass. Earlier, she had cajoled him into going to the pool for a swim, so now their bathing suits were draped over the railing, drying. Charlie watched them rustle in the warm breeze behind her, worrying they might blow away and be lost to the night, before she sighed and asked, "What do you mean, dear?"

Increasingly, following that doctor's visit a few winters before, Joy had developed a way of speaking to Charlie that irked him. It was as though she was talking to one of her students from Central High, and not a very bright one at that. Each morning, when she asked if he had taken his medicine, it was this tone she used. When explaining her need to sleep in a separate bed for the first time in their thirty-seven years of marriage, because of his newfound habit of tossing and turning, which kept her awake, it was this tone she used. And only days before that night on the terrace, when she sat Charlie down to inform him that it was time to take away the keys to the Oldsmobile, now that his little mental slips were becoming more worrisome, it was this same tone she used then as well.

"Stop talking to me like that."

"Like what?"

"Like I'm a kid."

"Well, I don't mean to, Charlie. But I don't understand what you're saying about not wanting this life anymore."

"You know what I mean," he said over the sound of that driver's clattering. He had made his delivery and was now rolling down the enormous back door then climbing into the truck, slamming the door shut. "You tricked me into living this life."

"Charlie, you're not making sense. I didn't *trick* you. We planned for this. It was our dream to be snowbirds."

"Well, I want to be a person again. Not some stupid fucking bird. Not any other animal either."

Joy looked at him, tilting her head. The candlelight had a way of erasing her wrinkles and making her appear younger, more like the woman he first saw when he took that job at Central High School years before and noticed her lifting boxes from her trunk and asked if she could use a hand. Behind her, those bathing suits still rustled on the railing while down below that truck was backing up to leave, releasing a series of automated warning beeps as it went.

"I know you can't help forgetting," Joy said, her pale eyes going damp with tears, "but we've had this conversation before, Charlie. Dozens of times, in fact. Last time, it ended with you screaming and breaking things. I found it quite frightening, all that pent-up rage I never knew you had, so I don't want to go through that again. Now, I need you to try hard and keep *this* thought in your head instead, because it will make things easier and be more pleasant for you than those other thoughts: *I like being a snowbird—and you like it too.*"

"No more driving for me," he told Tünde as she stood before him still in Joy's art room at the house on Arnold Street. He shook his head and sent that memory sailing away like those bathing suits had done later that night when the wind picked up and blew them from the railing so they seemed to dance in the air a moment before falling to the parking lot below. "Can you sit with me for a bit?"

"Sit? No. You pay me to clean. Now I must do, then go to other jobs."

Tünde left the room, and Charlie lingered behind for a while until he could not bear the silence any longer. That's when he carried The Pig to the kitchen and set it on the table. He began picking through the bags of groceries, ultimately making himself a roast beef sandwich with mayo, then swallowing the pills Tünde had dumped in his *Tuesday* compartment, chasing them with a sugary soda he did not recall writing on the list of things for her to buy. After that, he went in search of her, with the notion that he may as well take advantage of the company while there was another person in the house.

The narrow bathroom beneath the stairs—that's where he found her. She wore Joy's yellow cleaning gloves, which made her hands appear daintier than he knew them to be. Kneeling before the toilet, Tünde scrubbed with the same brute-force she brought to the kitchen table earlier. The woman did not so much as lift her head when he appeared in the doorway. Still, Charlie asked if she minded his sticking close by while she cleaned.

"You worry I break something?"

"No, not at all."

"You worry I steal something, like your wife thought me to do?"

"It's not that." And then, once more, he found himself admitting to something he had only ever told The Pig: "I'm just lonely without her around. She was the only person I ever loved. She took care of me. She understood me, at least until the last few years."

If Tünde had taken in those words spoken from the deep well of his broken heart, she didn't indicate as much. She gave a slight shrug, and then flushed the sudsy water down the toilet before turning her attention to the floor. And when she was done with the floor, she clomped up the stairs to the bathroom there. Next came the bedroom, where she ripped the sheets from the bed and carried them to the wash, before remaking it with fresh linens. At last came the dusting, which took her and Charlie all over the house and required a great deal of time since things were dirty after so many months with nobody home. Eventually, the wash was done and folded and the furniture polished and the air smelled like ammonia and bleach and all clean things. Tünde carted the smaller rugs to the patio out back, and Charlie watched from a window as she used a broom to beat them with the hardest of wallops. The rugs released what sounded like a pained grunt with each and every whack. After she returned inside to put them back in their places, she unpacked the last of the groceries, and then tackled her final bit of work: mopping the kitchen floor. As Charlie watched, he couldn't help but think it was just like the old days, with Tünde in her trancelike state pushing the dirty gray strings of that mop around.

"You were always so good at ignoring those kids," Charlie said after a long while, speaking his thoughts out loud without quite meaning to do so.

"What is this you are saying now?" Tünde asked.

She had finished mopping by then and was peeling off the yellow gloves, exposing her big, knuckly hands and chewed fingernails.

"I was watching you clean and thinking how you used to shut out those kids and all the bullshit they would pull back at that school. Like calling you that stupid name."

Tünde draped Joy's yellow gloves on the sides of the bucket she had just emptied. "They had name for you too," she said.

"I know they did. But unlike you, I could never tune it out. Their nastiness used to eat away at me. I think that's why I let a lot of anger build up inside over the years without even realizing it. Anyway, like I said, you handled them better than me."

"Maybe not so much as you think," she told Charlie. "Reason I was fired was for finally teaching one his lesson."

"What did you do?"

"I guess you don't read Providence newspaper. Big story few years back. I was like celebrity in this city. Well, bad celebrity. I choked one of those kids."

"*Choked?* Did you—"

"No. I did not kill him. I wanted to, but instead I just scared him plenty."

Charlie was quiet, staring at Joy's gloves clinging limply to the edge of the bucket. "Well, good for you. I'm sure the little bastard deserved it."

Tünde shrugged. "In the moment, yes. But now I have lawsuit. Which is why I need money. To leave town before they make me pay. Anyway, I must go to other job."

Charlie reached into his pocket and pulled out his wallet, carefully counting out the money he had agreed to pay her when they'd spoken on the phone the night before. When he handed it over, Tünde counted the bills again then pulled on her coat and scarf and walked to the back door. Things might have ended between them right then and there, but that's when she stopped. "Oh," she said, reaching into her pocket and turning around, holding something out to him. "I almost forgot. Receipt for groceries from the Whole Foods."

"Thanks," he said when she came closer again and he took it from her.

"You are welcome. But I think now you are the one forgetting something, yes?"

Charlie stared at her, then stared down at the receipt, trying to figure out what she meant. And then, all at once, he realized and reached into his wallet again, pulling out the amount equal to what it said on the receipt, rounding up a few dollars for change. When he handed the bills to Tünde, she smiled then turned again and walked to the door, pulling it open. At the sight of her about to leave, he braced himself for the silence and loneliness to follow, except there came a cloud of thought drifting through the blank blue sky of his mind just then. It made him say, "Wait."

She turned to look at Charlie. "Yes?"

"I think . . . No, I *know* that I already gave you the money for groceries before you left for the store."

"Of course you did not. I would remember."

"Well, you should remember. Because we stood right here in this kitchen, I'm sure of it, and I took out my wallet and handed you the money. So you need to give it back."

"You said yourself your head is not working in right way. I help you to straighten out your medicines. You swallow few pills and like that you have brain of Einstein. I don't think so. Now, I must go."

"No," Charlie told her.

"You are just like your wife," she said in a disgusted voice. "She accused me of stealing too. Then fired me. I did not steal then. I did not steal now."

The thunderbolt, the squiggly line—those things flashed in his mind, but Charlie tried not to get distracted. He glanced at the face of The Pig silently watching the moment unfold.

"I don't know what my wife accused you of stealing, but I

know I gave you the money. Give it back now and we'll both walk away. And I don't think you should come here anymore either."

Tünde closed the door. She walked slowly across the kitchen until she was standing impossibly close to him. Charlie looked up into those deep inset eyes of hers. His heart pounded in his chest. A buzzing rang in his ears until he heard those kids screaming in some long-ago memory: *In this corner, we have the Hungarian Barbarian! Standing at a hulking six-feet-one and built like a brick shithouse, the other ladies in the ring better get ready for an ass-whooping like they've never seen!*

"So," she said, "I ask you, Mr. Charlie Webster, are you calling me thief?"

"All I'm saying is that I already gave you the money. Maybe it was a simple mix-up. But I know that I did. My mind is not totally gone, after all. So you can't just—"

"Funny how you have so much to say now. But you never did then."

"What are you talking about?"

"Back at that school. Never once did you protect me from those kids. You just stood there. Watching like idiot. Doing nothing like coward. Those kids, they called you The Pig. And why? Because you were supposed to be cop of that school. But you were just coward. And then I come here and I think what joke is this that the man they called The Pig is carrying around pig with his dead wife inside! I laughed in my head at you! Laughed and laughed! But same time, I need money, so I keep quiet. I do what you ask. Clean. Shop. Fix pills. All that and now you make accusation at me. Well, let me tell you that I do not think you are very smart, Mr. Webster. No—Mr. *Pig*. No one knows you are here. No one knows I am here. And I have just cleaned this shit-house top to bottom with gloves on, so there is no trace of fingerprints from me anywhere but on door, which I can wipe off on way out.

So, Mr. Pig, since you are making me to be thief, I will be thief."

With that, she reached out and snatched the wallet from his hand, turning quickly and stomping back across the kitchen to the door. It was all happening too fast, and for an instant, Charlie just stared down at his empty hand. Those things she had said about him being an idiot and a coward all those years roiled inside him. He thought of the way he had lived his life, doing nothing but swallowing shit from a bunch of teenagers year after year after year, all the while biding his time and dreaming of some distant future life as a fucking snowbird. What a waste it had been since living that dream had not made him truly happy in the end! The only thing to ever make Charlie Webster happy had been Joy: her love, her kindness, her gentle laugh, the way she kissed his forehead every morning and every night. But now Joy was gone, all because of what he had done to her that night on the terrace—what his rage had led him to do—because with each passing day the disease rubbed away more memories and more brain capacity and even his ability to do simple things like drive a fucking car! Round and round those thoughts whipped in Charlie's mind until he looked up from his empty hand to see Tünde about to open the back door and walk away with his wallet.

The tiles were wet and slippery from all her mopping and when he charged across the floor his feet slid this way and that, but he managed to keep his balance. Charlie caught up with her. Her back was turned, and he lifted both hands, same as he remembered doing that night on the terrace in Florida, and shoved Tünde with all the strength he never used those years back at Central High. So tall and solid was the woman that what happened next was not unlike watching a tree come crashing down in one fell swoop after someone hacked away at it with an ax. There was no time for her to brace herself and her face struck the floor with the loudest of cracks. When she lifted her head, turning to look up at him, Charlie saw blood glistening on her lip and forehead. He didn't allow the sight to distract him and instead reached down and thrust his hands into her coat pockets even as her arms and legs thrashed about. When he felt his wallet, Charlie yanked it free. But that's when Tünde rolled onto her side and reached up to grab hold of his neck, doing her damnedest to pull him down with her. She might have succeeded if he hadn't managed to swing a leg around and mule-kick her with as much force as she brought to the beating of those rugs, and probably the choking of that student. When the heel of his foot landed on her stomach, Tünde released a surprised yelp and loosened her grip. Charlie slipped away, stumbling back as his feet slipped and slid on those slick tiles, until he grabbed hold of the table.

"Now get the fuck out of here, you crazy bitch!" he yelled, making his way to the phone on the wall. "I'm calling the police."

Tünde just watched him from her crumpled position on the floor, wiping that blood from her face with one hand while pressing the other to her stomach where he had kicked it. She gulped in air and said, "Good luck making call to other pigs. You don't think I know phone is not working. I discover that when I pick up to wipe earlier."

Charlie pressed the receiver to his ear, listening to all that nothingness shrieking back at him. How had he forgotten that it was disconnected? How had he forgotten so many things? He dropped the phone and let it fall to the floor. At the same instant, Tünde scrambled to her feet and came after him. Before she could close the distance between them, he darted to the opposite side of the table. Same as that morning, they stood across it, eyeing one another, but this time, Tünde reached out and grabbed the only remaining thing on that table: she grabbed The Pig.

As she raised it in both hands high above her head, there was a single frozen moment on that chilly March morning on

Arnold Street in Providence, Rhode Island, when all the faces in the kitchen—The Pig's face, Tünde's face, and Charlie Webster's face too—were wild with gaping eyes and flared nostrils and mouths full of gritted teeth. In that instant, as The Pig paused in the air above Charlie, he did his best to brace himself for the sight and feel of his wife's remains—her ashes, her tiny bits of bone, everything but her soul—raining down upon him. But really, how could anyone prepare for such a thing? And in the end, when The Pig hurtled in his direction and bashed against his skull, shattering instantly and sending Charlie's body slumping to the floor, it didn't matter because he saw and felt none of what he expected. Rather, Charlie heard what sounded like the heaviest of hailstorms pelting the roof of a car. It was a sound that amplified all around as he blinked open his eyes to see—not ash, not chips and slivers of bones—golf balls spilling from the shattered hull of The Pig. Dozens of them—in oranges and reds and blues and greens and whites—thudded against the wet kitchen floor, rolling away in all directions. When they came to a stop at last, the only thing he heard was the thumping of Tünde's boots moving away and the slamming of the door.

Early in Charlie and Joy Webster's retirement, back when they first signed the deed on their new apartment in Fort Lauderdale, they had not much more than a mattress ordered from an 800 number and a few stray pieces of furniture they'd managed to haul south in the Oldsmobile. A great deal of time during those initial weeks and months were spent shopping for a sofa and chairs and nightstands and lamps and all the many possessions people acquire to fill up a place and make it a home. Since they were always careful to stay within a budget, the couple took to exploring consignment shops in and around their new city. Something about hunting through those old things with the idea of putting them to new use gave them an unexpected thrill. If

they had thought much about it, Charlie and Joy might have realized that so much of the cast-off furniture had likely belonged
to other couples who came to the Sunshine State with the dream
of making a fresh beginning in their later years. But when that
beginning turned into an inevitable end, the things they owned
wound up in those drab shops with colorful names like The Prissy
Hen and Shades of the Past.

One afternoon, their search led them as far north as Palm
Beach, where they found a shop on Highway 1 called True Treasures. Most of the furniture in the place looked like something an
old movie star might have owned in a sprawling house high in the
Hollywood Hills. As Joy wandered among those curiosities, she
stopped to poke fun at the more outrageous pieces, like a four-
poster canopy bed with a glittery silver headboard and so many
layers of fabric that she dubbed it the Elizabeth Taylor Sleeper,
or an endlessly pillowed sectional sofa in clashing geometric pat-
terns that she called the Joan Crawford Couch. None of it fit
their taste, but that was okay since half the fun was laughing
about the things that were difficult to imagine being *anybody's*
taste. In the midst of all that, they laid eyes on a simple, soft blue
wrought-iron table and matching chairs tucked in the back of
the store. The set would fit perfectly on their little terrace, it was
decided, and money was handed over to the clerk. While Charlie
stood at the counter arranging the delivery, Joy wandered to a
shelf overflowing with dishes and vases and ashtrays.

"Look," she said.

Charlie turned and saw her pointing to an object high on a
shelf. When she pulled it down, he realized it was a bright pink
ceramic cookie jar made in the shape of a pig. Never once had Joy
mentioned the nickname those kids called him back at Central
High School, and yet he wondered for the briefest of moments if
she was making some joke about it for the first time by showing
him this pig. But at the end of the long hallway where the oasis

of her art classroom had been situated for so many years, Joy had managed to isolate herself from much of the unpleasant happenings at that school. Chances were, she never mentioned the name because she had never even *heard* it, which was just fine by Charlie. And so, he determined that she had pulled down the pig-shaped cookie jar simply because it called to her in that way certain objects have of calling to people. The moment became something akin to a person passing the window of a pet store and deciding they had to take home the puppy or kitten glimpsed on the other side—not at all necessary, but somehow completely necessary at the same time.

"This big guy is pretty cute, huh?" Joy said.

"More crazy than cute, I'd say. Look at those eyes. Those teeth."

Joy stared into that strange face a moment, before lifting its head from its plump body and peering at the emptiness inside. She put the head back on and looked up at Charlie. "Let's take him home."

"Okay, but you better feed him and walk him and deal with the neighbors when they complain about him oinking all the time."

She smiled and brought the cookie jar to the counter, letting the clerk know they'd carry it home in the car rather than have it delivered with the table. That's when Charlie thought to ask, "Do people who aren't allowed to eat cookies even *need* a cookie jar?"

"Oh, I allow you to eat cookies, Charlie," she replied in the same teasing tone of voice that he had asked the question.

"Right," he said. "One cookie. Once a year. At Christmas."

"What are you talking about? You just had those Mallomars when we stopped in Tennessee on the way down from Providence a few weeks ago."

"Mallomars? I don't remember any Mallomars."

"Probably because you ate them so fast."

Back and forth, they kept ribbing each other while the clerk wrapped the head of the pig in newspaper, then wrapped the body. Once they were rung up and finished with their business, Joy carried the bag with her new find out to the Oldsmobile, where she strapped it in the backseat with a seat belt rather than risk it rolling around and breaking in the trunk. When she climbed into the passenger seat and strapped herself in, she said, "I was just thinking, Charlie. You know those golf balls you keep bringing home from your walks the last few weeks?"

He started the car. "I do."

"Well, maybe you can put them inside the cookie jar instead of lining them up on the counter the way you've been doing?"

That is how The Pig found a home in Charlie and Joy's apartment in Fort Lauderdale. And that is how the golf balls found a home in The Pig.

So many years later, after Tünde brought it crashing down upon Charlie's head, then slammed the door and left him for dead, some part of the man's conscious kept flickering over that memory. All the while, his body lay still on the floor, surrounded by jagged pieces of ceramic and those golf balls brought home during the first winter of his retirement, which filled The Pig in no time, so he switched to tossing them in a drawer instead. Slowly, the light in the kitchen shifted, brightening with the high sun, then dimming as the sun went down. At some point, there came a distant knocking that grew more rapid-fire, before fading away. The memory of that store on Highway 1 faded too, as Charlie's mind moved from flashes of his past to a conjuring of his future. If he had indeed lived through the violence of that morning, he would need to make a new plan for his life without Joy. First, he would call his brother in Detroit, since there was no one else left for him to reach out to. He would explain that his mind was slipping away, not slowly as he hoped, but quite quickly, much to his dismay. Then he would sell the house in Providence, sell the apartment in Florida too. And if it came to it, which he knew it would, he'd allow himself to be put in some sort of home for people in his situation, where he would live out his final days in a lonely bed, staring out a window while waiting for the last of his mind to become one with that blank blue sky above.

Charlie thought about all of those things for some time, before accepting that the end had arrived for him in all the ways that really matter. Once he accepted that, at last there came the sound of a door opening somewhere in the house, then the sound of footsteps, familiar ones. He opened his eyes and lifted his head to see her standing before him. She had snapped on a light and, after all the darkness, it was so bright that it hurt his eyes. He squinted against it.

"Charlie," she said and came to him, kneeling on the floor.

"I killed you," he told her.

"No," she said.

"I killed you," Charlie repeated. "I pushed you from the terrace. And you fell. I lied to the police and to the people in our building. I told them it was an accident. I had your body cremated, and I came home."

She was quiet, slipping her arms under his shoulders and cradling his head in the warmth of her lap. She brushed her soft hands against the many cuts and bruises on his skull. She brought her soft lips there and kissed him, the way she used to do every morning and night during all the years of their marriage.

Then she said, "It's not your fault, Charlie, that you see things this way, but I want you to try hard and keep what I'm about to tell you in your mind, because it will make things easier and be more pleasant for you than those other thoughts: We had a fight on the terrace, and I went to bed. When I woke in the morning, you weren't there. I figured you had gone for a walk on the golf course until I saw our bathing suits had fallen from the railing, and I went down to the parking lot to get them. That's when I discovered the Oldsmobile was not in its usual spot. The keys, I realized when I came upstairs, were missing too. And so was that old pig. Oh, Charlie. I had the police searching for you down there. I kept calling your cell phone too, which turned up at a gas station not far from the apartment. Someone there said that they saw you fall and drop it in the bathroom. That you hit your head. But that's all they knew. And while the Florida police kept looking for you, I contacted the ones here in Providence in case somehow you'd made it all the way home. But they kept coming by the house and looking around, calling me back to say no one was here. I even sent that boy over who turns on the pipes and boiler for us, but Todd couldn't find the key so he left a note for you instead." She stopped and was silent for a moment, holding him still, caressing his head. She was crying now, but kept talking in the gentlest of voices: "Finally, since no one had any luck finding you, I gave up on you being down in Florida still. I had to do something, so I got on a plane and came here myself to see if you made it home. And now here you are. But what has happened to you? Are you all right?"

"I killed you," was all Charlie said again. He was as certain of it as he had been of the business with the money and the groceries. "I saw you fall."

"No," she responded, and hugged him close. "None of that happened."

He stared around at the pieces of the broken pig and the golf balls that filled the kitchen in their house, where they had lived happily for so many years before becoming snowbirds, moving north and south with the sun in an effort to dodge the cold and the gray winter skies over Providence and so many unpleasant elements of life in their final years. But there were some unpleasant things you could never outrun, no matter how hard you tried. And anyway, he thought, maybe all of it was just a trick of his mind. Maybe he was still back in Florida on that terrace watching their bathing suits blow away and dance in the wind before falling to earth. Maybe he was already in some Detroit nursing home where his brother had put him and everything that had happened was nothing more than a terrible vision out a window beside his bed. And there was another maybe, one he considered when he first saw that light she brought with her, when he felt the indelible softness of her skin and heard the sound of her voice comforting him when he never thought he would hear that voice again. This final maybe should have frightened him most of all, though it did not so long as Joy was with him. But how could he be sure she was? He looked up at her face, reached with his fingertips to try and feel her tears. He closed his eyes and opened them to see her there. He closed his eyes and opened them to see that she was not there. And in this way, Charlie Webster kept on blinking.

She was there. She wasn't there.

She was. She wasn't.

She was.

UNDER THE SHEPARD CLOCK
BY ANN HOOD
Downtown

The storm began as soon as I stepped out of the Shepard department store. I struggled to get my umbrella open, but the wind immediately blew it inside out, rendering it useless. Frustrated, I tossed it in the nearest trash can. The rain came down in horizontal sheets, wetting my shopping bag enough to cause it to give way and send my new, carefully chosen tube of Murderous Red tumbling out. I'd had my hair done the day before, and I could feel it deflate under the onslaught. The smell of hair spray mixed with spring rain.

In the middle of this calamity, I heard someone call my name.

I looked up from retrieving my stray lipstick and saw a man hurrying toward me. Tall, wearing a London Fog raincoat (I recognized the brand because my husband Jim had the identical one), and holding a large black umbrella aloft, he grinned at me from beneath a dark walrus mustache.

"Barbara!" he said again, and the voice made me feel flushed.

"Fred?" I asked, even though I knew for certain that this was indeed Fred Lancaster, the man who over the course of two decades had managed to break my heart, twice. The first time was when he left for the war, shipped out to the Pacific without ever looking back. The last time, he swept back into my life and out again so fast it felt like I'd dreamed his return. I'd vowed that if I ever I saw him again, I'd be sure to make him suffer. But Fred had moved out of the country, to Buenos Aires or some other hot South American city, and my fantasies about how to hurt him eventually faded in the chaos of Vietnam and assassinations and my own enormous grief.

Now here he stood.

In a storm like this, it was hard to say no to a man with an umbrella. I ducked beneath it, dripping rain on his wing tips.

"I can't believe I'm actually running into you," Fred said, shaking his head. "Just this morning I was wondering how I could find you."

"Really," I said, unable to hide my sarcasm.

"I heard about your daughter—" Fred began, but I held up my hand to shush him. I did not want Michelle's name coming out of his mouth.

With his free hand, he touched my wet cheek. "How are you, Barbara?" he asked tenderly.

I wish I had recoiled. Or stepped out into that storm. But instead I bent my head so that his hand cupped my face. Fred stroked my cheek, and traced my lips. I closed my eyes. When his fingers lingered on my mouth, I wanted to stand on tiptoe and kiss him. I wanted to let him hold me again.

Instead, I opened my eyes and stared straight up into his.

Then I bit him.

Hard. Enjoying the feel of bone, the skin breaking, and the metallic taste of blood.

"Hey!" he gasped, his hand jerking back, knocking against my teeth.

I smiled. Revenge felt sweet.

Fred assessed the damage to his finger. "Lucky for you, I think I'll live," he said.

That's when I noticed the thick gold wedding band on his ring finger. I ignored the pang of jealousy that cut through me, and said, "Lucky how?"

"Well," Fred answered slowly, "lucky because that means I can buy you dinner. Tomorrow night?"

I knew the response should be no. I knew that I should walk away, fast.

"Okay," I said.

"Okay," Fred said, his voice low.

He bent toward me. I didn't like the new style men were wearing, droopy mustaches and long sideburns. And Fred had both. Despite my protests, Jim had done the same thing.

"Maybe third time's the charm," he whispered, making me hate myself for the way those words and the smell of his Old Spice made my heart beat a little faster, made me want to rip off his London Fog and feel his skin beneath my hands again.

"Don't count on it," I said, surprising myself that I could pull off sassy.

In one swift motion, Fred straightened and yanked the umbrella shut. I could see small pinpricks of blood on his finger and they made me smile. The storm had ended as quickly as it began.

"We'll meet right here then?" he said, motioning with his chin toward the Shepard clock. "Six o'clock?"

Before I could answer, he simply walked off in the direction he'd come, leaving me wet and alone, my tube of lipstick still clutched in my hand.

We'd named her after the Beatles song. At night, we sang it to her to put her to sleep. *Michelle, ma belle* . . . When that song came on the radio now, I had to pull over, stop driving, until I could catch my breath again. Jim still played it on the stereo, over and over again in the living room with the shades pulled shut, a glass of bourbon by his side. That's where I found him when I got home, flopped in the easy chair, bourbon in hand, that hateful song's final chords playing.

"Please," I said, "don't put it on again."

He didn't respond, or even acknowledge me. But he stayed

seated at least, and let the needle on the record player keep skittering across the 45.

"Is there dinner?" I asked, already knowing the answer.

Maybe he shook his head no.

I didn't wait around, just went to the kitchen and peered into the near empty refrigerator. At first, people brought food: tuna casseroles and Chicken Divan, meatloaf and lasagna. But eventually those stopped, as if in half a year's time we should be better, over it, back to cooking dinner and living our life. Even though the high chair sat empty in the corner, and down the hall a room with lemon-yellow walls had a half-finished puzzle on the floor, a box of Crayola crayons opened, and an unmade big-girl bed. Even though, I thought as I opened a carton of cottage cheese, we had nothing to live for anymore.

Six o'clock on Westminster Mall is full of men in business suits, women in high heels, shoppers laden with shopping bags pushing through the revolving doors of Shepard's and The Outlet and Gladyings. I'd read in the *Evening Bulletin* that some politicians wanted to demolish the pedestrian mall and open it to automobile traffic. They wanted to enter the 1970s with an all-new Providence. But standing there on a warm April evening and watching life pass by me, I couldn't believe that anyone would let that happen. A policeman forced two long-haired college students in ripped jeans and T-shirts, holding signs that said *Hell No, We Won't Go!* to move along. Not for the first time, I found myself thankful that when I went to college, students still dressed for class—boys in ties and girls in skirts and sweater sets. We combed our hair and took baths and loved our country.

"You look deep in thought," Fred Lancaster's voice interrupted my silent rant.

I pointed to the two boys still lingering near The Outlet.

"I was reminiscing about my own college days," I said.

Fred smiled down at me. Had he always been so tall? I felt small beside him.

"We had our heads in the sand," he said, linking his arm in mine. "This generation is exciting, isn't it? They're thinking, questioning—"

"If we're going to have a pleasant dinner," I said, "maybe we should change the subject."

"Ah! You're one of those," he teased. "Please don't tell me you voted for Nixon."

"I think I'll take the fifth," I said, trying not to concentrate on the way our hips bumped pleasantly together as we walked.

"I seem to remember that you weren't quite such a straight arrow in college."

My cheeks burned, and I hoped he didn't notice.

"The night on my friend's boat," he said, as if I didn't remember.

"Well," I said, because I didn't know what else to say.

"And that weekend in Maine."

"Was that Maine?" I asked. "I don't think I saw anything except the inside of a bedroom." I could play this game too.

Fred stopped walking.

"The wallpaper had bluebirds on it," I said, flirting.

Without any warning, he tipped my chin up and kissed me full on the mouth. It was as good as I remembered. Only Fred could make my knees wobbly with one kiss.

"Cardinals," he said, his face still close to mine.

"What?"

"The wallpaper had cardinals," he said. "There was a red and gray and white–striped Pendleton blanket on the bed, and scratchy sheets by some Scandinavian designer."

"Marimekko," I said, remembering it all in one hot rush. Fred naked beside me, inside me. Kissing so much that my chin got red and chafed. Eating peanut butter on crackers so that we didn't have to leave that bed.

"We'll go to Maine again," Fred was saying. "This time I'll take you for lobster at this place right on the wharf—"

"You promised me that *last* time," I chuckled.

"Lobster is overrated," Fred grinned. "I'd probably not let you out of bed this time either."

"Except this time I'm married," I reminded him. Glancing at the wedding ring on his finger, I added, "*You're* married."

"Luau Hut or Ming Garden?" Fred asked. "Mai tais or chicken wings?"

I didn't answer.

"We go to the Luau Hut and have mai tais," he said, "I won't be responsible for my actions."

I thought of Jim back home in the dark living room. Funny, that room was anything but alive. It was death. It was Michelle's pictures on the mantle. It was the smell of bourbon and sweat and grief.

I said, "Luau Hut then."

I said, "And you'd better keep your promise to misbehave."

Pressed against the side of Luke's Restaurant after too many shared mai tais served in fake coconuts, I gave myself over to something I'd forgotten ever since the morning that Michelle died: pleasure. Upstairs from Luke's, the Luau Hut glowed. Against the wall, Fred kissed me in that way I'd forgotten people kissed. I found myself pressing against him too, meeting his tongue, whispering into his mouth, "Don't stop."

"Where can we go?" Fred asked, pulling back from me just enough so that our lips almost still touched.

"Your car?" I suggested.

I was drunk and stupid on mai tais and the promise of love. So much so that I forgot I hated Fred, forgot how he'd broken my heart twice, forgot my husband sitting in the dark crying.

Fred took me by the hand and led me down Westminster

Street, down Snow Street, to the almost empty parking lot where his Mustang sat, waiting for us. The attendant's booth was empty, though a bare bulb burned in it. *What time is it?* I wondered as Fred pulled me past it, so eager, so ready, his excitement fueling my own.

And then I was in the car, squeezing into the backseat with Fred following. He was kissing me, kissing me hard. I'd decided to keep my legs bare, and despite the cool April chill that had descended on the city, I was glad now for that.

Fred was saying all the right things. He'd thought of me so many times over the years. He remembered my smell.

"Oh, Barbara, this feels so good."

"Shut up," I said, pulling him closer. If I could have swallowed him whole, I would have.

"Shut up or I'll kill you," I said.

"Tell me about her," I said when we paused in the kissing.

"Not now," Fred said.

"Now."

Fred sighed. "She's crazy. She . . . drinks too much. She falls down and embarrasses herself. She rages at me, at the kids, at her miserable life. Then she passes out, and when she wakes up she acts like nothing happened. She makes us waffles and sausages like nothing happened."

"Oh, Fred," I said, "I'm sorry."

He shrugged. "And Jim?" he asked.

"Did I tell you his name was Jim?"

Fred laughed and poked me on the nose. "You *did* have a lot of mai tais, baby."

"Jim is sad," I said. "Terminally sad. Sometimes I'm afraid . . ." I shook my head.

"What?"

I hadn't said out loud what I was afraid of—that one day I

would come home and find Jim had shot himself. That Jim would decide he'd had enough of grief.

Instead of answering, I turned and kissed him.

"This is ridiculous," Fred murmured. "We're adults, making out in the backseat of a car."

I thought of the signs the college kids held. *Make Love, Not War*. My head hurt from those mai tais, my mouth tasted foreign.

Fred looked at me, took my face in both his hands. "Would you ever leave him? Would you?"

"Ouch," I said, trying to move free of his grasp. But he held on tight, his thumbs digging into my flesh. "You're hurting me."

"Would you?" he asked again. His eyes searched mine.

Could I leave Jim? He was there when Michelle was born, cradling her in his arms like the precious thing she was. And he was there beside me when she died. Funny how life and death were so similar, his face holding almost the same exact expression at both.

"I don't know," I said honestly.

Fred's jaw set.

"Could you leave . . ." Had he told me his wife's name?

"Angie," he said. "For you, I would."

Twice before, I'd let myself believe that Fred and I had a future. I'd imagined a house by the ocean, and kids with his blue eyes. I'd imagined growing old beside him.

"I don't know," I said again, not wanting to trust this feeling growing inside of me.

After all that had happened, how could I let myself hope again?

Fred turned so that he faced me squarely. There was a smudge of my new lipstick below his bottom lip. I didn't wipe it off.

"Then I'll have to convince you," he said. "Tomorrow night, Ming Garden. Chicken wings."

I had made that recipe at home once. The *Providence Journal* had run it at a reader's request. But the wings hadn't tasted the same.

"Barbara?" Fred was saying. "Tomorrow?"

I nodded. "Yes," I said.

To my surprise, Jim was awake when I got home, sitting in the kitchen with the table set: two plates, two napkins, two sets of silverware.

"I made lamb chops," he said. "They're probably dried out by now . . ."

"I'm sorry," I said. "I ate."

Jim nodded, studying my face. "I made potatoes too, little roasted ones."

I shrugged apologetically.

"Wine?" he asked me, holding up a bottle. He didn't wait for me to answer, just cut the foil from its neck and yanked out the cork.

I took the glass he offered and sat at the empty place setting.

"I made peas too," Jim said. "With the pearl onions. You like those."

"Yes."

Jim sipped his wine. "Funny day today," he said.

"How so?"

He hadn't talked this much of his own accord in almost a year. It should have made me glad, but instead I felt suspicious. Maybe that was guilt.

"Someone was poking around our life insurance policies," Jim said. "Charlie called me and said some guy called the office yesterday, pretending to be me, asking if our premiums were paid up and what the policies paid out."

"That's weird."

"You think so?"

"Well, of course I do."

Jim nodded. "Asked if the policy paid out in case of suicide—"

"What?"

"And in case we both died—"

"Jim, you're scaring me." I wondered if there really had been such a call, or if Jim was trying to tell me something.

"Charlie said, *You have a copy of the policy yourself*, and the guy said he'd misplaced it."

"But he didn't give out any information, did he?"

Jim refilled my wineglass. "Where have you been until almost midnight, Barbara?" he asked.

"Down city," I said. "I met Betty and Dorothy for Chinese."

"Ming Garden?"

"The Luau Hut. I had one mai tai too many, I'm afraid."

"Girls' night out," Jim said.

I could smell the lamb, acrid, almost like urine.

"Thanks for making dinner," I said. "It's been so long."

"We'll have it tomorrow night. If it's salvageable."

I thought about Fred. Somehow he seemed more familiar, more intimate, than my own husband. Did grief alienate people like this? Could we ever go back to how we'd been?

"Tomorrow night . . ." I began, but I couldn't think of a good excuse for being out again.

"If the lamb's ruined, I'll make pork chops . . . All right?"

"Yes. Either way," I said, forcing a smile.

Of course I didn't meet Fred the following night. How could I? But as I sat across from my husband, eating Shake 'n Bake pork chops and Rice-a-Roni and applesauce, I thought of him waiting under the Shepard clock for me. How long did he stand there, looking expectant at first, watching the stream of people moving toward him, thinking one of them would be me? Like Jim, Fred is a tall man, tall enough to see over the heads of the crowd; he would have spotted me right away. How often did he glance at his watch, wondering what was keeping me? How long did he stand there, waiting?

I sipped the cold Chablis Jim had bought, and ate my dinner, and thought about Fred under the clock, maybe worried by now, maybe angry.

Jim's voice broke into my reverie: "I think what unnerved me the most is that I did think about it."

He was talking about the caller yesterday. He was talking about killing himself.

"But I didn't want to leave you," he said, and reached across the table and took my hand in his. "I couldn't . . ." His voice broke and he didn't continue.

Was this the beginning? I wondered. Were we starting to emerge from our fog of grief? Starting to make our way back to each other? I looked around the dining room, acutely aware of how quiet the house was. It had been that way ever since Michelle died, like it was holding its breath.

"Could you do it?" Jim asked me.

"Kill myself?" I said, surprised. "I don't think so."

"Could you kill someone else?"

I laughed nervously. "I admit it," I said, "I have had murderous thoughts."

We chewed our dinner in silence for a bit, and then Jim said, "I think we should leave. This house. Providence. We should go away and start over."

I squeezed my eyes shut to block out the images of Michelle here. Here at this table smearing mashed sweet potatoes on her face. Crawling in the odd, army-style crawl she had, like Vic Morrow at the beginning of *Combat*. Taking her first bold steps across this threshold, nothing tentative about our daughter. She pulled herself to standing, walked into the room, then fell down hard on her diapered bottom.

"Leave," I repeated, opening my eyes. "How?"

* * *

The next night I made excuses, an overdue library book, a sale at Cherry & Webb. Jim frowned at me but said nothing. Outside, the wind had picked up and dark clouds swept across the evening sky. April had certainly come in like a lion, I thought as I walked quickly across the Westminster Mall to the clock. Foolishly, I had forgotten an umbrella. The first fat drops of rain began to fall. The mall emptied fast. Was I also foolish for expecting Fred to show up?

But no sooner did I have the thought than I saw him, with his purposeful stride, moving toward me. He had on his London Fog, belted loosely.

"I thought you'd changed your mind," he said when he reached me, pulling me into a long hard hug.

"I can't stay," I said, moving out of his arms. "Jim . . . he's suspicious, I think."

Fred nodded. Then he took my arm and tugged me along.

"Really," I said. "He's making meatloaf. I told him I was going to the library."

Fred didn't answer. He just led me back to Luke's, and upstairs to the Luau Hut. Despite my protestations, he ordered us two mai tais and a pupu platter. Once they were delivered, he lifted his glass and slid the napkin from beneath it.

"You guys have life insurance?" he asked, taking a Cross pen from his inside jacket pocket.

A shiver ran up my arms.

"Of course," I said. "Doesn't everybody?"

Fred was writing something, but he laughed. "Not everybody. I had some hard luck, nothing serious, down in Buenos Aires. That's why I came back here."

"So you don't have a job?"

"Not exactly," Fred said. "But I do have a plan."

He turned the napkin around and moved it closer to me.

The mai tai tasted overly sweet tonight, and I bit into an egg roll dipped in hot mustard to get the taste out of my mouth. Immediately, my eyes began to tear.

"What is it?" I asked, coughing.

"A," he said, pointing to the napkin, "you do something to upset him—"

"Who? Jim?"

"—then you leave the house. See, you'll be out of it."

"Out of what?"

"But you leave the door open, see?" He pointed to the letter B on the napkin. "So that I can slip in . . . Don't worry," Fred continued, looking me right in the eye, "he won't suffer. Hell, he's suffering now, isn't he? With grief? We'll be doing him a favor."

"How did you know about Michelle?" I asked Fred suddenly.

"Who?"

"My daughter," I said softly.

"I ran into Simone . . . what's her last name? Your old friend from college?"

I took another sip of my drink, trying to make sense of what he was saying. Simone married a guy from Australia and moved there a million years ago. After one Christmas card with a picture of kangaroos pulling Santa's sleigh, I never heard from her again.

"How else can we be together?" he asked me.

"But your wife . . ."

He grinned. "That's what I wanted to tell you. She's agreed to a divorce. She thinks I'm a no-good son of a bitch, and she said good riddance." Fred reached across the table and took both of my hand in his. "I came looking for you. Third time's the charm, babe."

I didn't know what to say. I stared at Fred, the man I had loved more than anyone ever. I stared at that napkin.

"You come straight here, and I'll meet you under the clock."

It felt like a dream. My whole life—Fred and Jim and even Michelle—all of it.

"We wait until the insurance pays off, then we go."

"Go where?" I asked him. A plan was taking hold.

"Anywhere," he said, smiling. "Where do you want to go?"

I shrugged. "Hawaii?"

"Sure, I like that."

"Kiss me," I said.

He leaned in.

"Not like that," I said, and I moved to sit beside him in the red booth.

"Like this," I said, kissing him until he couldn't catch his breath.

The rain was cold and hard.

The next evening, I stood nervously under the Shepard clock, my umbrella clutched tight in my hand. The wind tugged it, and I couldn't help but think of how Fred had saved me.

I felt like I waited forever before I spotted him approaching, his head bent beneath his own umbrella. I could make out those ridiculous sideburns, the mustache. His London Fog was belted tight against the storm. Already his wing tips looked soggy.

"Is it done?" I asked him when he reached me.

He lifted his face. He was still beautiful, I thought.

"Done," he said.

"Do you think—" I began.

But he held up one finger and pressed it to my lip. "Believe me," he said, "they won't be able to recognize him."

I nodded, trying to steady myself.

"It's time to call," he said.

I went to the phone booth and stepped inside. I dialed 911.

"My husband!" I said, trying to sound panicked. "I came home and found him. He shot himself! He's dead!"

I broke into sobs, real ones, as if everything I'd had in me all this time was finally freed. The woman calmed me, asked for my address, said help was on the way.

When I stepped out of the phone booth, he reached into his inside pocket and pulled out the airline tickets, just enough so I could see them.

"Honolulu," he said.

I thought of mai tais on the beach. I thought of the ocean pounding the shore, washing away memories and pain and grief.

"The flight leaves at nine. We have plenty of time to get to Logan."

"Kiss me," I said.

My husband bent his face to mine and kissed me. We had not kissed in longer than I could remember and it felt good, right.

Jim hooked his elbow in mine, and we walked together through the cold April rain. I thought I could almost hear the faint sounds of the song "Michelle" playing in an empty house.

THE VENGEANCE TAKER

BY ROBERT LEUCI

Olneyville

*While there are several names in this story from the public re-
cord, this is a fictional tale. The story is completely a creation
of my imagination. —R.L.*

T ommy Boyle, restless for life, a young man of twenty-four
who had learned to live on his family's connections, his
nerves, and his boundless energy, made his way from his
three-room apartment in Olneyville Square to the Federal Hill
section of Providence. Once there, Tommy would borrow money,
twenty thousand dollars, from a man some referred to as the Old
Man, others called him George. His name was Raymond Patriarca, a mighty Mafia don and bon vivant. Tommy was hoping
to launch a spectacular diner with the borrowed money. It was
money for which he would pay a vigorish 20 percent weekly, a
loan shark's interest, collected with a half-smile and a baseball
bat.

A brutal world the don lived in, but of course it didn't seem
that way to Tommy Boyle. Tommy had set his mind on being rich
and famous—if it took a Faustian committment to the don, then
so be it. It was uncontrolled enthusiasm, a twenty-four-year-old
grafter's vow.

A product of the state's thriving special-education program, Tommy had a natural inclination for business, according
to his friends. Blond and well-built, his ice-blue eyes burned

with a fierce desire to accomplish great things. Some suspected that at times he suffered minor emotional disturbances. Tommy was, they said, a dreamer. He could be accident prone, forgetful. Sometimes he would pass into a kind of trance for twenty-four hours straight with a blankness in his eyes that many found alarming. His father had warned him to be especially careful, that things among the gangsters had started to go funny. All the mobsters, it seemed, had lost their sense of irony. But Tommy remained positive. Borrow money, pay it back with interest, simple.

He'd sit for hours with a yellow pad and black and red pens, sketching out ideas for a menu. New York–style wieners, french fries with vinegar, tuna club, turkey club, steak sandwiches, grilled chicken club, bacon-and-egg western sandwiches, and the pièce de résistance: coffee milk served from a magnificent, polished copper dispenser liberated by his grandfather from a destroyed hotel in Calvados, France.

Recently, due to the toxic combination of his infernal horniness and late-night drinking, Tommy had impregnated his girlfriend. A woman with whom he had nothing and everything in common, and they'd just married. A pregnant wife and no job. Tommy felt incredibly unlucky and hoped that maybe dealing with the don would change all that.

In those days his Olneyville neighborhood was a desolate area of rundown, multifamily triple-decker homes and small manufacturing shops, which sat in a valley across an overpass that ran above the Route 10 connector to I-95. It was a short walk from the Italian Federal Hill section of the city. There were no signs showing the demarcation points, differentiating one neighborhood from the other, and none were needed. The intersection of Atwells and Harris was the boundary. Along Atwells up on Federal Hill sat cafés, restaurants, salumarias, social clubs, laundromats, pastry shops, and live-poultry markets; all part of the don's fiefdom. When gang-banging street criminals considered edging out of their Olneyville neighborhood and moving toward the Hill, the thought was a fleeting one. The don deplored any and all street crime unless, of course, he himself ordered it. Brainless violence was bad for business; it brought unwanted attention from the police. Olneyville gangsters did their dealing in Olneyville; it was safer.

Not long after opening the diner to outrageously favorable reviews, Tommy suddenly felt an enormous inner brightness. Mighty success smiled and the money rolled in. On weekend nights lines circled the block, wieners by the thousand were consumed. During that heady time, in a spurt of passionate gusto, Tommy finally fell madly in love with his wife Callie. Dark brown skin, part Japanese and part Brazilian with a round pretty face, Callie delivered a baby girl they named Lara. All seemed perfect. Until it was not.

With the don, Tommy shared an interest in contact sports, recreational drugs, experimental sex, and a need to amass a huge amount of money. It took him only a few months to pay off the loan, 20 percent interest and all. Then, on a bright summer Wednesday in July, Tommy was startled to learn that the don, in the precise middle of a ridiculously slow fellatio, had an enormous ejaculation. It was said that the Old Man called on God, grabbed at his chest, and died. In that one luxurious moment, Tommy Boyle's protection was gone and all changed.

Twelve years later

Her name is Lara Boyle. She is twelve years old, sitting on the top step of the stoop in front of her family's house. She waits for her babysitter. The blue sleeveless sundress she wears is embroidered with tiny yellow tulips. Lara is as neat as a pin; being neat and well-groomed is a permanent character trait that will follow her all the days of her life.

The family car is parked in the driveway, and her father is putting cardboard boxes, one at a time, into the backseat. The boxes are heavy and she notices the patches of sweat staining the light brown shirt he wears, she thinks from the heat of the morning. Lara does not know that her father's sweat flows with nervousness and fear.

"Callie!" her father shouts, drawing Lara's attention. He runs his hands through his hair, shouting for her mother again, and then he slowly brings his hands to his face, calling out once more. When he turns to look at Lara she sees a small, sad smile form, and in that moment her mother comes out of the house, moving quickly, as if angry or afraid.

"Vanessa is on her way," her mother says.

Her father nods, then bends and puts his hands on his knees, holds them there as though he is in pain, rocking. "Call her, Callie, call her again."

"She'll be right here," her mother says. "Tommy, I don't understand why I need to go with you. Is there no end to this?"

Her father seems to weigh the question as he picks up the last of the boxes, staring at it as if waiting for a sign. And then, nodding, he places it alongside the others on the car's backseat.

"I want you with me," he tells her.

Lara notices Vanessa's small red car breaking out of traffic, pulling to the curb, and parking on the opposite side of the street. And then for one long moment she thinks of the night before, the way her mother cried into her father's shoulder. She understands that something her father said made her mother cry. Her mother crosses the front yard quickly, her father is already in the car, his hands holding the steering wheel. He throws Lara a kiss, she is expected to return it, just as she is expected to sit and wait on the stoop.

"C'mon, Lara," her father shouts, "be nice and throw your daddy a kiss! Daddy loves you."

She does.

Lara watches her mother now, the way the back of her hand moves across her lips, how fast she walks. And then, as her mother opens the car door and sits beside her father, Lara hears the ignition as her father turns the key, distinctly hears it.

And then Lara hears the explosion.

The morning erupts in thunder, shattering steel and glass. Lara hears her mother's shriek, a sound like crazy laughter. After the blast, the erupting glass and flying steel, she sees an orange-red flash of fire and then there is silence.

Lara's father, Tommy Boyle, somehow stumbles out of the silver car. His body is smoking and he is coughing blood, the glare of the sun all around him. He makes a noise Lara cannot understand, drops to his knees, his hand extended toward her as he falls to the grass.

Her mother is gone. There is nothing but a drowsy hissing sound coming through the smoke and fire. Lara puts her hands over her ears and shuts her eyes. In the middle of the street, Vanessa screams.

Sometime after noon, Lara is sitting shoulder to shoulder with Vanessa on her bed. The babysitter's arm is around Lara's back, her hand cupping the child's shoulder. There are a number of strange men and women in the house now, moving around as though they belong. Her mother would not be happy.

From the street there have been the sounds of fire engines, police cars, and an ambulance. Lara keeps her eyes shut tight and her hands cover her ears; in the closing off of all light and sound, maybe she can change what happened. She allows herself to go with that feeling, that none of the horror happened.

Lara hears the door to her bedroom open. She uncovers her eyes and sees two men step in and stop. The men stand three feet from her. She moves her hands toward her face and worries that she might start to cry.

"Is the child being cared for?" the one with a mess of blond hair asks softly. "Does she need anything?"

"She's in shock," Vanessa explains.

The man nods. "Yeah, well, of course," he says, then he points to the man standing beside him. "This is Brendan McKenna. He's a state police investigator. My name is Mark Perino, I work for the FBI. Lara, your mom and dad were on their way to meet with us when the accident happened."

Hearing this, Vanessa begins crying out loud.

Accident? Lara thinks. *It was an accident?*

Things come to Lara now without her knowing how or why. She remembers her father and mother arguing about gangsters, the looks they exchanged, and she understands now that in those looks there was dread. It was the way they touched each other, the way her father hugged her mother, the way her mother gave in. And, in the remembering, she wonders what the blond man, whose name is Mark, meant by *accident*. And considering that, Lara feels sorry for herself. She realizes that everything has changed, that there is no one left, that she is alone. She sits on the edge of the bed and stares at the blond man. His gaze goes through her like a breeze.

"Does the child want something to drink? Juice or soda? We'll get her whatever she wants," the blond man says.

"She won't speak to me. She hasn't said a word," Vanessa says. Her voice is trembling and filled with panic.

Lara hears herself mutter, "Please," and wonders where the word comes from. She wants to scream but she is too frozen with fear. A tiny "please" is all she can manage.

A woman in uniform has joined the men in the room. She is not as tall as Vanessa and she is serious and hard-faced. Her voice, her tone, gets Lara's attention. "We need to place her," the woman is saying. "Apparently, there is no family."

Tears come again to Lara's eyes, run down her cheeks onto

her hands that are folded in her lap. She does not cry out loud, just sits, silently weeping.

The guy standing next to the blue-eyed man rubs his elbow, saying, "Whadaya mean, no family? No one? How can there be no one at all?" He looks at Lara in a strange way, and she thinks: *There is no one.*

"There is no family," Mark Perino says. "Tommy and Callie were the last Boyles. Now listen," he tells them, "this child, this beautiful little girl, is not going to any state facility, no foster home. I couldn't answer to my conscience if I allowed that."

The uniformed woman smiles, a sad smile, Lara thinks. "What do you mean?" she says. "You won't allow it? C'mon, you know better."

"I gave Tommy Boyle my word. I told him, God forbid anything happens, I'll take care of his wife and daughter."

"I doubt you have that authority," the woman says.

The blond man smiles. Lara sees that his, too, is a sad smile and guesses that it was meant to be. "I represent the government," he says, "my word is backed up by the United States of America."

Something in that makes the woman shake her head.

"It makes no difference to me what you think," he says. "Tell your superiors, the child is going with me. I'll take care of her."

The woman tries to step around him, but Mark Perino grabs her shoulder, stopping her.

"I'm calling my superiors," the woman says. "I don't want any problems here."

He doesn't seem to hear her. He reaches down and puts his hands on Lara's shoulders then slides them under her arms and lifts her. Walking, he is gentle, lifting her with one arm and moving the uniformed woman out of the way with the other. And all the time, the woman is talking.

"I don't think you can do this," she says. "There are rules and procedures, state laws."

When he speaks his tone is all business: "I don't care about your rules and procedures. You're going to get out of my way. Later, when the child is settled, I'll call your boss."

He puts a hand on the uniformed woman's shoulder and pushes her toward the door. Everyone in the room gives him nervous looks, as if they are not sure of what to do, whether to get involved or not.

"You pack her some things," he says to Vanessa. "Be quick. Don't get fancy, just essentials."

In her mind, Lara wavers between the bittersweet joy of having someone strong hold and protect her, and the crushing certainty that she will never see her mother and father again. He is gone. Her father is gone forever, and that is a concept she finds impossible to comprehend. Lara wipes her eyes and flattens her cheek against Mark Perino's shoulder. He breathes out heavily and then pulls her closer to his chest, hugging her so tightly she can hear his heart beat.

"I honestly don't think you can do this," the uniformed woman is saying.

Lara hears Mark reply: "I know what you think. I know your attitudes. I even know the movies you watch."

Lara thinks of all the strangers in her house who will not go away. She hears one say, "If it were me, there would be blood for blood." Lara thinks about that, blood for blood.

She leaves Mark and walks to her bedroom window, looks down onto the driveway and sees the family car. All at once she wants her mother and father, wants to touch her mother's skirt, smell her father's aftershave, feel her mother's long fingers stroke her cheek. Lara senses her mother and father know this, that now they both know all there is to know, and in the quiet that consumes the house, Lara is aware that her parents are watching her. Then it comes to her like a blow, a phantom rage that brings her upright.

There are voices, her mother's and father's, at first roaring, then gentle whispers. Music, she can hear someone giggle, she is certain she hears someone cry.

The voices have found her. It is the first time, but they will come again, and again. In the not-so-distant future they will take up permanent residence in her brain. Lara lowers her head and puts her finger across her lips. "Be quiet," she whispers to the voices that shout, *Murder!*

Fifteen minutes later Lara is sitting in the front seat of an un-marked government car as it rolls slowly up the street. Her gaze moves to the smoldering hulk on the driveway and then to her family's house. Mark slows the car a moment, deciding some-thing, and then picks up speed.

"Will I ever come back here?" Lara asks.

"Sure you will," Mark tells her.

"Where are we going?"

Mark glances at her. "I know that your mom and dad would want you to be with me."

They ride south on the interstate, the late afternoon turning dark. They stop at a McDonald's for Lara to use the restroom and get something to drink. Then they drive into darkness.

"It's okay," Mark says.

Lara has been weeping quietly for most of the ride. "I'll never see my parents again." The thought oppresses her; there is no promise of relief. "Never ever," she says.

"Close your eyes. Concentrate on your mom and dad. Con-centrate. Can you see them now?"

Lara nods.

"Grab onto that. Believe they are here. I promise you," Mark says to her, "you will never have to go through anything like this again."

A moment drifts by, neither of them speaking.

"I promise you," he repeats.

The whispering voices come to her again, like insects buzzing around her head. *Murder*, she hears, *no accident, murder.*

"It was not an accident," she tells Mark.

Mark, Lara, and Hannah stood awkwardly on the porch of Mark's house. Hannah Perino was medicated—not heavily, just enough so her expression seemed as though she was hearing pleasant music in her head.

What truly infuriated Hannah was the loss of her thick, lustrous strawberry-blond hair, taken by the radiation and chemo. She had a face as pale and beautiful as any Lara had seen. Even with the silk black scarf covering her head, you could see this. Hannah Perino's eyes locked with hers and all at once something shifted inside Lara. She remembered that her mother was gone and felt a horrible thrill of grief.

"Lara will be staying with us for a bit," Mark said.

"Well then, c'mon in, sweetie." Hannah held the door for Lara.

Up close Hannah smelled familiar. White Linen, Lara's mother's favorite. Inside the large colonial room with a fireplace and bookshelves, a sad Sinatra song played. She was aware of the exhaustion now. After a short time, she followed Mark to the guest room.

Mark explained to Hannah that Lara's parents had been killed that morning. He told her, "She saw her parents burn alive."

"The poor child," she said, "my God."

"There is no family. Do you know what the system will do with her?"

"We can't keep her forever," Hannah told him.

"No, just long enough for me to figure out my next move."

"I'll be okay. You'll do what you have to do, what is right. You talked to them, the police and the Bureau?"

"They talked to me."

"And you're going to try to hang onto the girl?"

"For the time being."

Hannah seemed to understand.

Lara rested for a few days, Mark made clear that they needed the solitude, he did and Hannah did and certainly Lara did. They pretended that in time life could go on in an almost normal fashion. Within a day or two, Mark found that Lara was no ordinary twelve-year-old. There was a touch of caution and a certain menace in her.

After the third day, Hannah asked, "Do you think we can keep her?" Mark liked the question and liked the way Hannah smiled when she asked it.

On their fifth night together, not quite a week after the bombing, Lara sat at the dinner table and said, "I think you know something you're not telling me."

"Like what?"

"Like who killed my mother and father. I mean, you're an FBI agent."

Mark explained that he couldn't be positive, not yet, but he'd know soon enough. It was proof, Lara thought. The murder of her parents was proof positive that what the nuns had told her was true. Satan's evil grip was running free in the world. The voices confirmed it.

Hannah complained that rainy night—her sickness, the awful pain of it, drained her of all faith, all belief, she told them.

In the ensuing weeks Mark got himself an expensive and cunning lawyer; together they fought off all attempts to turn Lara over to the state.

In Lara's heart there was space set aside for her mother and father; as things began to go bad for Hannah, she found space for her as well.

In Lara's teetering mind all this was one bad dream. "Why?" she asked Hannah over and over again. "Why you?"

Drugs were Hannah's only answer for her pain. Morphine was good, but the Olneyville street heroin was better. Carboplatin was forced on her. Poison. It killed cells, all her cells. It was a magnificent killer. The doctors said that it was up to her to go on with this.

With what?

For many months Hannah had been a fighter; then abruptly the battle was over. She could no longer take the pain in her back and stomach. Her day was: lay down, vomit, get up, diarrhea, again and again. Everything closing down, the last stages. Mark shouting at God: "Heartless bastard! You do this to a good woman?" The shouting made Lara cry.

Near the end, they kept her at home. Lara and Mark together held her close, turned up the morphine and the heroin. Then in the center of one night, a sudden storm, fingers of lightning, thunder; in the excruciating rapture of a heroin OD, Hannah reached out and grabbed Mark's and Lara's hands. She looked at their tear-lined faces and smiled a medicated smile. Sinatra sang in the background, and Hannah, just like that, was gone.

The following morning, Brendan McKenna, the narcotics officer, called. He was beside himself. "You better sit down," he said. "We identified the bombers."

Mark told him that during the night, they had lost Hannah.

"Oh Mark," Brendan gasped over the phone, "I am so sorry, what a horror." For years after Brendan had stopped drinking he could be easily brought to tears. "Would you like me to come by?" he asked.

"We're okay, I've been expecting this for a while," Mark told him.

"The Boyle girl, she's still with you?"

"Lara is part of my family now, Brendan. So tell me," Mark said, "can we put these animals in the penitentiary?"

"We know who they are Mark, it's who we expected." Then he added in a particularly cynical way, "There's not another FBI agent in the world I'd tell this to."

Mark cleared his throat to remain calm. "C'mon, cut it out, what is it?"

"The information came off a bad wire, a narcotics tap without a court order. We collar them, they'll walk. We have nothing—no witnesses, not one forensic that ties them to the killing. Zero."

"Mickey Reno," Mark said.

"Right, and two of his slammers, Sonny Mullen and Freddie Bordure."

Mark was quiet for a long time, then, "Ahhhh—this is bullshit," he snarled into the phone, "murdering bastards, evil sonsabitches."

"You'll get no argument from me, pal," Brendan replied.

One morning, Mark awoke to find Lara in his study; somehow she had gotten hold of his case folder. There were photographs of Tommy and Callie Boyle, pictures of their incineration. Composed, Lara fingered one of his guns. Although Mark had locked it away, she'd found the key to his safe.

Suicide, he thought. Lara was about to shoot herself. She sat cross-legged on the sofa, looking at pictures of her parents and studying the nine millimeter in her hand. "You're not thinking of hurting yourself, are you?" Mark said, taking the gun from her.

"Them," she responded. "I want to shoot the people that did this to my mother and father. I want them to suffer and I want them dead, I want to help make them dead."

"You're twelve years old," he told her.

"I'll be thirteen in a month. I can do it."

Mark believed her.

During the ensuing days and painful, sleepless nights, no matter how he asked himself the question, he kept coming back to the same conclusion: he would become his own government, dispensing his own justice. It was what he and Lara both wanted. What Lara wanted was what he wanted, and he said it out loud now, because he felt it deep in the marrow of his being, a need to say it, as much for Lara as for himself. Justice, pure and simple. Honorable vengeance was what they both needed.

The following week in Olneyville, Sonny Mullen stalked the street like a hunter on a track. Head bowed, he moved slowly to Olneyville Square. He found a bench and sat. His eyes were black, a gold chain hung from his neck. He was nicely exhausted with little energy to bring to bear. Two days and nights at Foxwoods, and he'd won big time.

He lit a cigarette.

Sonny had been sitting for a short while when Lara walked up to him.

"Please, can you help me?" she said.

His fatigued, tanned face put on a show of weary amusement.

Lara showed him a dog's leash, then pointed to a nearby alleyway and looked as though something had made her suddenly sad. "My dog ran off, he's hurt, he's down there and I can't carry him."

"Your dog?"

"She's strong."

"It's not a pit bull?"

"A yellow lab."

He folded his arms and leaned back against the bench.

"I don't like dogs and they don't like me. Maybe you should call your folks. Or the cops." An unhurried hoarse voice with that Providence tough-guy street accent he'd picked up at the ACI.

"I thought you'd help me," Lara said, her voice catching.

He looked around to see if anyone was watching, then quickly got to his feet. "Oh man, fuck it," he said. "C'mon, let's go and get your stupid mutt."

Lara smiled and handed him the leash.

It was quiet in the alleyway and the far end was dark as a mineshaft. Sonny sensed something was prowling and hiding out among the cardboard boxes behind the dumpster.

"Hey, kid, this mutt of yours, what is it, a male or a female?"

Sonny heard, "Why would it matter to you, hot shot? You got no problem killing either one."

Instantly, Sonny's mind went to the gun in his pocket, then he thought he recognized the man standing next to the dumpster, the guy holding the nine millimeter like he knew how to use it. The nine millimeter with a professionally fashioned silencer attached.

The kid smiled at him.

"Do you know who I am?" Sonny said.

"You think that makes a difference to me?" the man answered.

"You're not fucking with some bullshit guy, some bust-out nobody." Sonny put his hand in his coat pocket, slowly felt his automatic, knew he'd have to push the safety off and then cock it. It would take way too long. He knew that too. "You want to tell me what this is about?"

"Take your hand out of your pocket," Mark said.

Sonny brought his hand from his coat pocket to his side.

"It's about you and two of your buddies, Reno and Freddie Bordure. Your lunatic band of killers," Mark said.

Sonny folded his arms, looking down the alley then out toward the street, wondering where everyone was. "Don't know who you're talking about, never heard of those guys."

"You killed my mother and father," the kid said. "I was there, you put a bomb in our . . ." In that moment she heard the voices gather, soft sounds of laughter or wailing.

Sonny said, "I got my ATM card. I could probably get you a few thousand, maybe more. This way everybody earns and just goes home."

Mark said, "Not about money."

"The fuck it's about then?"

"You have a filthy mouth," Mark said. And then he fired his gun.

Lara watched Sonny, his eyes wide open, spring back, hit the ground, and roll over. There was an anguished and fearful sound and Mark shot him again.

After pulling and dragging Sonny behind the dumpster, Lara said, "He was scared, I like that he was scared."

It was almost dark when Lara knocked on the door to apartment 2B. Nothing. She knocked again, harder this time. Mark stood nearby, out of sight. The fish-eye in the door slid open. A voice from behind the door, a woman's voice: "Whadaya want?" There was a dog barking a tiny bark, a puppy's bark. The voice saying, "Adorable uniform, you a Girl Scout?"

The door opened halfway, a redheaded woman stood leaning against the doorframe, smiling. "Aren't you a cute one," she said.

Lara said, "It's my last box. Chocolate mint. Everybody loves them."

A man's voice mumbled angry things. "Ey," he said, "tell her we already gave; tell her, will ya?"

Lara handed her the box, "Open it," she said. She paused with her hands on the door, then brought them together as if in prayer.

A man sitting across the room on a sofa shouted, "Freddie, come out here and give this kid a few bucks, get her the hell outta here!"

The woman said, "Look here, check this out, there's a wedding picture in the cookie box, a beautiful couple."

"My mom and dad," Lara said.

The man on the sofa stood up and walked to the woman, took the photo from her hand, went back to the sofa, and sat down. At first he seemed calm. But as soon as he looked at the photo, he didn't seem calm anymore.

Freddie came in from the bedroom, a puppy tumbling around his feet. "Smokey," he said, "cut it out." The puppy was gray and black, a pit bull.

Freddie, his hands on his hips, saying, "What's goin' on?" The man on the sofa wiped his mouth with his forearm, looked up as Mark came though the door and shot him in the neck right below his chin.

The woman put both hands over her mouth and held her scream. Freddie reached for the pistol he had tucked in his belt. Mark took him with a clean blast in the forehead, proving once more that Mark Perino was one hell of a pistol shot.

The bookkeeping was real, all debts were paid. Lara picked up the puppy.

"Please don't shoot me," the woman begged.

"She saw our faces," Lara said.

"I didn't see any faces, I wasn't even here, how could I see a face?"

"What are you doing with these animals?" Mark said.

"Earning five hundred dollars, thank you very much. And, by the way, there's a suitcase full of cash in the bedroom. Take it."

"You take it," Mark told her. "Give us twenty minutes before you call anyone."

"I'll give you twenty years, I'm calling no one."

Lara saying now, "Your friends murdered my mother and father."

"My friends," the woman countered, throwing her arms in the air, "no, no, no, not friends. You can trust me, trust me, you can trust me. I'm going to throw up."

Mark said, "We're not murderers."

"I hear you. I'm so happy to hear you. Maybe God is with me today, maybe God has finally shown up. I've been waiting a long time."

"You give him some of that money," Mark said.

"You bet I will. Yes, I certainly will."

Lara said, "I'm taking the puppy."

Five minutes later they were in the car heading south. The pit bull sat in Lara's lap, licking, squirming. She held him tight to her breast. "I feel good, I feel good now."

Mark took a moment then said, "Lara, I know, I know how you feel."

A motorcycle sped past, swerving close to their car. Lara turned and set a rigid stare on the driver, pointed her index finger at him, went, "*Boom*."

The puppy growled.

Mark's attention fixed on the highway in front of him, an odd sense of uncertainty began to rise. He could feel it taking hold. "Lara," he said, "I love you. Please believe that I love you. I want you to know that no matter what, we share this road together."

When he turned to her, Lara was staring at him. Her stare made him feel cold and he shuddered. She frowned and pulled at her collar. Her expression was entirely without emotion, without sentiment. He might have been a total stranger. She stroked the dog in her lap.

WALTZ ME ONCE AGAIN

BY LaShonda Katrice Barnett

Mount Hope

When the shot went off and R.C. fell to the floor, Gussie shook awake.

Min lay beside her, reading with the penlight required in early-autumn New England mornings, strangely comforted by the little noises of their Mount Hope home: the *drip-drip* faucet in the en suite bath, the sputtering hot-water tank off the kitchen in what used to be the maid's room, back in 1886 when the house was built. The curtains behind their bed, slightly parted, let through enough light to tell on their recent household neglect. Min could live with the dust but knew Gussie would have to go over every piece of furniture with a rag and a little Lemon Pledge before the sun set that day.

"Same dream?" Min said, touching Gussie's shoulder.

"It's Willadeene's boy. He's in our house. Don't know why he's here, but he's asking for trouble and you give it to him. You shoot him, Min."

"What you dreaming like that for?" Min said in agitated Kriolu, the Cape Verdean dialect Gussie had fallen in love with. "You know I've never fired that gun. Only reason I hold onto it is 'cause it meant so much to Daddy. I don't even know where the damned thing is."

"Watch it now. Don't go starting the day off with ugly language."

"It just makes me nervous, Gussie—you dreaming something like that. Make it so bad, you keep dreaming it over and over. Just gets me riled up."

Gussie raised a large veiny hand to work at the kink in her neck. "I don't know why I'm dreaming it either. Maybe I feel bad for Willadeene. Bragged on that boy so tough when he finally got himself situated at the halfway house over on Friendship Street. Now he's back home. She says he on that stuff. Say he's lost his mind. Cracked out. That's what the youngsters call it. Cracked out."

"R.C.'s dough never was quite done but I don't think he's on that stuff. Just can't handle his liquor," Min said, drawing the curtains. "But R.C.'s not behind your nightmares, Gussie. Willadeene neither. You know I told you to stop eating after eight o'clock. You can't sit up all hours of the night, watch reruns of no-good shows, and eat too."

"I been snacking well into the night all my life."

"You call what you do snacking?"

"I tell you that ain't got nothing to do with it." Gussie threw back her half of the quilt and frowned. Everything was dull and gray, even her toenails, she thought, wiggling her feet. Did Father Time really think he could win without a fight? Might not dye my hair 'cause it can't take it, thin as it is, she thought. But I can paint these yellow toes staring up at me, making me feel old.

"That was my cachupa you got into last night, wasn't it? You think I could sleep through that aroma? The spices in the linguica could wake the dead. With your indigestion you'd think you'd know better than to fool with sausage after eleven o'clock."

Gussie yanked the covers, disgusted she had finished the delicious soup and none remained for today's lunch, but grateful Min hadn't also smelled the peach cobbler.

"Eating late doesn't have anything to do with anything. That's just something folks say to keep old folks from enjoying the little bit of juice left to squeeze out of life. Now if I tell you a hen dips snuff, look under her wing: I'm not dreaming that dream in vain. Something's going on with R.C."

"What's on your dance card today?" Min asked.

"Thought I'd shovel the drive. Don't feel like doing much of nothing, but somebody needs to do some dusting." Catching another glimpse of her toes, she added in a disgusted tone, "Need to go over to White Cross and pick up my prescriptions and some nail polish."

Why a woman needed to polish her toes when everybody was in boots was beyond Min. "If you're going to Randall Square, could you pick up my eyeglass prescription?"

Gussie nodded. "Well, *minha flor*, you ready to go get this day?"

"I'm ready and I ain't gonna let nothing get in my way."

The two took their time getting out of bed, little chuckles for all the effort it required—the twinge of muscles still asleep; the memory of a time those creaks didn't fill the room or the bones. Min paused at the dresser crammed with treasures—perfumes and lotion decanted in ornate crystal bottles, a jewelry box filled with little value except for the pair of sapphire rings they had exchanged years ago—to glance in the mirror and pat down the cropped downy hair framing her smooth brown face. Gussie—apt to catch a chill no matter the season (for thirty-two years she had complained their stately Greek Revival had never been "wired right"; she blamed Min for insisting they buy an historic home, which had made foreign travel nearly impossible)—tied the belt of a mint-green robe around her thick waist. From the doorway they went separate ways: Min to the kitchen, Gussie to the bathroom.

Second on the list of life's most important things, after welcoming each new day with Gussie, was brewing coffee. Min dumped three scoops of Brasileiro Cerrado—how anybody in Providence could buy coffee sold anywhere other than the Coffee Exchange was lost on her—into the filter, added water, and turned on the radio. After starting her bath, Gussie joined Min in the kitchen to set the table, then poured herself a cup and returned to the bathroom. She placed her mug on the corner of the tub then gripped the long chrome handle recently installed on the tiled wall. She leaned back in a bergamot-scented bath, closed her eyes, and listened as the radio announcer finished the harrowing report. Yesterday's news was today's blues—that made two black boys taken in a couple of months by two white cops and no indictments. The ticking of the stove top went on too long because Min either liked to annoy her or needed reminding to gauge the fire under the skillet. Soon after, though, Min started to hum because breakfast could not come together without a song.

Min sang "Polka Dots and Moonbeams" with such feeling it made up for all of the missed notes. "*Now in a cottage filled with lilacs and laughter. I know the meaning of the words ever after. And I'll always see polka dots and moonbeams. When I kiss my pug-nosed dream.*"

Gussie liked to recall the day she first heard that song.

After graduating from Rhode Island College, she had filled a post at Moses Brown, the Quaker school. In her apartment that August, the mercury climbed to 103 while one oscillating fan took on a job for a 5,000-Btu air conditioner. Too hot to think, let alone read, she had laid her book aside and reached for the envelope on the table to fan herself. She reread the Women's Auxiliary Mission's invitation given to her by a student's mother, which promised "a break from the heat and plenty to eat" that day. Later, as Willadeene Rutherford, proud Tennessee transplant, ushered her through the air-conditioned foyer straight to the patio, it was hard to hide her disappointment.

"Miss Hewett, I want you to know I don't blame you the teensiest bit for giving up my Robert Calvin to that remedial program. The head of the school himself explained it to me. It just seems to me they should've let R.C. finish the year out. But what

do I know? Now don't you be shy, Miss Hewett. Go on. You'll
fit right in. Sure hope you'll want to join the church and WAM
one of these days. If you need anything, tap on the kitchen window and I'll run out," the happy hostess said, leaving her in the
middle of the garden. Gussie had dabbed at the corners of her
forehead with a handkerchief, listening as a woman came to Willadeene's defense.

"You know with Willadeene everything has to be *just so*. She
wants to keep the house nice and fresh for Reverend Porter. I
imagine we'll be allowed back inside once he arrives," she said
to a gaggle of women standing between the hollyhock and New
England Aster.

Nearby, Min stood with both hands fastened on the strap of
the 35mm range finder suspended from her neck. Gussie walked
over.

"Willadeene called the *Journal* and insisted someone come
out. Made such a fuss over Reverend Porter funding the new
day care at the church," Min explained. In dungarees and a crisp
white oxford shirt, she was the only woman there not dressed to
impress.

"At least you're getting paid to be here."

Twenty minutes later Gussie tried to unpuzzle why it felt she
had known Min all of her life. "I taught Willadeene's son, R.C. I
didn't want to disappoint her by not showing up," she said. Min
looked dubious so she drew in closer and twisted her mouth to
the side and whispered, "I don't have air-conditioning. And I
hate to cook."

"The truth shall set you free," Min replied, offering a sly
smile and, after they'd eaten plenty, a ride home.

The scent of violas had wafted into Min's light-green Po-
lara as they coasted along Memorial Boulevard, Gussie tapping
her feet against the car floor to Tommy Dorsey's band, Sinatra
crooning "Polka Dots and Moonbeams."

"What a storybook evening," Gussie began, leaning her head out the window. "I betcha the temperature hasn't dropped on account of all these stars. I mean it's nothing out here but stars; the sky's just full of them!"

All except the two in your eyes, Min wanted to say, but then she thought, *Too much, too soon.*

Min pulled along the curb trying to figure out how to start a friendship. "I don't know if you're planning to take a vacation this summer, but I'm heading west—through the Black Hills, on down to Colorado, winding up in the Sierra Nevada," she said, pleased at how free and easy the plans for her dream vacation had come together on the spot. She patted the dash of the Dodge. "She's brand new, and I've always wanted to shoot Yosemite"—a truth she had never said aloud before.

"When you plan on leaving?"

"July. I figure August'll be too crowded. What do you think?"

"July'll be just as crowded," Gussie said, turning to face her new friend. "Why don't you give me your number so we can plan this trip the right way."

Min topped off Gussie's mug at the table filled with rye toast stacked high, gooseberry jam, turkey bacon fried perfectly flat and crisp, scrambled eggs, and sliced cantaloupe. "We are officially off of real eggs. May I introduce you to Egg Beaters," she quipped.

Gussie waved a hand, as if shooing a fly. "Problem with the stand-your-ground shit is the children don't have any ground to stand 'cause they're *children*! They should lower the voting age and the gun permit age. Level the ground! Adults running 'round with guns, picking off these black boys with impunity. Trayvon Benjamin Martin. Need I say more?"

Min flashed on a terse exchange she'd had with a reporter at the newspaper. *Be sure you include his middle name,* she'd said to the guy who was writing about a black boy killed by cop a little south of Providence, in Bristol. *A middle name reminds people of all the thought a parent put into naming a child.*

"And now Jordan Russell Davis—for playing his music too loud. The day after Thanksgiving. Jesus."

"Burns my ass," Min said.

"They ought to level that ground down in Florida. Let the boys vote and carry a gun, die like a citizen, not some dog in the street. It's like Daddy used to say, we didn't invent the world or its trouble, but we gotta keep on living or die trying."

"My daddy didn't put it quite that way. Whenever there was talk around Fox Point about somebody being wronged on account of their color or accent, he'd say to me, '*Minha flor*, you just remember you are as high above them as cake is over shit.'"

A hard knock on the kitchen door made Gussie jump.

"You expecting somebody?" Min asked, standing up from the table.

Gussie shook her head no.

Min looked out the window over the sink, wondering why on earth Willadeene Rutherford's son was standing on her back porch wearing nothing but a cardigan on such a cold day. "It's R.C.—with miles of smiles."

Gussie choked a little, clenching the front of her housecoat.

The man just didn't look right. Still, that was no reason to mistreat a soul or forget your manners. "Morning, R.C.," Min said, trying to fix his shifting eyes with her own steady gaze.

The young man grunted something. Whether it was a *Good morning* or whatever hip greeting the young folks used these days, she didn't know. But she heard his question clear as a bell: "Can I shovel your walk for twenty dollars?"

"No thank you. We planned on doing it today ourselves. We need the exercise. Besides, you're not dressed properly, R.C. You'll catch pneumonia like that."

"Don't worry about me, Miss Min. I'm what they call hot-blooded. Hotheaded too. Least that's what they said at the last group home I was at. Won't take me long. You and Miss Gussie don't have no business out here in this mess. It's real icy. Hate for Miss Gussie or you to break your hip. Mama broke hers two winters ago and she still ain't right."

"Well, okay then. You shovel the drive and the sidewalk out front."

"You don't listen, Minrose," Gussie began no sooner than the door closed. "I told you I'd do the shoveling."

"That was before I looked out there. You don't have sense enough in that hen head of yours not to go outta here on a day the devil himself wouldn't walk around. You courting a hospital stay? R.C.'s right about that hip business."

"What about my dream?"

"Gussie, it was a dream, darling. Just a dream."

"And you think it's fine to give him beer money, or money for that stuff?"

"Even a fool makes sense some of the time. He had a point about the ice." Min looked out the window. She could see the open door of the toolshed. Where was R.C.? She left the kitchen for the living room. None of the windows gave sight of him, so she stepped out on the front porch. No R.C.

A few days later, when the snow nearly reached their knees and neither the snowblower nor the shovel could be found, Willa-deene Rutherford paid Gussie and Min a visit.

"I envy you and Minrose. At least it's two of you. That sure do make things a lot easier. I have to struggle to make ends meet all by myself." She fumbled with the clasp on her black patent-leather pocketbook. "I sure wish I could do more. It's aw-fully hard without a husband—being on a fixed income and all."

Gussie tugged at the envelope clenched between Willadeene's fat fingers, thinking the foolish woman's ends would meet just fine if her son stopped robbing the neighborhood. She could feel Min leaning against her back, fighting to quell her laughter. They had stood in the exact same pose a year ago at the side of Herbert Rutherford's gilded casket lined with scarlet crushed velvet.

After the passing of Willadeene's husband, Gussie and Min had paid her a visit only to find the woman did not have time. She cut them off at the door when the Bell Funeral Home van pulled into her driveway. Motioning for Gussie and Min to step aside, she'd instructed the three young men charged with the delivery of the casket to put it on the picnic table in the backyard.

"Herbert was too good a man to go down in the earth in just anything," Willadeene had explained to her neighbors. "Now, you all have to excuse me. I must go and pick up a special order of gold paint."

Over the next several days, between writing and rewriting the eulogy, ordering the flowers, selecting the perfect hymn, and placing the announcement of Herbert Rutherford's "Home-going Celebration" in the *Providence Journal*, Willadeene Rutherford primed, painted, and appliquéd plastic gems on the once plain coffin. Gussie and Min would stand tippy-toe on their back porch, craning their necks to see over the silvery Andorra shrubs as the busy widow transformed her backyard into Designer Coffins "R" Us.

Now Willadeene dabbed at her brow. "Fifty dollars is all I can spare."

"Thank you," Min replied over Gussie's shoulder.

As soon as Willadeene had departed, Gussie remarked, "Guess you're satisfied. You gave a wino permission to go into our toolshed and pawn the snowblower."

On an errands spree the week before Christmas, Min and Gussie huddled close with Maudetha Blake as she recounted a scene in the parking lot of Whole Foods.

"Last summer I was having a good time at WaterFire—just standing there watching the street performers, getting excited by the craft and food vendors, and who did I happen to see riding by on my grandson's ten speed? I tell you, R.C.'s nothing but the devil. Nothing but."

Min reminded Maudetha of her high blood pressure, but Gussie commiserated: "Let him keep on stealing from folks. It's bound to come back on him. You mark my words. Can't do wrong but for so long before the sin finds you out."

Maudetha admired Min's fur coat, told her she just looked "delicious" in it. Gussie rolled her eyes because she hated what was coming. Min didn't know how to give a simple thanks for a compliment. On the way to the car, Gussie said, "Maudetha didn't ask you how old you are. Anybody who stands still long enough and you have to blurt out, *I'll be seventy-four in such-and-such days.* You ought not to carry on so, as if getting old is something to be proud of. Any fool can do it."

"I wouldn't be so sure . . . with these police going off half-cocked," Min said.

The late-December moon waxed full at half past eleven several nights later and Gussie couldn't sleep. She blamed the insomnia on Min's cooking—the evening's fish cakes and tasty *jag* called to her.

She was carrying the cod cakes into the den when Min entered the kitchen and picked up the large bowl of grapes she'd left uncovered on the counter, a vain attempt to encourage her partner to snack healthfully. When Gussie brought her first forkful to her mouth, Min reached over her and snatched away the Tupperware dish.

"Shiiiit! You like an old sneaky cat, woman," Gussie hissed, accepting the bowl of grapes Min handed to her.

"Scoot over. I can't sleep. And I'd appreciate it if you'd find a decent picture for us to watch. None of that Jimmy Fallon or other foolishness."

They were settling into the worn sofa and *All About Eve* when a knock thundered on the wooden frame of the door, startling Gussie. Min looked at her and wondered if this was the woman she would know for the rest of their lives—so nervous, so jumpy all the time.

"Who makes a social call at this time of night?" Min said.

Under the porch light stood R.C. Rutherford. Min didn't know what to say.

"I know it's late. I been away. Just come back to town. My own mama don't know I'm back yet. I feel mighty bad about what I did to you and Miss Gussie."

"Min?" Gussie called out in a frail voice.

"Yes?"

"Who is it?"

"R.C." Min stared into his eyes in search of truth, and thought she saw some.

"Now, I know what you thinking, Miss Min. You wondering why you should listen to a thief."

Gussie entered the kitchen and listened from behind the door.

"You don't have to tell me, I know I've split my britches with everybody on Larch Street—wait a minute. Here, I brought you something." He dug into the pocket of his jacket and pulled out a crumpled envelope. "Please take it. I want you to buy a new snowblower." The hand clutching the envelope trembled a little; with his other hand, he reached out and grabbed the handle of a shovel propped against the house. "Wish I could get you one of those snowblowers you ride around on."

"Thank you, R.C. This'll go with the money Willadeene gave us too. Now you take that shovel and put it back where you got it from. Now let me close this door before we both catch pneumonia."

A look of disappointment flashed on R.C.'s face. Min knew he wanted her to invite him in, but he launched into the story anyway, right there on the porch in the dead of winter. He was twenty-seven and for the first time in his life he had a good plan. The waitress at the IHOP on Pleasant Valley Parkway, where he'd stopped for country fried steak, told him it was a good plan so he knew it had to be. He didn't need his mama's home or a halfway house. He would go to clown school and entertain children. But first he had to get the money together.

Min told him, "Good luck," edging the door closed.

"It's gonna be harder than I thought, huh, Miss Min?"

"You know bad news, R.C.—ain't no speed it won't drive. Travels fast. And good news barely moves at all. Get yourself together and know it's going to take a little time before folks trust you again."

"I'm real sorry about what I done. Please tell Miss Gussie I said so. I'm gonna find a way to make it up to you."

"Well don't think too hard on it tonight, R.C. Go on home."

When they finally climbed into bed at two in the morning, Gussie turned on public radio and got excited by the voice that came out. "There he is. My, it's been a long time since we heard him."

"Bobby Blue Bland," Min said. "That album *Dreamer* . . . what was the song you used to wear out? Named after some woman, I think. Yvette?"

"Yolanda! Driving around Charleston in a bright red cadillac. She took his money and left him crying."

Min started to sing, "*Oh Yolanda, why you forsake me? Why you just lay, lay, lay my body down? Oh Yolanda, why did you leave me? In this wilderness with no money down.*"

"You remember that summer we drove to the Shenandoah Valley and just happened to catch Mr. Bland at that dive in Staunton?"

"You said that was the best barbecue you ever tasted in your life."

"It was."

"You drank too much beer."

"I did."

"Sat with you in the car with your head in my lap for a couple of hours before you could drive us back to the hotel."

"Yeah, so, what does this story prove except you love me? Tell me something I don't know."

Gussie slept fitfully. When the shot went off and R.C. fell to the floor, she shook awake and opened her eyes to Min's steady breathing. The room was still dark but she sensed sunrise was not far off. She pulled the quilt up higher when she heard a loud thud. On her way to the kitchen, Gussie stopped at the basement door. She could hear someone singing "Silent Night."

The door swung open and Gussie stumbled and braced herself, stunned to see R.C. standing there in her hallway, smelling like a saloon, snot eddying in the gulch just below his nose, just as it had been every day she taught him the first quarter of fourth grade.

"I was just coming to get you and Miss Min up. I've searched everywhere that I would think to hide something valuable and can't find anything worth a damn. So I figured I just better get you two up and ask you."

Gussie thought about the storm doors outside that led down to their basement and how she and Min never locked them. This probably wasn't the first time he had been inside their home.

"R.C., what in the world is going on here?"

"We not in your class anymore, Miss Gussie. You go sit in the kitchen. I'm gonna get Miss Min up. We gonna talk about this the way I wanted to when I came a few hours ago."

Gussie was unmoved until R.C. pulled from his pocket the little six-shooter that had belonged to Min's father.

"I found this in one of the boxes. I don't plan to use it but it comes in handy for scaring folks. Now you go on in the kitchen and sit down."

"What has your life come to, R.C.?" Min said, appearing out of the shadows.

R.C. scratched his head and tugged at his left earlobe, gestures Gussie remembered from when he was unable to answer questions in class. He pushed both women into the kitchen, flipped on the light, and ordered them to sit down at the table. Under his baleful gaze Gussie felt her heart jackknife in her chest as her bladder released.

"What do you want, R.C.?" Min's voice was flat and disgusted.

Gussie groaned as two urine rivulets became one at the cleft between her pressed-together knees.

R.C. looked at Gussie's hands shaking on the table and Min's still as a frozen pond. "You all used to have rings—I remember that—just like you was man and wife. Where they at?" He smirked and wiped his runny nose with the back of his hand.

Min saw the rings in her mind's eye, white gold with baguette-cut sapphire inlay, in a little black velvet bag in the third drawer of the jewelry box, where they'd kept them when both of their knuckles had swollen too large to wear them.

With a captive audience, R.C. launched into his plan to become Rhode Island's top clown, and his need for money. He asked about the rings a second time—calm, almost friendly—but neither woman said anything until he waved the pistol in the air.

Gussie began to cry.

"You won't give me no money so I need those rings—for clown school, I've already told you. You think the Boy Scouts of Providence would ever hire me? You know, to entertain the troops? I never did earn any badges for my mama. Planned to but didn't. Never did bring home no As either. Matter of fact, after your class, Miss Gussie, my report cards didn't have no letters on them at all. Checks. Just checks. No letters. That's why I always said you was my favorite. Between me, y'all, and the gatepost, I don't think you have to be too sharp to put checks on a piece of paper. I still got the report card Miss Gussie gave me, framed, hanging on the wall. Four Ds . . . an F in math . . . and a C in physical education. I think they let me into the Scouts on account of that C in gym. I think I took a shine to you, Miss Gussie, right then. Sky-blue eyes, big, wide smile, tall as a sycamore tree. Made it awfully hard when I got up in age and people started saying funny things about you and Miss Min. Even though I wasn't yet tall, I wasn't ashamed to stand up for you. I told them just 'cause you was kinda built like a fella didn't mean you made believe like you was one in the bed with Miss Min. Problem was, the boy I mouthed off to was a whole bunch bigger than me. He asked me if I was calling him a liar. I told him if the shoes fit he didn't have to buy them but he had to walk around the store in them. After I got my behind beat for you—all shades of blue—I asked my mama if what folks said about you and Miss Min was true. *I imagine it is*, she said. How my own mama imagined something like that was beyond me. Men got pricks and ladies got cooters and that's just the way it goes. Who ever heard of two cooters— didn't make no sense. Still don't. One or both of you is gonna have to get right with God. Anyway, the way I see it, Miss Gussie chased my luck from bad to good with that report card, which is probably how I ended up in the Scouts. No other club took me before then or since. And all I'm saying now is that I need for her to do that for me again—be my luck, Miss Gussie."

Gussie vaguely recalled that R.C. had been on medication when she taught him. She thought he must be on something now too. "If it's money for medication, I'm sure your mother would help you."

"Oh, I've got a special card for the drugs they want me to take. But I don't never take them—" He fished around the inside of his jacket pocket, pulled out a small folded card, and tossed it on the table. Gussie could make out a blue anchor but the writing was too tiny to read. "'Cause the pills give me runs."

"Clown school?" Min said, merely to say something. And she regretted it.

"At least give me one of the rings," he said, growing agitated.

Gussie sobbed that she couldn't do that.

"Alright then." R.C. stood up and walked over to the kitchen door, grumbling.

He opened the door, complained that it was too damn hot, and what kind of heater did they have anyway? He pulled a long wool scarf off the hook and tied Gussie's hands behind her back, looping the ends of it through the bars of the chair, a tight, sophisticated knot learned in the Scouts. When Min protested, he paused long enough to point to the gun tucked, temporarily, between his bare belly and his jeans.

"Funny how a thought will come to you, don't matter where you at or what you're doing," he said, settling back down at the table with the gun before him like a plate of food. "You know what I was thinking about when I climbed into your basement? You 'member that talent show we had at the church? Miss Gussie, you had on a pretty white dress with a red carnation pinned up high. Pretty enough to frame. I couldn't believe you was my teacher. Now, Miss Min, I didn't know what to make of you—dressed up in a man's suit—but I thought those red and white wing-tipped shoes was real sharp. Sharp as two tacks. 'The Jitterbug Waltz'—that's the song you two danced to. Maybe if you sing it for me, Miss Min, I'll think about untying Miss Gussie so she can go get me one of those rings."

Usually Min's voice was an above-average soprano. Now, with a nervous stomach, she couldn't breath right, and it sounded like a falsetto. A poor one at that. *"The night is getting on, the band is getting slow, the crowd is almost gone, but here we are still dancing . . ."*

R.C. jumped up and spun around, belting out: *"Nothing to do but waltz!"* He laughed, then turned sour, his words curling like the fingers of a fist. "Sounded better back in the nineties. What year was it, Miss Gussie?"

"Can't say I remember exactly, R.C."

"Miss Min, then."

"Nineteen ninety-eight, R.C. Nineteen ninety-eight."

"Well, make like it's 1998, Miss Min. Put your proper singing voice on."

It turned out R.C. had talent for something besides mischief. His tenor was clear as crystal, unwavering like the man Min had stood next to in the church choir. *"I'm tired and out of juice and yet from head to toe, my body's feeling loose and warm and kind of supple . . . Nothing to do but waltz . . .* Naw, that don't sound right. I skipped a verse or two, didn't I, Miss Min?"

"I'm tired of playing this game now, R.C. I'm not going to speak to you again until you untie her."

"Min, please," Gussie whispered.

Min could see that her partner was petrified, the proof of which had gathered around the heels of her new slippers in a neon-yellow pool. "R.C.! You untie Gussie right this instant!" Then she reached across the table and grabbed the gun.

R.C. gave Gussie's chair a mighty kick, sending her down to the floor in a crash.

The narrator pauses here—'cause Min would want it—to say that no one should ever come to know what it feels like when the shadow of many years of togetherness descends and you're looking dead at the person shutting off the light.

Gussie's tears couldn't be stopped; she trembled horribly watching her wife dial 911 with a steady hand.

"This is Minrose Andrade at 28 Larch Street. I've just shot Robert Calvin Rutherford . . ."

PART II

WHAT CHEER

ONCE, AT TRINITY REP

BY ELIZABETH STROUT

Trinity Repertory Company

There it stands, on the corner of Washington Street, the pride of Providence. Trinity Rep has been in that old building for almost fifty years. Before that, the theater was used for vaudeville shows. I am an old lady, and my father used to speak of them; and I think that for a long time almost everyone who entered the place seemed to feel the history of past performances, the excitement of the unknown. Even with the beginning of Trinity Rep, how it did so well with the old chestnuts, or new unknown pieces, or the annual rendition of *A Christmas Carol*, the theater itself offered what theatergoers wanted: a promise of emotion. But after what happened, happened, it took people awhile to get back that feeling enough to abandon their guard, I think, and just enjoy the show. Season ticket subscriptions were down for years. And I've noticed, though no one mentions it anymore, that they have never staged an Ibsen play since, and this is no small thing in the life of a regional theater.

Let me say this: the lead in *A Doll's House* was a darling girl. That is how she was described later, by her mother: "A darling girl, with a heart of gold." The poor mother was a mere sixteen years older than her daughter Lena, and Lena was an only child, so they were more like sisters. A number of people who knew them agreed with this. I knew them myself, and I agree with it too; they were as close as twins. Whatever living arrangements Trinity had made for Lena Lochsheldrake fell through at the last minute, and the directors approached me, knowing my rooming house—later I would call it a bed-and-breakfast—had few guests; people know things in a small town, which Providence is.

So Lena Lochsheldrake and her mother stayed with me; they'd sit at my breakfast table for hours—they both loved to talk—and I would leave something in the refrigerator for Lena when she came in late at night, and I served her breakfast any time she wanted, and made snacks for her to take to the theater.

"Oh, thank you," she always said, her brown eyes sparkling. "Thank you. Look at this, Mother, what she's done"—holding out the custard, wrapped in foil. "Oh, you're just the *best.*"

Lena did not have those perfect teeth you see on all the young people today; her teeth were slightly indented and crooked, and this was very endearing somehow, her smile. And yet I often could not help but see those teeth and think of the word *rabid.* I assume because they were pointed and made me think of a fox. But she was a darling girl, really, just as her mother said.

Lena had been born Hope Mayhew. Her mother sent out birth announcements saying: *Hope Has Arrived.* They loved telling me this story; they loved any story about themselves. Once they asked if I'd been close to my own mother, and I said my mother had died when I was young. This was true, and enough truth as needed, so when their faces clouded and they said they were sorry, I looked away and they asked me nothing more. I'd not have told them anyway. I had learned long ago that no one wants to hear the story of an ambulance in a driveway when a child gets home from school—of a mother's furious screeches that she only wanted to die, had been acted upon. It is the darkest story in the world.

But these two! Chattering like birds, fluffing their feathers. Of each other they could not get enough, and I learned how the young girl took the name "Lena" because she thought it was stagelike, and later Lochsheldrake because she'd been born in upstate New York not far from the town with that name. Lena

Lochsheldrake. That's who she was, in theater programs and on posters and spelled out with lights on the marquee. But her friends, the ones from the cast who came to see her in my home, always slightly shy and always polite, referred to her as Lena Lock.

According to the papers and police reports, Lena had hundreds of friends all over the country. This was before the days of Facebook, which would have undoubtedly added thousands more, but still, each friend had to be accounted for, and this took a great deal of time. One newspaper was not so friendly after a bit, and clearly had some connection in the investigator's office, because reports began to appear that Lena Lock had *quite* a reputation, particularly with older men. This caused her mother Carina to be even more distressed, if such a thing was possible, and I'd have taken care of Carina had she not chosen to return home after the first few days, after the police released all the business in their rooms at my B&B—the clothes and jewelry and letters and stuffed animals, which Lena always took with her on the road. A man named Luther arrived, and Carina, poor stunned thing, climbed into his car with Lena's belongings and drove away. I missed them terribly. I was stunned myself. Well, the whole town was.

It turned out that Carina Mayhew could not stay away from television, going on any station that would have her, saying her daughter was a darling girl with a heart of gold, and that in such a business as show business, a pretty, darling girl had admirers of all ages. Nothing could possibly account for the tragedy done to her, and it *was* done to her—this part the poor woman cried out again and again from the television studios. And after a while, Carina Mayhew got a famous woman lawyer who began to appear on these shows with her, saying that a blame-the-victim mentality had plagued women for years; that everyone should be ashamed. Ashamed. That lawyer was frightening looking, like an eagle with a wig of dark hair. Of course this lawyer was looking for libel suits and money, and poor Carina eventually became someone who people in town here lost interest in sooner rather than later. This is New England, after all, and incontinence is not a virtue. But I have not forgotten Carina. I have not forgotten Lena. Not for one day.

And the men—*they* could not forget so easily! I could see that. Certainly not the men who had seen Lena perform, not the men who had staged the show, not the men who had paid her rent in the past, or paid for trips to Europe with her mother (they called my home in such distress, these men, telling me things I should not know, did not want to know, but they could not forget her). And not the men, either, who had seen her walking down the street while she was in town, or in the restaurants, or at the stage door at night signing programs; and not the man who helped her with a costume change backstage and was the last to have had a "real" conversation with her before she returned to the spotlight in her sweet little dress and character shoes, and touched her rather flat chest in front of a full house and collapsed. The costume changer's name was Kip and his proximity caused him to be the first suspect. Photographs of this young man sobbing on the front page of the morning newspapers didn't help with his public image. (Speaking of incontinence.) And he was gay. There were, don't *not* believe this for a minute, people in neighborhoods of Providence who thought that a gay man in the theater was as likely a culprit as anyone else; after all, weren't there reports that some of these individuals had anonymous sex in public places, particularly at the YMCA? Oh, lives in town were destroyed before this whole thing was over. If anything is ever over. You decide that one.

But back up and picture this: Fantastic reviews when the show opened. Lena's face all over town on posters and on television—such a lovely interview she gave the local TV station, saying she did not think of her character Laura as a feminist, she thought of her as a woman deeply in love with her husband; in other words, Lena charmingly gave answers no one expected. She did have this "thing"—that could not be denied.

The "thing" was not traditional star power. It was sweeter than that sort of blazing charisma. She was, as her poor mother said, darling. She was adorable. She was disarming. Her active, pretty face held genuine expressions as she spoke of her past, how she had been Miss Cornflower at the age of three, how she had been Miss Baton Champion at the age of five, how she had been the mascot to the football's marching band at Buffalo State when she was seven—all accompanied by snapshots moving across the television screen of this darling little girl raising that tiny leg with the tasseled boot. Some people you can't stop looking at, and you don't know why. This was the case with Lena.

It was raining the night of the incident, as nature would have it. Pouring from the heavens in sheets. And yet the house was full. People checked their umbrellas and coats with the sopping wet shoulders, or else folded those coats under their seats, though there was barely room. The place smelled a bit like boiled wool and wet dogs—I hate that smell.

The lights went down, the stage lights came up on the rather traditional set. But they did not have a curtain for the show, it was at a time when curtains were going out of fashion; that attempt to keep the audience in the dark, so to speak, was going out of fashion; the idea was to make things more intimate with the audience, not to leave them out of the make-believe. Or so Lena said. You would have thought she was the first person to have heard of any of this—she got a little high on her horse when she spoke to me about it—and I did not tell her that these changes had been going on for decades before her. But young people are like that, and her mother was like that too, only worse, because she knew less. The only thing Carina knew was what her daughter needed: the face lotion, how much to eat, how much to sleep, how to put hemorrhoid cream below her eyes after a night of drinking. Close as two peas in a pod, that's how they were.

Carina was at the show that night too. She almost always went, so she and Lena could talk the next day, or maybe well into the night, about every line, every audience reaction; they loved it all, I will say. I don't know that I'd have had the energy, had I been a mother, though undeniably Lena was more needy than most daughters would be. I thought about it sometimes, how could I not, their infectious love and excitement right there in my house.

Do you have children? Lena had early on turned and asked me one night, her brown eyes round and warm and curious. I told her I did not, and she said she was sorry. No need to be sorry, I said. Life hands you what it hands you, and in that department it handed me an empty plate. They exchanged a fleeting glance then, mother and daughter, and it was hard to be seen as I felt they saw me, a barren woman with a thickening waist serving people oatmeal every morning. And then Carina couldn't help herself and asked if I had been married, and they got the story out of me, my twenty-year marriage, all the miscarriages, my husband endlessly kind and then distant and off with a woman half his age—I became a statistic; you never expect to, but you become a statistic, and yes, before Lena and Carina could ask, I said yes, yes, he had his children now. It's a story to scare any woman, I know that. And they laughed and said, oh, men are so awful, just awful, they only want one thing, and I began to think these two were not my . . . caliber. Well, I had known that all along. But I had to take an extra sleeping pill that night, one of the many I got in Mexico on a vacation there, since there is no need for anyone in this talking town to know the B&B proprietor needs nerve assistance some nights. I could hear them whispering late, on and on, and perhaps it was egotistical of me, but it was my life I felt they were discussing with that energy. On and on it went.

So that rainy night Carina was in the audience with a friend she had made here in town, a woman who brought the muffins to my house when I had more than a few guests; Carina had struck up a silly, girlish friendship with her, and there they sat in their complimentary house seats, dead center. Carina turned and waved at me. Her eyes were brown like her daughter's, and in some ways her face was a more conventionally pretty face, but she did not have that "thing" that Lena had.

When the show began and Lena appeared, there was a hearty applause at the mere sight of her; that is how much she was already loved in this town and on this stage. She did a nice freezing thing, the way they must teach actors when this happens, to just stop herself—in character of course—and then sail into her line. I had not seen her perform before, though she had offered me tickets on opening night two weeks earlier. I had turned her down then with a vague excuse, but really I had no one to go with, and as much as I was mesmerized—oh, that is too strong a word—by this pair in my house, I had not wanted to sit next to Carina, knowing that I would have to breathe toward her and receive from her a cloying adoration regarding her girl. I should not have worried; I did adore seeing the show. I watched far more attentively than I had imagined I would, and I sat next to the one woman in town I can claim as a friend, though much of the time she tires me, this friend—a school librarian who had also found herself alone in midlife. She was wearing a scent that night I had not noticed on her before; it gently came through the smell of dampness all around.

At intermission my friend wanted a glass of wine, or rather a plastic cup of wine, and I stood with her in the lobby and introduced her to the sparkling-eyed Carina who was filled with liveliness at the success of the whole show, and most especially of course with the success of her daughter. I believe I drank from a bottle of water I bought when my friend got her wine. And then a drowsiness came over me, as though I had had the wine, and not my friend, but it was distinct and peculiar, to feel so apart from the bustle of everyone else as they took their seats for the final act.

Lena, as Laura, told her stage husband she was leaving, and off she went, and then she returned in her thin dress, holding her coat, her dainty feet in their shoes, and I watched as she began to sway, putting her hand to her rather flat chest, and her words became incoherent, and for a few seconds, or minutes, I sim-ply can't tell, looking back, I think we all thought it was part of her performance. I think it was Carina who caught on first that something was wrong, for in my memory she stood, and started to move past all the people in their seats; and by the time Lena was slumped over, just motionless, Carina was already calling out, "Get a doctor, get a doctor!"

I suspect I am not alone in saying that I have never been in a theater when such a thing has happened, and there was great confusion, onstage as well as in the house; and because there was no curtain we saw the agitation of her fellow actors building, with great speed, as they were pulled out of their characters and began to call out for help. Lena stayed completely motionless, she had fallen in such a way that her head hit the stage and her hair somehow flew from its pins. Oh, it was unnerving. Unnerving.

No one, I believe, expected the worst, although Carina later said on one of her television interviews that she had known right away. The rest of the audience, according to those who spoke to reporters later, thought she had collapsed from exhaustion or a sudden illness, or even, though it seemed unlikely, a terrible and savage onset of stage fright.

There was chaos, naturally there would be. And it must have been the stage manager who finally got people organized and asked them to leave in an orderly fashion. There was an understudy—Lena had never thought much of her—but there was no talk of the show going on, so I learned that shows do not always go on. I went back to my house straight away, thinking that would be the place to help the most in whatever capacity I could, but Lena and her mother did not make any appearance, and in the morning I learned that poor Lena had died, right there onstage. There would be an autopsy, perhaps a sudden blood clot or aneurism, of course nobody knew, and when Carina finally appeared back at my B&B she was drugged to the gills and in the company of the muffin maker who had stayed all night with her at the hospital. And the waiting began. Endless cups of tea for Carina and the muffin maker, and for a friend of Carina's who arrived from upstate, and then the police—oh, they tramped through the house and were terribly officious; it was all dreamlike. It still is, really, a lot of the time, for me.

Finally the preliminary reports of drugs, of poison perhaps, but no, not that after all, back to drugs, and Carina just went wild because there was talk immediately, I suppose as there would be, of suicide. Almost as much as the death itself, this suggestion threw poor Carina into higher fits of hysteria. No. No. No. Lena loved life. She loved her life, her mother's life, the life of her friends, and her men friends, *no no no no*. To be truthful, I was not sorry to see Carina go when that fellow Luther finally showed up.

Again: the show did not go on. The rest of the run was cancelled. The town was thunderstruck.

And then eventually, sooner than you would think, the town became un-thunderstruck and routine took over once again. Even for me, routine took over once again. I had guests calling, reserving, but always in paltry numbers—I am only ever full when it's graduation time. Not until everything went on the Internet did I see feedback from guests who had stayed here, and many of these postings, "reviews" they are called, were mean. So mean. Adequate service, but the proprietor does not bring a cheerful atmosphere to the place, et cetera. Well, I have no heart for it anymore.

I wait. I still wait.

And I still, in the middle of the night, look through what somehow the police never found, and poor Carina never knew she'd left behind: one of the scrapbooks they always had with them when they traveled, showing clipping after clipping of this little brown-eyed girl winning Miss Cornflower, Best Baton Twirler, beauty pageant winner, mascot for the Buffalo football team. All of it is recorded here, in this scrapbook with the tape yellowed, the clippings yellowed, and in almost every clipping there is Carina, the mother, clapping her hands, smiling radiantly, both of them—sun.

THE AUTOBIOGRAPHICAL HOUSE

BY AMITY GAIGE

College Hill

I moved into the Armory District in the springtime of my fourth year of college. A handwritten sign on the door of a beat-up china-blue historic home on Dexter Street: *Attic/One Bedroom*. At the time, the area was full of dropouts like me—storied young people, generously tattooed. I like to think it had a tang of Berlin to it, circa 1990—I mean the contradictions, especially between Broadway and Westminster: RISD types mixed with Dominican muscle men mixed with gay professionals, with a couple defiant elderly people lording over each block. It reminded me a little of old Woonsocket, a place I no longer felt I could return to. For the several months before Dad and Ma discovered I'd left Brown, I walked the district, content to be alone. What I loved best was the building itself—the Armory—a castle-like structure running an entire block of Cranston Street, bookended by two crenellated turrets. In the daylight its bricks were tacky yellow, but in the nighttime the Armory building filled up the West End with its medieval shadow, and remained, since it had been in disrepair for decades, unlit; you could almost hear the dripping of pipes in the great hall. Nobody came in or out.

I had been happy once or twice, and these moments were also associated with large buildings.

1999: The Metropolitan Opera House. Mémé in a stole. I was ten. "Champagne for me," Mémé had whispered to the barman in her Woonsocket French accent, "and champagne for the child." I did not watch the ballet; I watched the hall itself, five fan-shaped levels studded with gold lights, red velvet everywhere, a thousand rapt faces and no one looking back at me. The air was smoky with rapture. As the starburst chandeliers rose up on their pulleys I knew they would rise up in my dreams for years afterward. Was it the champagne? I don't think so. Later, when I was inside other big buildings, not nearly as pretty as that, I felt a similar weightlessness, a deep, wheezy, excited freedom, tinged with the illicit. I am a watcher. I don't like to *be* watched. Mémé would put her two fingers to her eyes, then move those fingers to my own. *I know you.* Later, this identification made me quite uncomfortable.

How I got from Woonsocket High to College Hill is a short story. I worked like the devil is how I did it. I studied until bedtime and set the alarm for four a.m. and got up and studied again. Every once in a while the gatekeepers at Brown would admit a Rhode Island native for good measure, and one year in the early aughts, that native was me. Mom and Dad shelled out for a party at Amvets, and all of Woonsocket came. Brown hadn't taken a single kid from Woonsocket since Frannie Archambeault in 1994. A great party except for when Ma raised a shaky glass to Mémé, and Dad had to shoo her into the powder room, both of them drunk on muscatel. Of course, come September, I was glad to be gone.

They didn't know what to make of me at Brown. Ma had taken me shopping for clothes but our approximation of what a Brown student would wear turned out to be pretty badly off the mark. I showed up with half a dozen cardigans from Apex, but they didn't suit my low-class haircut nor cover my jaw-dropping chest, which was, to be honest, an attribute my family discussed openly, because it presented many problems, some of them just logistical, like how to get a seat belt over it or how to buy a jacket for it, and some problems historical, because my Mémé had exactly the same legendary bust size, and consensus was that it had ruined her life. I had worked so hard to be a good girl. In high school, I'd worn the Woonsocket version of a burka—shapeless tunics over cotton leggings, everything a couple sizes too big. It was within me, always in my mind, that I should work extra hard against whatever it was Mémé recognized in me.

Professor K—— was my freshman advisor. Dad and Ma were happy about Professor K—— because he was a famous architectural scholar (they read this on the website), and ever since I was a kid I'd said I wanted to be an architect. In photographs, he looked like a cross between Albert Camus and a *Dukes of Hazzard*–era Tom Wopat. He was forty-two at the time I came under his influence, walking straight up to his desk with my hand out, like Dad had instructed me, my notebook pressed against my chest. I might as well have said, *Here I am, the dope you have been waiting for, an absolute fool*. His smile, after a pause, was warm and youthful. He was a very warm man when you first met him, and naturally, he had a brilliant mind. He had written a seminal text on Walter Gropius; I'd read it closely, at age sixteen, and upon hearing this he signed me up for his popular lecture course, The Autobiographical House.

He was Viennese. When he first referred to himself with the term, I didn't know what it meant. I thought maybe it meant he was from Venice, but he sounded like a German. Why not just call yourself an Austrian? But this was the first of many such moments at Brown. Words in English that were not in my vocabulary. Everyday allusions more difficult to parse than anything out of *The Wasteland*. Every time I pretended to understand was a minor betrayal of myself, and all the people of Woonsocket, but it never once occurred to me to ask anyone to clarify. Looking back now, there was a lot of buried anger, layer under layer, but I did not feel any anger at all until I left school and moved to the Armory. And then I felt a lot, quite a lot.

Anyone but me would have seen it coming. Any girl who'd read the right Thomas Hardy novels or attended private school or owned a passport would have read the signs. Not me. Once, he even grabbed my wrist as I tried to leave Sayles Hall after The Autobiographical House, whispering, "Stay." Another time, during one of our meetings, he'd langorously opened a coffee-table book of Franz von Bayros's erotic paintings and asked me what I thought of them. ("Technically proficient.") Yet I persisted in seeing ours as a collegial relationship. I struggled quite a bit, however, once he finally got me down on the floor. There was strenuous physical resistance and clear use of triggering words. So it was a violent coupling—the only pause originating in his awestruck expression upon penetration—and after that, well, I never struggled again. We had both experienced revelations: his, that I was a virgin, and mine, that my personal sovereignty was completely irrelevant. The situation dragged on, and on, and on—three years—a month off here and there, one semester of liberation (Austrian sabbatical), all of it a marathon of denial. As a junior, I suffered through one excruciating semester as his TA in Vienna: City of Dreams, during which I developed a case of eczema so profound that I felt I was cursed. Who'd cursed me—his wife? God? I never had any sexual pleasure. He was always rough and loveless. I told no one, and did not pursue other boys. Back in Woonsocket for holidays, I took my place around that noisy table, drawing a blank when anyone asked how school was going.

"She's too modest," Ma said, dragging on her cigarette. "So smart they made her an assistant to the *teacher*."

Faces flipped toward me like dominoes: eyes, nostrils, mouth—five holes.

I tipped back my glass of muscatel.

"Jake, Jake," my aunt said to my cousin, waving, "tell the story of how you got arrested at Brown."

"Not arrested—"

"He was on a *job*," my aunt said. "A couple weeks ago. A raccoon or something got into a crawl space so they called us. Some chick called the campus police and said an unidentified white male was trying to dig his way into the building. Unidentified white male!"

"That's me," said Jake. "Unidentified."

"Fucking eggheads."

I believe that I know what a *relationship* is. I know that it implies two people with individual wills meeting one another in some kind of mutually-agreed-upon psychic territory, and in the material world, at certain places and times, i.e., "Let's meet at two o'clock at the Coffee Exchange." I even understand that a relationship can encompass moments of sacrifice and duty and even unhappiness and still be mutual. But then there are relationships that mimic relationships, and even if you are one of the parties involved, you have no clue that you are not, in fact, in a relationship. You are in a kind of excruciatingly convincing performance.

It was not until my junior year, when, pausing outside a plate-glass window on Thames Street in Newport, I experienced a moment of clarity on this point. I stood in an oversized raincoat, my hair in the kind of childish kinks it develops in humidity, and a man came up behind me and stood there breathing over my shoulder. I thought we were both looking at our reflection, the two of us. A calliope hooted eerily from somewhere in the fog-bound bay. By then, I was skinny and pale and miserable and so self-hating as to be radioactive, and I thought, *I am so terribly unhappy. I am going to have to kill myself. I am going to have to kill myself if I don't get out of this.*

Professor K—— put one aged hand on my shoulder. "I will buy it for you," he said. I blinked. *What?* He gestured at the charm bracelet that now appeared to me on the other side of my reflection. "I will buy it for you on one condition," he said. "I will tell you when we get back to the hotel room." I nodded, though I had not been listening, and he disappeared inside the store.

In the chronology of things, I do not believe that what he did to me in the hotel room in Newport had any sort of bearing on subsequent events. It hurt me, and I bled. But I was from Woonsocket. I'd blinded myself throughout my life there, but suddenly I realized that all the violence was inside me anyway, a branching map of transgressions, crimes, betrayals. The community was full of the passions of any semi-isolated cultural subgroup on the economic downslope. We were full of rage. We were trying to kill one another as a form of relief. I remember what my own father had said of Mémé the morning after we returned from the ballet those years ago. "She got you drunk? She got you *drunk?*" He ripped open the front curtains, as if she'd still be standing on the porch hours later. "Where is she? I'm going to kill her. I'm going to do to her what she did to Claude. That crazy fucking Nipmuc."

A shame, really. Uncle Sam was wasting forty-two grand on my senior year. Palid, unwashed, I stalked the edges of that aristocratic campus, moving around largely at night. I was a ghoul. I clung to the low wall that ran along Charlesfield, I watched normal boys hee-hawing through the windows of the social dorms (*that's* how you wear a cardigan), I watched attractive semiotics majors smoking Gauloises. And then I just left. Left my things in my room and rented my place on Dexter Street which remained, for years, almost completely unfurnished.

I met Edgar in the park near the Armory. He owned an ugly dog back then, something he'd rescued, and the mutt dragged himself around Dexter Field with the other dogs at the end of the workday. I was sitting on the swing set—no real kids ever used it—and watched the beauty with which Edgar threw the mutt a stick. He was a tall, broad man with a very neat trim of dark hair, the tattoo of a tentacle or a vine reaching out from under his collar and up the side of his neck. He flapped his Carhartt coat open and closed when he talked with the others. He was very expressive, and the cluster of people laughed whenever he joined them. He looked like any other twenty-something day laborer, but later, from the shadows across the street, I saw him step out of his house in tight black pants and a fierce trench with a fur collar, swinging an actual cane around his arm and singing—loud—some kind of bachata; he was probably the most attractive man I'd ever seen.

He was the sort of man who had deep, destroying affairs, and I loved hearing about them, my head against his chest, and after a while we both started to suspect that the best part of the affairs was talking about them afterward, together, under the oblique streetlight, on the mattress, in the dark—with the *stories*, the violence, the kisses, the breaking glass, the running, the crying, the begging. I was not at all surprised when he told me what his uncle did to him as a boy. I think I knew this the first moment I saw him in his Carhartt and work boots making people laugh in the park. Ours was a deep fidelity and a complete exception to our otherwise brutalizing relationships—his, in their number, mine, in their absence. Because I loved him, I hated his pederast of an uncle. One day I told him that I wanted to find his uncle and do to him what my Mémé had done to her long-ago lover Claude. I told him what I would do with the knife.

"Ah," he sighed, "my darling. You can't. Somebody already had the pleasure, when he was in prison for something else."

I imagined this, and felt relieved that the man was gone from the world, but also disappointed.

"Too bad," I said. "Don't you wish you could have watched?"

It did not take us long to get around to Professor K——, and

for me to pour out the sad story I had never uttered to anyone. After that, all we had to do was formulate the terms of restitution. Edgar really had nothing—less than nothing—to lose. As for me, I'd been paralyzed for nearly four years, estranged from my family, my architectural dreams reduced to breaking into the Armory to sit in its great, leaking hall. I was an expert on this building—I could have told you where the structure needed maintenance and where the steel trusses would first collapse— but I knew nobody would ever ask me what I thought about this or anything else.

We caught up with him in the late afternoon of an astonishing autumn. He was leaving his office, and I was right to assume his attachment to a regular schedule would be unchanged four years later. He was, naturally, on his way home to dinner with his wife. Edgar came up and slipped his arm companionably through the professor's, and I did the same. Professor K—— was tall, but Edgar was taller, and had about fifty pounds on him. Edgar smiled winningly as I'd seen him do so many times, so many people in awe of him physically, and him just having the time of his life, knowing it all leads to death—even pleasure. The professor's expression, of course, was one of confusion. We walked together, arm in arm, like chums. The professor looked from Edgar to me, and back to Edgar, then me.

"How are you?" I asked him.

"He's great," said Edgar.

"He'd have to be, on a day like this," I said, whistling. "What a stunner."

"What are you doing?" the professor whispered.

"Yes siree, he's feeling great," Edgar continued. "He's blessed with so much. A high-class job. Summers off. A loving wife."

Professor K——'s expression clouded. He pulled back on our arms, but of course we did not give him any slack.

"Our car is just over there," I said. "Don't worry. It's not far."

"He doesn't think it's far," said Edgar. "He's happy to walk. On a day like this. He knows how lucky he is. And look at his shoes. Comfortable. European."

"Viennese," I said.

"He doesn't look Vietnamese," said Edgar.

"Oh poo," I said.

"You *cannot*," said the professor. "You can*not*—"

Edgar opened the door to his Charger, arm still hooked through Professor K——'s, whose mouth was opening and closing in disbelief.

"We can't?" Edgar smiled at me tenderly. "What was Obama's slogan, honey?"

I smiled at Edgar. We were going to heal ourselves. "*Yes we can.*"

Plans had been laid and abandoned for the Armory building numerous times. Given up by the National Guard due to upkeep, it functioned, for a time, as a soundstage for a couple Hollywood movies. In 2004, a proposed bond issue to finance renovation was placed on the ballot; it did not pass. Standing inside of it, feeling the dank, perpetually wet air, one realizes that it will never be renovated because there is something *wrong* about it, something dark and un-American. It brings to mind torture. It reminds me in design of the Stasi building in Stuttgart, a building on which I'd written a paper for—who else?—Professor K——.

Had he ever been inside before? I asked him, when we were settled.

He did not answer me. He was sitting on a folding chair with his hands clasped together, looking at his shoes. He hadn't said anything in a while, and looked a little pathetic, so small in that grand space, storage containers stacked to the windows on either side, with only a camp light to see by in the falling light. Edgar approached and stood behind him. I winced, but all he did was cup the professor's neck lightly with one hand. He bent down and whispered, "Are you all right?"

Professor K—— laughed shortly. "No," he said. "No, I am not."

"Okay, okay." Edgar began to rub his shoulders. "It's okay."

Edgar looked at me and smiled sympathetically. I alone knew what this smile meant. It meant it was time to go forward, to live. Before I knew it, he'd led the professor over to an old industrial desk—some remnant from the National Guard—and softly instructed him to grab onto it.

Did I want to watch? No.

I just wanted to listen.

There were no words at all, of course, only the shuffling of feet, the friction of clothing, the occasional sound of Edgar's murmur, and a cry or two—the professor—something like the cry of a person stumbling upon an unspeakable vision. Watching the last of the sun fade through the western windows, I thought about what the professor had really taught me: he'd taught me that the body was a *design*. A brilliant design, a very tidy machine, a collaboration of limbs and joints, all working together to get itself down the street, or to raise a glass to its lips, or to crouch in a corner and hide. No need to get too emotional about it or march around campuses and in general take things too much to heart. A belt buckle clattered to the floor. The desk juddered as it was pushed a little further. The professor cried out again, a warble of pain. I wondered how Edgar and I would speak of this later, on the mattress, under the streetlight.

We drove the professor back to College Hill. Up onto Benefit Street, left at the Athaneaum, arriving at the back gates of the main quad, where graduates egress with diplomas each May. He sat in the back, not saying a word.

When we pulled in front of the professor's building on George Street, Edgar turned and put his hand over the seat bench.

"Which one's your car, honey?" he asked Professor K———.

Professor K——— stayed silent.

"Hey," Edgar said, swatting his leg.

The professor jumped. He looked at me. "I don't understand this," he said, and started to cry.

"I know you don't," I said. "I know you don't."

"Which one is your car?" growled Edgar.

The professor looked around. He started shivering. "That one," he said.

"Good," said Edgar, leaning over the backseat and opening the professor's door for him. "See you next week."

"What?" said the professor.

"We'd like to see you again," said Edgar. "Does next week work for you?"

"Again?"

I turned around. George Street was behind us, leading gently uphill to the heart of the campus, a bower of aged trees, a vision of New England worthiness.

I said, "If you don't show up here again this same time next week, I will tell your wife what you did to me, and I will tell the chair of your department what you did to me."

Professor K——— looked at me without recognition.

"He understands," said Edgar. "He understands the terms. After all, he's a very smart man. He's an expert. He's a professor."

Not unfrequently, in these relationships-that-are-not-relationships, there can be very graceful victims. That is, people who can smile and appear happy and even grateful, even when there's a meta-phorical gun to their ribs. I used to think these people were all women. But recently I have come to think, no, men can do it too, men can be graceful victims, and it has made me feel more warmly toward them, actually. Every time Edgar and I pick up Professor K———, I feel a rush of sympathy for him, the way he stands with one hand cinching his coat together against the cold, or when he troubles to bring an umbrella, and as we pull up in front of his office on George Street, he looks off into the treetops, almost politely, as if he is writing poetry in his head, as if things are going precisely as he planned.

FEMUR

BY HESTER KAPLAN

Butler Hospital

Gordon, down on his knees in the dirt and muck, wind shrieking at his neck, the pose of disgrace. His father would definitely approve—his only child ordered to the Siberian task of clearing the slope of its brambles. There was zero point to it; no one ever stepped foot here. Behind him, past the leafless trees where men cruised men in the camouflaged months, was the Seekonk River, a smudgy gray this November afternoon, and the jaws of the railroad bridge frozen in a wide gape. In front of him, on the far side of the parking lot, was the psychiatric hospital. That was what he was supposed to call it, but to him it would always be the loony bin. He looked to the upper floors but saw no one behind the dark, captive panes.

Maybe none of the windows actually opened, not a terrible thing since it meant that his sketches on the cafeteria panes with a black marker would stick around for a while. Two weeks ago he'd drawn a man with a noose around his neck, a girl jamming her fingers down her throat, another guy screwing a sheep that ended up looking more like a poodle. Late at night, the cafeteria had been closed and black inside until the flashlight of a security guard had pinned him to the glass and made shadows shiver and dart inside. Gordon's friends, who'd come to watch him, had gone for their bikes and sped away, while he couldn't figure out why he wasn't fleeing too. The guard, a young Dominican guy, recognized his last name.

"Yeah, my father's a shrink here," Gordon had admitted. He

was vaguely insulted that the guard didn't find him threatening, worth calling for backup. He would always be too small, too delicate looking, like his father.

The guard swept his flashlight over the drawings. The ink had a phosphorescent quality; the figures throbbed. "Shit. Really? Doing this where your old man works? That's harsh."

"He's an asshole," Gordon had said.

The guard laughed and put up his hands. "Hey, that's between you and him. Not my business."

Gordon's punishment had been worked out privately between his father and Mr. Baranek—Fat John, head of facilities management. No police, no charges, just forty hours of outdoor clearing, cleaning, the worst shit work, penance in the cold dreamed up by the two colluding men. Only sixteen more hours to go. They could make him do it, but they couldn't make him feel guilty or even regretful, and he held on to his crime like it was his last supper.

He gathered a fistful of hard red berries from the bramble. If they happened to be poisonous, he could coat them with chocolate and serve them to his father, one each day, a gradual sickening, a drawn-out misery. When he threw them over his shoulder instead, he lost his footing, slid backward down the slope, grabbing for anything that would stop him. His tailbone skimmed a rock and nausea ticked through his body. He was almost at the bottom by then and the river's edge; he stood uncertainly to watch the rowers and listen to the lonely slurp of their lifting oars. Maybe, if he was very lucky, he'd see Ellen, his father's last girlfriend, out rowing on the water again—but he also knew that was impossible. She'd left Providence three months ago, though he didn't know where she'd gone or why; today she'd be only a mirage of his missing her.

He wasn't going to climb back up the same way he'd come down, so he walked far along the dimming bank of the river to where the woods came down to the shore and blocked his path. The rowers had all gone in by then, and high above him the loony bin glowed over the tangled trees. He clawed his way through the chaotic density, ankles torn by thorns, his hands on fire, freezing, and sorry now that he hadn't taken the gloves Fat John had told him he was going to need, sorry now that he mostly knew what was right but he always did the wrong thing anyway, sorry that he'd been kicked out of two schools, that his mother didn't like him enough to live on this continent or talk to him, that even Ellen was gone, gone, gone. Oh, he missed her; he didn't understand why she'd left him too. He was crying, being a seventeen-year-old pussy, he scolded himself, but he couldn't help it. Everything hurt. Sometimes—sometimes, he felt like nothing more than someone's careless exhale. He jammed his hands into the earth to stop his idiot tears.

His fingers found warmer purchase, something faintly textured, almost silky, and he dug further, still sniffling at his sorry-ass self, and pulled out a bone. His eyes stuttered and he dropped it. The thing was about eighteen inches long, knobbed at both ends, a silvery, porous white. This was no chicken bone, no bird bone—but maybe a dog bone, or a coyote's? The loony bin campus was full of them, he'd been warned, animals that howled through the grounds performing their nightly soundtrack. He catalogued the possibilities to quiet his mind, but he knew this was a human bone. Not because he knew what it was called or which part of the body it came from, but because it lay there with the certainty of something wicked and secretive. He considered taking a picture of it for his friends, but he was too spooked. The whole place creeped him out enough already—and always had.

He picked up the bone with his sweatshirt and made his way back to the grounds. In the long shed of the maintenance building, Fat John was at his desk, his chair surrounded by soft flesh, as if the furniture had sunk into his quicksand body and not the other way around. A few of the maintenance guys were getting ready to go home, banging lockers, swinging lunchboxes, calling Gordon *mijo* and smacking him too hard on the back.

Fat John smirked at him, the pink lower lids of his eyes pulled down by the weight of his florid cheeks. "Ah, the little artist returns," he said, "the little felon. What's up?"

"I have to show you something," Gordon said breathlessly when the others had finally cleared out. He unswaddled the bone on the desk and took a step back. His pulse thundered in his ears.

Fat John shot up and the bone fell to the floor. "Jesus Christ. Where the hell did you find this?" The man's face had gone gray-white.

"On the slope," Gordon said, and added, to bolster his minor untruth: "Where you sent me to clear those brambles."

"On the slope," the man repeated.

"Weird, right?" Salt flooded Gordon's mouth. He wondered why he hadn't just left the bone where he'd found it. "Do you think maybe someone was murdered?"

Fat John didn't respond but wheezed as he bent over to hastily reswaddle the bone. He threw it in a locker, which he secured with a padlock.

"Hey, what about my sweatshirt?" Gordon said.

"Forget your fucking sweatshirt. And forget this." Fat John gripped the padlock and wouldn't look at Gordon. "It's a deer bone. We've found them before. Now go home."

"Are you serious? I think it could be human."

"Do I seem like I'm joking? Get the hell out of here and keep your mouth shut."

The man was usually playful, always in a slightly menacing way, but now something rank rose off him, the contagious musk of fucking up, of being afraid. Gordon was both assured and alarmed by how familiar the smell was; it was his own too often. He felt robbed of some information he wasn't sure he really wanted to know in the first place. He was sorry he'd found the bone at all because he wouldn't be able to forget about it now, especially after Fat John's evasion, his mind drawn to everything that was trouble and troubling.

And his sweatshirt was a total loss—he wasn't going to get *that* back. He biked home through the hospital's vast and winding campus designed by someone famous and dreamy—a man who'd ended up in a loony bin himself, he'd heard—past heavy strokes of black winter green and low, badly lit brick buildings, the wood houses with their frenzied details like torn nightgowns, the clapboard barn, the stone walls like a million knuckles. He'd known kids who had ended up here for a stay, parents too, teachers. Every neighborhood should have a nuthouse down the street, like a 7-Eleven, for emergencies. If he were ever put in here, he knew that all he'd want would be to sleep for a long time, for days or maybe years. He'd give in to giving up for a bit. He'd force his mind to be a room where the windows didn't open. He swerved around a dead squirrel fallen from a wire, its tail bristling in the wind.

Out on Blackstone Boulevard amid the roaring buses, and then up the hill to his house, his lungs froze with the cold, but his ears burned with Fat John's weird warning. As usual, his father wasn't home, but there was a supermarket roast chicken in the fridge for his dinner (the second time that week), a note reminding him to work on his college applications and to feed the half-dead dog his mother had left them a decade ago. He didn't like the pooch with its dirty white fur and its trails of pink tears. He ate cereal from the box, sipped some of his father's scotch, did not touch the chicken in its plastic coffin, or his homework, or his applications, his father's delusion of his future fanned out on the dining room table. He fell asleep on the couch.

* * *

He woke to his father standing over him. "You were supposed to walk the dog earlier. She defecated in the kitchen." He handed Gordon the dejected animal on the leash.

"Defecated? Do you mean *shit*, by any chance?"

His father blinked wearily. His face was lined but stony. "I spoke with Baranek earlier. He says you aren't doing what he tells you to do, says you fool around. Is this true?"

"What? That's so not true." Fucking Baranek, a fink, definitely not on his side. Gordon had an instant flash of Fat John raking leaves in the backyard into piles the wind kept blowing apart, his father watching, nodding. Master and servant. He shook it out of his head, a strange misfiring of his memory.

"Gordon, listen to me. I am—we are—cutting you a break here." His father was still in his suit, though he'd taken off his tie. He radiated a disheartening stink: something cheap and sweet, like soap from a gas station bathroom. His eyes were womanish, long-lashed and a deep, cold blue. "It's important you hold up your end of the deal you made."

"I didn't make the deal," Gordon said. "You made the deal, remember? You and Fat John. I'm doing everything I'm told. And anyway, why are you checking up on me?"

"Checking in, not checking up. Baranek claims you went where you weren't supposed to be this afternoon."

Gordon stood and nudged the dog with his foot. He hesitated. "Is this about the bone?" He felt its textured life against his fingertips again.

His father's expression shuttled between neutrality and accusation. "I don't know anything about a bone. This is about you."

Gordon opened the front door and let the cold air stampede in. "I stopped by the river to watch the rowers for a minute, okay? I wanted to see if Ellen was out on the water." He hoped to hear his father's breath catch at her name, like a hangnail on his heart, but there was nothing.

"But you knew that wasn't going to happen," his father said, his expression blank.

"How would I know? How would I know anything?"

And maybe I did know, but I still *wanted*, Gordon told himself, and slammed the door behind him. Didn't his father understand what longing was about, that it was not always about something real? From the sidewalk, he saw his father's bedroom light go on, saw the man's fastidious closing of the curtains. He didn't know how patients or even the idiot Baranek could stand the man; his mother clearly couldn't. Ellen couldn't either, finally. No woman could. But his father kept souvenirs from the one's he'd screwed, as though this was all he could keep of them; Gordon had found their panties, some with tiny bows or hearts, neatly rolled like pastel cigars and lined up behind his father's socks. He was ashamed to have evidence of his father's hidden desires and small crimes.

He dragged the dog around the neighborhood. Didn't his father worry about him getting jumped at this hour? He passed the house where a wife had supposedly shot and killed her husband years before, though she never went to prison. The bushes creaked in front, the dog tiptoed and whined as though it knew to hurry past. Gordon recalled the sound of the rowers' oars moving in and out of the water earlier, the sound of Ellen's dipping oars on the days she'd taken him down to the river so he could watch her train. He'd been happy then, squinting at the sun sliding along her boat. Sleek-haired, athletic Ellen with her spandex rowing outfits and long legs. One day she was there in the house, teasing Gordon and letting him fall in love with her, letting her bare arm fall across his shoulders, letting him relax into her affection, a consolation for his motherless self for the first time, and the next she and her almond milk were gone. His father had offered no explanation. Ellen had left his father—that made sense, because who wouldn't?—but she'd left Gordon as well, and that he would never understand. With her around, he'd thought he might actually survive.

Once, after he'd watched her race, she'd explained that her power came from her thighs, and she let him touch the muscles that bound her femur. *The longest bone in the human body,* she'd said, *perfectly constructed, my secret weapon.* The bone he'd found that afternoon: a femur. He knew it now. He shivered at the confluence of bones. Ahead of him a tunnel of black branches hung over the street, and he picked up the sad dog and ran.

In the morning, his father kissed the top of his head and asked, "Scrambled or fried?"

The sun was a false beam of light in the kitchen; his father, as usual, was not the man he'd been the night before. Gordon hated this daily confusion, but allowed himself for those brief morning moments to love his father just a bit, even though it was a weakness, even though it was a waste. He couldn't help himself; he would die if there were no one at all he could love. By evening, though, the man would be an asshole all over again. Sleep washed his mind clean, but the day's patients, the fuck-up son, the runaway wife and deserting girlfriend, would dirty it once more.

"Fried, please," Gordon said. Every morning he made the tentative decision to be his father's son once more.

They talked about Gordon's day ahead, conversation as seemingly benign as a baked potato. His father slid the eggs out of the pan onto Gordon's plate and then brought last night's untouched chicken to the table. He surgically sliced the meat from the breast without ever nicking the bone, peeled off the skin and draped it on his plate. The wishbone was a mysterious bracket waiting to be filled. Runny yolk clogged Gordon's throat and he couldn't swallow.

His father looked over at him, grease winking on his upper lip. "Everything okay?" There was something different about the man this morning, his knife poised in the air stilled with fierce intent. "Something you want to talk about?"

Gordon shook his head.

"You do know Ellen doesn't live in Providence anymore, right?"

Gordon's voice was strangled. He nodded. He thought he might be sick, the food beginning to rise. It was likely last night's scotch revisiting.

"Good. Because last night you mentioned looking for her on the river, so I wanted to make sure."

His father's words hung over the table, a caution to not confuse desire with reality, because where would that lead you except straight to the loony bin? Gordon knew his father was examining him, but he couldn't look back. He made a show about not being late for school, and as he left the room he had the chilling sense that his father knew everything about where Ellen had gone, and that he, Gordon, should know nothing, ask nothing, think nothing. Forget everything. But there it all was—the woman gone, his father still there, the unexplained. And the femur he couldn't stop thinking about. It knocked against his head, his chest. Yes, he was sure his father knew all about the bone. But *what* about it?

After school, he rode across the highway, through downtown, and over to the boulevard. A bike lane had been put in the previous spring, but he still rode provocatively down the center of the street, comforted by the train of irritated drivers stacking up behind him. Let them wait, be late, be pissed. When he went to the maintenance building for his work assignment, a few of the regular guys were standing outside—not by choice, it appeared, given their glares and how they slapped the cold off their biceps. Fat John was waiting for him, his soccer-ball face pulsing with rage.

"You got me into a shitload of trouble with your father last night," Fat John said, slamming a clipboard against Gordon's chest. "He ripped me a new one. Called me late and I was asleep. Do I need this? No, I do not need your father on my case."

"What the hell did I do?" Gordon asked. His chest stung from where it had been whapped, but he'd grown a skin so thick he wondered if anything could ever really penetrate him anymore.

"Didn't I tell you to keep your mouth shut about that god-damn bone?" Fat John said.

"I just asked him—"

"I was looking out for you before, but I'm done now. I have one piece of advice for you: don't ask questions and do what you're told." When the man's weight plummeted to the chair, he seemed, for a moment, defeated.

"That's two pieces of advice," Gordon mumbled.

He was sure that for once, just once, he hadn't done anything wrong—or not very much wrong, in any case—but the indictment was simpler and bigger than that: *he* was wrong. And clearly everyone knew it. He imagined his unattached heart out bobbing on the Seekonk River's surface, tepidly hopeful air keeping it afloat for a minute before it sank, the people in the loony bin watching the drowning without emotion. Fuck them. He looked at the clipboard. His assignment for the day was to pick up the goose shit on the side of the main entry road. There were always geese hanging out there, convincing the people arriving that they were entering serenity. Convincing people leaving that life was a scene out of a children's book.

"You're kidding, right?" Gordon said. "I clean it up and the geese just come back and do it again? Is there a point?"

When Fat John didn't look up, Gordon gathered the wheel-barrow, a shovel, and an empty garbage can and made his way down the long drive. He parked his equipment on the swooping land by the side of the road. At first glance, there didn't seem to be much goose shit, but the more he looked, the more there was, until it seemed that the stiff grass was dotted with a billion frozen pellets. Five geese eyed him warily.

Soon, his gloveless hands throbbed from shoveling, and his knuckles cracked and ached from the cold. He leaned on the shovel to watch cars entering and leaving. The security guard who had caught him the night of the graffiti slowed his prissy electric car as he passed, and then spoke into a cell phone. Gordon gave him the finger, and didn't go back to work. He felt conspired against, watched from every branch by his father's agents. When he stopped to zip his windbreaker against a sudden dampness, he spotted a group of patients his age leaving the low building set back in the trees. They followed a man, straggling alone or in pairs, toward the main building. He knew they'd given in, these kids, they'd given up, and he winced in envy. For some, their thinking was out of their control, and that was okay too. *That* was real bravery, not this fake bravado of his, his smart-ass-ness.

A girl who had been at the back of the group veered off into the deeper pines unnoticed. She crouched low, then ducked behind trees while the others continued on. When she emerged onto the side of the road, she looked right toward the boulevard and her escape. As if she were unsure what she wanted now that she saw her way out, she peered ahead, maybe hoping to see the bucolic geese and some comforting meaning in the ancient stone walls, maybe to take a deep breath and decide what to do next. She saw Gordon instead. He was shocked to find that they knew each other, not by name, but from the hallways at school. She was perfect, pretty but gaunt now in the dim afternoon light, untouchable by boys like him, and if she recognized him, she wasn't going to show it. By the way she wiped her implacable eyes with her sleeve, it was as if she'd seen no one at all and nothing but the troubled and frightening minutes ahead. She pivoted and hurried back through the trees to join the frayed end of the group again.

He wanted to tell her that he knew how confusion some-times felt like the deepest sorrow—and hadn't she been aban-doned too?—but the words *my father* and *femur* agitated in his mouth like prisoners clawing to get out and tell their version of the truth. Behind him, the hissing geese advanced, urging him to find her, and he grabbed the shovel, crossed the road, and slipped into the tensely hushed grounds. It was almost dark by then and he'd lost the last glimpse of her red coat. He crept through the rose garden, all thorns and stubs in the cold. The grounds were a maze, each building he passed named for someone—Sawyer, Kane, Lippitt—whose life had been saved or destroyed here. It amazed him to realize that he didn't know which building his father worked in, and that instead he'd pictured him in all of them, the harsh fluorescent lights in the hallways and rooms his own private and blameless guidance.

Gordon had stayed away from the cafeteria since the graffiti episode, not sure if he wanted to see his drawings gone or still there, but now he crouched below the large windows that faced the woods. It was blaringly light on the other side of the spotless glass and he knew he couldn't be seen. Inside, a few people ate at tables, while the woman at the register slept with her mouth open. Light rain made a whisking sound against his windbreaker and the cold rose up from beneath his sneakers. When he blew on his hands to keep them warm, he smelled blood on his knuckles. He smelled macaroni and cheese and the unmistakable muck of fish sticks from the exhaust fan. He hadn't remembered until then how he'd eaten dinner there with his father in the months just af-ter his mother had fled—hadn't remembered even as he'd drawn such distress on the windows weeks earlier. He hadn't thought about the metal tracks you pushed your tray along, a kind of consoling roller coaster for a seven-year-old. One night, looking back at the table where his father sat moving food around on his plate, Gordon had seen the man's deadened expression, and it had entered his body and never left him. It was the same expression he'd seen when he asked his father about Ellen—why she'd left, where she'd gone—and had gotten no answer. His father was not grieving then—or now, Gordon suddenly understood with a sickening recall of the warmth he'd felt in the femur—but was the source of all grief itself.

He left the cafeteria window and ran to the back of the farthest building, tumbling down the slope where he'd cleared the brambles. At the bottom, he retraced his steps along the river's bank to the woods where he'd found the bone. He'd left the earth exposed the day before, but even in the near dark he could see that someone had filled in the bone's shallow grave and scattered leaves to hide it. He aimed the shovel at the dirt, turning over clods and rocks and roots, the smell of wet nature like his father's breath hanging over him. Pearlescent blisters appeared on his palms. There was a condom shed like snakeskin, and a piece of torn cotton, rusty with dirt, one edge puckered with elastic. He could pretend once more that he didn't know exactly what he was seeing, but he knew. He stopped digging; he didn't want to find anything else. When he reached the parking lot and the last building, he saw a body move behind a window, maybe the girl. Maybe she'd been watching him, waiting for him.

It was dark when he approached the maintenance shed. Despite the cold, the front door was open and Fat John was bent in the light, sweeping the floor in a rhythm of subjugation, just as he'd been raking leaves in Gordon's backyard years before.

"You weren't over by the main road where you were supposed to be." His father had come up behind Gordon, and clapped a hand on his shoulder.

The shock made his legs go watery. In the doorway, Fat John had stopped sweeping.

"Yes, I was." Gordon's hand tightened on the shovel. He didn't turn around.

"No, that's not true. I was just there looking for you."

"Then you didn't look hard enough. Why don't you ask the security guy you sent to check on me? He'll tell you I was there." He walked away from his father to the side of the building, and with his mouth now almost pressed against the brick siding, he realized he was trapped, hemmed in by equipment and his father.

"You're cold," his father said. "You're shivering. You should wear a coat. You're too old for me to have to remind you about these things."

"I found the bone."

"What bone, sweetheart? I still don't know what you're talking about."

"Yes, you do." His heart pounded monstrously. "What happened to Ellen?"

"Happened? Why do you think something *happened* to her? Let's go inside. I'm worried about you."

"The bone. Ellen's bone. You know all about it."

When he turned to face his father, it seemed that they both realized at the same instant that Gordon was now the taller and stronger one.

"I'm not going crazy," Gordon said. "I'm not going crazy."

"No, you're just confused. And sad. I understand, it's okay. You'll be okay." His voice was so soft Gordon wasn't sure he hadn't imagined those words.

"You killed her," Gordon said. "You know it and Fat John knows it and I know it. You killed Ellen."

His father inhaled sharply. "Stop it, Gordon. Stop it now."

"Then where did she go?" he demanded. "She left *you*, she didn't leave me." He lifted the shovel above his head, forcing his father to walk backward toward the trees. His father said his name, and his gaze slid for a second to the white-black sky and the rain. Gordon wanted to walk his father all the way to the river, but he also wanted to lean against his chest and blubber. His hands burned at the shovel's handle. They'd both been left, deserted and unloved by women, but they were nothing alike. His father was telling him to stop, to put the shovel down.

Something yanked Gordon from behind and, with effortless power, threw him onto the ground several feet away. His head smacked the dirt and he bit his tongue.

"What are you doing?" His father charged Fat John, a small body against a bigger one. "What the hell is wrong with you, Baranek?"

Fat John appeared stunned by his own action, a dumb animal trained to save his master. Both men looked down at Gordon. His head felt split open and he wanted to sleep there on the cold ground, but he got to his feet and ran. He could save himself, even though he was stumbling, bumping into things, his father calling after him.

Every building he tried was locked, but the back door to the cafeteria was propped open with a can of tomatoes. He slipped inside, the sound of the rain fading behind him. To the few people at the tables, he probably looked no different from the friends or relatives they were there to visit—confused, sick, grieving, terrified, sad. Maybe there was nothing strange to anyone sitting there about a wet, shivering boy who'd bitten his tongue, who was wandering through, then wandering out, shuffling up and down stairs, trying every door. Gordon knew that if he were asked who or what he was looking for, he might say *femur*, but he might also say *father, mother, girl,* or even *future.*

MISSING SRI

BY MARIE MYUNG-OK LEE

Brown University

"Sussannah!"

The sun glinted off the awnings on Thayer Street, temporarily blinding her. Bead Store, hookah bar, Urban Outfitters, movie theater—practically a movie set of a college town.

Brent was running from across the street. He was a big goof, did things like call her Soo-JZAH-nah after he noticed that's how her Korean immigrant parents pronounced it (and probably why they accidentally put an extra *s* in *Sussannah* when filling out the birth certificate). But right now he looked dead serious.

Brent had to pause, hands on his knees, and catch his breath next to a sign that said, *Congratulations Brown seniors! We have mango bubble tea!!!!* "It's Sri . . ." he panted.

Sri? Her heart jumped. "Is he okay? Did something happen?"

"He's missing."

"Missing . . ." She paused. Sri was always missing. As recently as Friday night, in fact. His best one so far. They'd all gone to a campus party. Only he'd left without telling anyone, sidled into the Rock—dead drunk—right before closing, curled himself like a chipmunk into a carrel, and somehow slept undetected by library security until morning. In the meantime, they couldn't find him, panicked, called Brown security, fanned out looking for him all night, yelling his name—they'd done everything but dredged the shore off India Point Park. "Don't you have any consideration for others' feelings?" she'd screamed at him when they found him (adorably, she had to admit) disheveled, stumbling into the bright sunlight of day out of the world's ugliest college library. "I got bored," he had replied, as if that were a perfectly reasonable explanation. "I ran out of pot, and I couldn't find any of you, so I left."

Sussannah disliked poseurs who used their so-called artistic proclivities and vices as a lazy excuse to forego basic social niceties, but Sri really was moody, mysterious, easily absorbed and distracted, exactly the kind of person who might follow a butterfly for miles, miss lunch and dinner, just to see where it would end up. (That, and he was also a pothead.)

"Text someone next time," she'd said, as if that would help. Sri hated technology and was convinced cell phones cooked your insides like microwaves. So even if he had his phone, he'd never turn it on. Not helpful. But very Sri.

So she wasn't panicked now. Not yet.

"I had dinner with him at the Ratty yesterday"—and she had actually seen him later than that, but not in a context she wanted to mention.

"April said she didn't hear him come in last night."

"*April*," Sussannah groaned. "Great." April, the old lurker of Environmental House.

Sussannah and her best friend Marla had ended up at Environmental House only because they'd gone into the junior housing lottery together and were awarded the worst—*the worst*—numbers probably in the history of the lottery. This meant the old janitor's closet in Pembroke or something. Then Marla, who had a campus job in admissions, was tipped off from her friend who worked in housing that Brown was opening up a new residence: Environmental House. A refurbished Victorian that had once been the Slavic Studies office. It would mean a real bedroom in a real house. Some shared housework, but they could still be on the meal plan *and* cook if they wanted to avoid "Jambalaya Nite" at the Ratty (there was a reason students since the 1800s referred to the Refectory as the RatFactory, Ratty for short). So attractive an option that they talked Sri and Brent into joining them in the coed house. The only problem was none of them were particularly environmental. But no one asked them to swear on a Bible that they would devote their lives to Greenpeace ("I don't club seals," Sri affirmed), and they got in.

At "home," they felt no need to fake it. Their housemate Sam was an environmental studies concentrator and an aspiring documentary filmmaker (working on something about how gas drilling in Wyoming was poisoning local aquifers), and this meant he was almost never home. The other housemate was April. April was practically an ecoterrorist. Forget absentmindedly tossing a Chobani container in the garbage and not in the recycling bin (Marla) or trying to slip nonorganic blueberries into the compost (Sussannah) or using paper towels (Sri). April, when she wasn't yelling at them, was stomping out the door with this or that MassPIRG clean-water petition on her clipboard; her VW Golf was held together by rust and bumper stickers: *Save the Whales*, *Greenpeace*, *Coexist*, and the *Don't Tread on Me* flag that the Tea Partiers were now using for their illogical statementing (was there something ironic Sussannah was missing?).

April was also in her thirties (they guessed), a Resumed Undergraduate Education student. During Sussannah's first year, budding journalist that she was, she had done an article on RUE students and therefore knew the biggest majority were former professional ballet dancers who'd needed those years to dance. There was also an Amish guy who'd decided to become un-Amish (there was some name for doing that, which she couldn't recall), an Iraq vet who'd become a super-pacifist Buddhist. But it was a tiny, self-selecting program and you had to have a compelling reason why you delayed your education. All the RUEs she'd interviewed lived off campus, being kind of beyond the dorm thing, especially the Amish guy who had three kids and also worked at the Job Lot. But what April's deal was and why as a thirtyish (most of the RUEs were still twentyish) adult she was living in a house with undergrads were questions that no one wanted to ask. The best they'd ever gotten was, "I got into Brown because I have a terminal disease." Were they supposed to politely laugh? Was this more irony or what?

"April said *you* came in at 4:53 this morn, Soo-JZAH-nah, you hussy."

"Yes, I was bedding the *Brown Daily Herald*," she said quickly, a bit breathlessly, even though it was true. "Um, that's accurate but übercreepy—does April sit at the door with a little clicker or something?" April was mysterious like Sri, but in an erratic way that felt ominous to Sussannah.

"So you saw Sri at dinner, but then he didn't come in last night—"

"It's barely lunchtime," she said. "I really think he's okay." Saying it was so was going to make it so, right? The gears in her head were whirring. There was "missing," as in temporarily (if not salubriously) self-extracted from the stream of undergraduate life, versus "*missing* missing"—Amber Alerts and all that. She had to believe Sri was off somewhere writing and didn't want to be disturbed. Maybe he was even in some weird place in the house, like that roof cupola that was being refurbished and had yellow *Danger No Entry* tape across the doorway, that would be irresistible to him. "I think that lady at Brown security wanted to kill all of us when she saw Sri come out of the Rock basically okay except for his massive hangover. Can you imagine if we came in again like three days later?"

But then she considered: the first twenty-four hours of a crime with a missing person were the most crucial. What if . . . "Oh, man," she said, suddenly emotional.

Brent made his empathy-eyes at her, inviting her to step into his ursine arms. She wasn't going to fall into that trap. She'd been very aware that Brent had had a crush on her from their days in the first-year unit. His dark good looks made him the object of interest to some of the other girls, but not her.

He looked the tiniest bit disappointed. "Hey, isn't Sri's play-writing class today?"

"Yes, it's at four."

"So you've memorized his schedule, like April."

"Shut *up*," she said, hitting his arm. "I just know because . . . Marla has her orgo lab in Arnold at the same time. And you know what? I think today his piece is up in workshop. He won't miss it."

"Okay, okay. If he misses that, we'll know—"

"We'll know he still wants to be a writer and piss his parents off. No worries, Brent, okay?"

"Okay," Brent said. But his eyes were dark, watchful. He was worried. It was touching how close those two unlikelies were, the South Asian kid rebelling against his physician parents by taking mostly writing classes that were graded only Satisfactory/No Credit—bye bye, medical school—paired with the goofball "Portagee from Pawtucket," as Brent Duarte called himself. He'd grown up just a few miles from here, never flown on an airplane, and was one of the smartest people she knew.

She accepted a goodbye hug. Brent was occasionally hooking up with Naran, a girl from Mongolia who nonetheless looked strikingly Korean. He didn't try to hide it: "She reminds me of you." Sussannah found this both touching and stupid. With the guileless Brent, the Asian fetish was a lukewarm annoyance, never approaching the level of creepy. But the move to Environmental House had had unexpected benefits: one of the house rules was, *Residents shall maintain a strict gender-neutral space at all times,* i.e., they were supposed to eliminate housemates as potential sexual partners so as to promote an easeful "sibling-like atmosphere."

* * *

They texted Sri their plans to meet at Nice Slice for dinner after his workshop (as if he would ever see such a message) and arranged for Marla to drop by the classroom and pick him up. Sussannah looked forward to fighting over the hot pepper shaker with him, each of them coating their pieces with flakes. "Who's hotter?" he'd say with a wink.

"According to that sign, they have gluten-free pizzas now," Brent said listlessly. "What the hell is gluten?"

"Calm down, he's just late," Sussannah said, toying with the squat hot pepper dispenser.

Brent glanced at his phone, then put it down. Then picked it up again.

"Would you cut it out?"

He put it down. He picked it back up. He bent his head to stare at the screen.

He looked up, mozzarella-pale. "No," he said. "He didn't show."

The two pushed through the hungry dinnertime crowd. They left a wake of surprised students and locals behind, almost upended a stroller in their haste, but didn't hear all the people yelling, "Hey!" and, "Watch it!" behind them.

Sri could disappear like a magician. He could secret himself in his room, writing for hours, and they wouldn't even know he was home. But his playwriting class would always flush him out. Your work only came up twice a semester, and there's no way he would miss it, short of—

Sussannah, Marla, and Brent burst into his room, a complete breach of house rules (*No house member shall enter the room of another for any reason without the permission of the inhabitant*) because they knew he wasn't going to be there.

On his desk, laid out like a still life: ID, keys, his wallet, some wooden coins that you could use at the campus farmers' market, a wristband from last week's Thursday Night Fishco outing, a few dollar bills, his phone.

"Shit," said Brent, and Sussannah knew what he was thinking: Marla's first-year roommate (that ill-fated Ophelia named Ethel) had left a similar tableau, a runic pattern that screamed (in retrospect): *I now need nothing.* For a full twenty-four hours, Brown security had told them not to panic: "Left her ID and wallet behind? Maybe she's just gone for a jog." By the time they started looking for her seriously, she'd been dead for a day.

But was Sri a suicide risk? Ethel (what kind of parents name their daughter Ethel?) had been ill-suited to college life from the start. She'd come in all prim and proper, a little gold cross around her neck, giving Marla the fish-eye when she walked around in just her bra, seeming aghast at the candy-colored condoms given out during study break by an older lady who may have been a professor. But then Ethel started disappearing, staying out all night—this was just during orientation week—kept coming in looking like hell, wouldn't talk to anyone (granted, Marla didn't try too hard). And then she'd disappear again.

"Are you sure he hasn't just gone off for a jog or something?"

Marla snorted in anger and tried too late to turn it into a cough. Sussannah didn't dare look at her. Also, *was* this the same security lady from Friday? Regulation, middle-aged-lady pageboy, those navy-blue uniforms with work pants (universally unflattering to all women, even the young one with the blond ponytail) . . . she couldn't tell.

"He's been missing for more than twenty-four hours now," Marla said.

Sussannah bit her lip. Okay, not quite, but now was not the time to bring that up.

"We can't violate this student's privacy, looking into his ID trail unnecessarily," said the lady. She gave them both the stink-eye. Same lady. On Friday, they'd found Sri, simply enough, by tracing his ID swipes to the Rock. Sussannah had visions of him bound and gagged in the stacks, but he had stumbled out, reeking like a still, just as they arrived there with the Brown rent-a-cops.

"But that might be the easiest thing to do, to eliminate foul play. We've already called his parents. And the *BDH*—" Marla pointed to Sussannah. "She's one of their top investigative reporters."

The lady sighed, disappeared into the room marked *Chief.* She soon returned, wordlessly typed into the computer, her fingers slamming the keys, repeating on several, 0-0-0-0-1-1-1-0-0-0, as if she were playing a ragtime piece on the piano. "Do you have *any* reason to think your friend's met with foul play?"

"It's really impossible to know." Sussannah found herself tearing up unexpectedly. She didn't look toward Brent, because she already had a feeling he was watching her face very, very closely.

"Well, here's his ID trail." They all craned their heads forward.

"Last night he entered the Sciences Library at 10:15 and left at 10:56."

Sussannah thought he was going to stay up there and write. But he'd left not long after she had. She found herself blushing.

"That's it. No meals swiped. So no one's seen him since you, Miss Park, at dinner at the Sharpe Refectory?"

She nodded.

"No," April said, in her robot monotone. "He hasn't come by. But you guys might want to do something about those little kids. I keep telling them to leave, but they won't."

"Little kids?" said Brent.

"*There*," she said impatiently. She pointed to a corner of the living room where there was nothing but an *Earth Day 2011* poster and the phone, an actual landline tethered to the wall by its jack.

"April," he laughed, "are you mainlining shrooms or something?"

"*There*," she repeated, then added, "I'd *never* do drugs. Plus, you don't mainline shrooms, that's heroin. You eat shrooms." On her heavy feet, she swayed a bit, started to dance around as if she were at a Grateful Dead concert. Without the music, however, it just looked weird.

The three housemates looked at each other. What do you do with a housemate like April Blaine? Sussannah recalled her chewing out Sri: "Do you have any idea how many trees were murdered for that stupid little paper towel you're using?" "But it's a Seventh Generation paper towel!" he'd yelped. "It's recycled!" Sussannah couldn't help smiling at the memory.

"So, April," said Brent, "you're sure he never came in last night?"

"I said I was sure."

"So you were, like, up all night?"

"I'm a very, very light sleeper." Her voice creaked, like a door opening.

The next day, Sri's parents arrived from California. They set up a war room in their hotel downtown, having brought dozens of flyers (the vivid color photo of Sri in a Brown sweatshirt, joyously smiling, was painful to look at). They spent the day plastering the entire College Hill. But no Sri. More posters (Amtrak station, the seedier areas of downtown, one friend brought them as far away as Boston), a Facebook page was set up, the posts and shares multiplied as they watched. People were shocked and interested. His disappearance made the Boston news.

But.

"We haven't even gotten any hoax calls," Brent complained.

How could there not even be a trace? Sussannah wondered. Could he, in this connected age, somehow just disappear?

One week, then two. While each day made them more frantic, other bits of shiny and urgent news had come in, and the outside world loosened its grip. The digital photo stopped replicating, the virus went dormant. He was no longer of interest as the missing Ivy League student. His clueless PoliSci TA even called to say he was going to flunk the class if he didn't show up soon.

Sri had become yesterday's news. It would be a mighty fight to keep him in the today, to not become accustomed to the idea that he was missing, that this was simply his new state of being.

Then Brent texted Sussannah: *A fucking bomb went off at the Boston Marathon.*

And: *All the cell phone towers are down.*

She didn't have to think as she typed back: *Marla . . .*

Marla had gone to Boston to watch her cousin run his first Boston Marathon.

Sussannah could hardly stay still as Brent drove.

"Look, I'm sure she's all right," he said.

"How the hell can you say that? Like you know anything." She glared at him. She was mad at him. Well, not *him* exactly. But she was mad at a world where Sri and Marla could both disappear. She should apologize.

Brent didn't say anything. He reached over and put his hand, warm and comforting as a worn-in softball mitt, on her knee. As a form of apology, she allowed it to remain.

"Her cell working yet?" asked Brent.

"No."

"Call her parents."

"Do you think she'd somehow call her parents and not us?"

"Uh, yeah?"

She dialed.

Marla's northern Alabama parents had syrup-sweet accents. "We can't get through either," her mother Janelle explained. "But she said she was planning to watch Jimmy run at the girls' school, Websley?"

"Wellesley," Sussannah said with relief.

Wellesley was so far away from Boston, you couldn't tell anything was amiss. The only sign today was different was the sea of trampled Dixie cups on the road where the runners had gone by. The campus was beautiful.

"You guys came!" Marla cried when she saw them. "Did you hear about the bombing—"

"Of course, you silly," said Sussannah, hugging her friend for extra long. "What, were we just going to sit around while you were in the middle of this? They still don't really know what's going on. I'll feel better when we're all back in Providence."

"Yeah, but I wish . . ." she said. "I wish . . ."

"Yeah, I know," said Brent. "I wish Sri was coming home with us too."

Some crazy person had detonated several crude bombs right at the finish line. Apparently spectators and runners alike were blown to pieces, limbs and blood flying everywhere; the bombs were particularly cruel, designed to destroy at leg-level. In the paper, Sussannah had seen a picture of a man rushing an ashen-faced runner out in a wheelchair. If you looked closer, in place of the runner's lower leg, all you saw were some ribbons of flesh maypoling a broken-off tibia, the one long, white bone splinter looking sharp as a shiv.

Brown canceled classes so they could have a day to work

through what had happened. But how do you work through something like that?

"How can this be happening on top of Sri missing?" Marla wailed. Her cousin had been close enough to the finish line to be knocked down by the blast, but he was okay (except that his ears were still ringing). Thank God for that.

Sri's parents had now moved to a B&B near campus; the owner had declared she'd keep the room open as long as they needed it. The Patils were, like everyone else, horrified by the Boston bombing. But Sussannah could tell they felt a little bit like she did: the bombing was an expression on a massive scale of how their tiny group suffered; and maybe now the whole world needed to pay attention to the fact that Sri was missing, that things in this world could actually break.

Environmental House had a tiny TV in the common room. On the news, the Boston police were saying they probably had photos of the bomber.

"I told you, the government is always watching us," said April. "Even while we sleep." Sussannah rolled her eyes—April was still ranting about the kids playing in the living room. She claimed they made a lot of noise at night.

"They said it was some kind of bomb made with a rice cooker, like the one you have, Soo-JZAH-nah," said Brent.

"Did it have pink flowers on it?" She rolled her eyes again. "How's a rice cooker going to kill someone?"

"That's what the FBI says." He click-clacked into Google. "Oh, wait, it was a pressure cooker that had a detonator. I guess that makes more sense. Remember that movie we saw, *The Hurt Locker*? How they activated the bombs with a cell phone?"

"Vaguely." She imagined the police having to tackle every single person carrying a cell phone in Copley Square.

"And here are the first pictures of the suspect." Brent swiveled his laptop screen toward her.

Sussannah leaned, squinted. Young guy, track suit, a baseball cap with its bill obscuring most of his face, a bit of dark hair peeking out. "He looks like a generic marathoner, or someone in the lacrosse frat."

The phone rang. April was closest, so she got up.

"No. He's not here. DON'T YOU KNOW HE'S BEEN MISSING FOR ALMOST A MONTH?"

"Wow," said Sussannah. "Sri's TA *again*? He hasn't seen one of those *Missing* signs?"

The phone rang again. April swiped it up.

"NO. SRI HAS NOT BEEN SEEN FOR OVER A MONTH. HE IS NOT HERE. NOT HERE!"

Again.

"NO, HE IS NOT HERE. NO, THERE IS NO ONE TO TALK TO YOU ABOUT IT . . . OH YEAH? THEN GO TALK TO THE FEDS."

"What the—?" said Brent.

The phone rang and rang. Like it was broken, stuck on *ring*. Like it would never stop ringing unless they took it outside and killed it. Sussannah ran upstairs and grabbed the other extension. "Hello," she said, her voice overlaying April's. "*WHAT NOW? WHO ARE YOU?*"

"This is the Associated Press calling. Is this the residence of Sri Patil?"

"Yes," Sussannah said automatically. Speechless, she listened. After three minutes, April started yelling again—Sussannah could hear her through both the receiver and her free ear. She hung up the phone, her face pale.

Brent's eyes widened when he saw her. He looked sick. "Did they find Sri?"

She shook her head. How to choke this out?

"What?" said Brent. "Then what?"

"They think he's involved in the Boston bombing."

"*What?*" Brent's mouth popped open.

"Because he disappeared, because . . . They're saying he probably went underground and was plotting all this time, that his whole coming to Brown was just a cover and that—" Sussannah couldn't think. The media was hinting Sri was Muslim. She was pretty sure he wasn't. But what if he was? Should that matter?

April was hauling the phone over to Brent, handing him the receiver. "This one's for *you.*" Brent's mouth was still open in shock. When he took the phone, he gargled out, "Hello?" Glancing through the window, Sussannah saw the first news van slide into the parking spot in front of the house, its conical satellite tipped to the air like they would be transmitting to some far-off solar system. She shut the curtain, which April had made out of recycled rice bags.

"Yes . . . um . . . yes, well . . . Um, sure, okay . . . Where? Should I— Oh, okay. Yes, I will." Brent looked like he might cry.

Now the police wanted to question them.

They questioned Sri's family first. Sussannah learned this on TV. Sri's parents looked like normal American parents. His dad, partial to golf shirts. His mother, pretty with long black hair and wearing a burnt-orange sari. But if she didn't know them as Sri's parents, Sussannah wondered if she'd think, *Of course his mommy thinks he's not a terrorist!* In these situations, it was standard journalistic practice to find a neighbor to say, "Gee, he was a quiet guy, but I never would have thought that he would . . ."

She noticed, too, they broadcasted a lot more pictures of his mom wearing the sari than his dad in the golf shirt, and they'd also dug up some photo of Sri in traditional garb at a cousin's wedding in India. He looked so handsome, a garland of flowers around his neck.

Sussannah wanted to scream. There was no way Sri could do something like this. They made it sound like he was some bored Ivy League kid who'd gone underground, become radicalized, and started to kill. How insane was that?

"How can you be so sure?" Sussannah's mother said. "He's just a boy in your house."

He was much more than just a boy in Environmental House.

"This is doubly insane," she complained to Brent. "Did you know that Sri's family is Hindu? Not only vegetarian, they practice ahimsa, respect to all living beings, that's why Sri can't even bring himself to kill a bug, much less—"

"Sussannah," Brent interrupted. "So what's up?"

"What do you mean, what's up?"

"You know something, don't you? About Sri . . ."

She could feel her eyes flashing. "Why would I know something and not tell you, or the police, or anyone? No one wants to find him more than I do."

"I know. That's what I'm curious about."

"There's nothing to be curious about," she said.

The Boston surveillance cameras had picked up images of two young men placing duffle bags on the sidewalk, right where the blasts went off. Sri didn't wear track suits or baseball caps, a fact the media ignored. But Brent did. And suddenly he became the "second dark-skinned accomplice."

"Un-fucking-believable," he said. "My late-spring olive complexion." On the news, the reporters pronounced his name, the Portuguese Du-ART, as Doo-ar-TAY, as if making him sound Mexican would make him more suspicious.

Sussannah was surprised the phone's bell hadn't given out: *ring, ring, ring*. They couldn't unplug it, of course, *just in case*. "Yes, I was in Boston that day," she heard Brent say on the phone. "I got as far as Wellesley, to pick up my friend—" Sussannah, scribbling on a piece of paper, reminded him that they'd been advised by the Brown lawyers to speak to no one. "Also, I don't look like the guy in the picture at all—I never wear white sneakers, what is this, the '90s? Jeesh! And lastly, it's *Patil* not Patel. P-A-T-I-L . . ."

Given the resurgence in interest, the Facebook page sprang back to life. There were some terrible trolls making terrible comments, but Sussannah took charge, deleting things before Sri's parents would see. No new leads, but at least people were thinking about Sri again. They even had a one-inch article in the *New York Times*.

"Yes, he did own a cell phone," she told the detective. She, Marla, and Brent had agreed to be questioned together. The detective assured Brent he was no longer a "person of interest."

"That day he disappeared," said Brent, "you'll note that while we texted him, we also texted Marla in order to actually deliver the message—we didn't assume he had his phone. And he didn't."

"He hated cell phones, thought they irradiated you or something. He would have never spent hours tinkering on some bomb," added Marla.

"Maybe he wasn't worried about long-term health consequences anymore," said the detective, his hair close-cut like the bristles of a brush, like the stereotype of a hard-boiled detective or a slightly cleaned-up Boston cop. Sussannah realized that pretty much anything they said could be twisted around to make Sri sound guilty. The cop probably felt that in their vigorous, clamorous defense of Sri, they *must* be covering something up.

"Moving on, he spent a lot of time in the Sciences Library," said the man. "Even though he was an English major."

"Not English, he was a Literary Arts concentrator—that's creative writing," Marla corrected, as if the guy would know, or care. "Really—our friend is missing. You guys should be helping *us* look for him, not give us the third degree."

The cop had probably not gone to college, or maybe not a college where you all live together like they did; could he understand the incredible closeness that developed between people like them? The three years they'd spent together—morning, noon, and night—added up to several lifetimes stitched together.

"So he's a writing major or whatnot, but the interesting thing is he's in the Sciences Library all the time. And according to this log, in December he spent almost five hours at one stretch, didn't check out a single book." Sussannah almost expected him to end with, *So whaddaya think of that, huh? Sound like an innocent man to you?* Sam Spade style.

"People study in the library too," said Marla, with enormous reserves of patience. "The SciLi is very quiet and has the best views in town."

Sussannah remembered, also: "In December, I bet it was because Sri was helping his engineering friends set up their *Tetris* game." Using colored Christmas lights, the students had made the grid of windows of the SciLi's south face into a gigantic *Tetris* game that you played from the ground. What did they use as a controller? she wondered. Cell phone? She then decided the Brown lawyers were right: speaking less would be better.

"On the night before he disappeared, he signed in to the Sciences Library at 10:15, left the library at 10:56," the detective said. "No ID, he signed in manually." He showed them a slide with Sri's recognizably teeny writing, *Sri Patil 10:15*, done in the special pen that could write from any angle, in any weather.

Sri was casual about his ID. Some people bought special holders to carry them around their necks via lanyard. He found that so sheeplike and summer-campish. At best, he put his in his pocket and forgot to take it out of the wash, or he just left it behind and signed in everywhere.

"Again, he didn't check out any books. And it didn't corre-late with anything else."

Sussannah stared at him. What was he implying?

"The only thing it even vaguely correlates with is Miss Park."

She was startled to hear her name.

"You checked into the Sciences Library with him at 10:15 and left at 10:51."

Sussannah stiffened. She pictured herself swiping with a flourish, maybe giving the attendant a bullish *Hello!* She'd been so—what?—happy that night. She didn't look at Brent or Marla. Didn't want to give anything away. What was there to give away? Was it a crime to go to the SciLi together? *No!*

"You were the last one to see him, correct?"

"Yes."

Brent didn't say anything in front of the detective. She felt grateful for that.

In fact, Brent didn't say anything at all after the detective left. Marla did, though.

"Suse, you said dinner was the last time you saw him."

"Yeah, well . . ." Could she say she'd just somehow spaced on the library meet-up? Or maybe they just happened to go around the same time. One could theoretically be on the stairs (if you walked fast) within sixty seconds. But why spend so much energy making up a lie? What would this new information add? This wasn't about her—this was about Sri.

"Let me take the fifth—a friend-fifth on that," she said.

"Self-incrimination," muttered April. She'd been lurking in the wings the whole time.

Sri was not the bomber, he was not the bomber. Sussannah tossed and turned. But how well did she know him? she won-dered. Could it be possible? Like that guy John Walker Lindh. He was some rich kid from Marin County who could have probably gone to Brown as easily as he'd gone all jihad. Sri did indeed hate the war. Could it be possible that he hated it enough to—

No. Not possible.

They had only two weeks left of classes. Brent was exhausted by his double concentration in bio and public health. He wanted to be a doctor. "After all, there's already Dr. in Duarte," he had joked, back when they used to joke. But he also wondered if he could pursue public health without spending four years and the six figures on an MD. For a few hours a week he shadowed Al, a fourth-year med student who was doing work for immigrants with obesity in North Providence.

Al was sitting at Environmental House's kitchen table, his short blazer-style *Brown University Alpert Medical School* white coat flung across a chair, a cold Naragansett beading with condensation in front of him. "Med school is stressful," he said, nodding toward the beer, his second.

"I promised Al I'd make him Portagee food," said Brent, covering some pieces of fish in lemon, garlic, and about half a bottle of olive oil. "So you all will get Portagee food as well unless you prefer the Ratty's Jambalaya-Is-a-Fancy-Word-for-Botulism Nite. *Bom apetite!*"

Sam brought *Vinho Verde*, Marla and Sussannah procured a mushroom cloud–shaped sweet bread from the Silver Star. It was like old times, eating, drinking, huddling close, happy just to be with each other. Nothing felt so right, and so forever.

Except. Sussannah could feel them holding back, like someone who never quite draws a full breath. Holding back, saving a little something. Like they'd never laugh as loud and with such abandon as they once did. Like they were each subtracting a little bit of their own life out of respect for Sri.

"April, you want to join us?" Brent did this too, out of respect for Sri. Sri liked everyone, no matter what. Sussannah and Marla tended to be scared of April and impatient in equal measure. But when they were all sitting around the house—eating, drinking, watching TV—if Sri was there, he would invariably reach out to April, with a kindness that made Sussannah's eyes tear up at the memory.

"Uh, sure," April said, a bit to their surprise. She paused in front of the table and did her soundless dance, arms akimbo. She backed away two steps, then rushed the table so hard the utensils clattered. She took a bite of food, then pushed away from the table like she was launching a boat (clattering utensils once again) and staggered to her room even though she hadn't had any *Vinho Verde*. Within minutes, the sweetish scent of pot wafted out.

"RUE student," explained Marla to Al. "Although kinda old to be such a pothead. She smokes so much she hallucinates—she's always going on about the little kids playing in the house."

"Oh my, I can't believe it: we just learned about that," said Al. "And cannabis—ah, that makes sense."

"About RUE students?"

"No, no. The little kids. And chorea."

"Korea?" Marla echoed. Sussannah shrugged when everyone looked at her.

"No, c-h-o-r-e-a, which means 'dance' in Greek. It's a symptom, along with seeing little kids: a dopamine thing. And lots of people with that self-medicate with cannabis. So, how long have you all known that April has Huntington's?"

Huntington's disease! They'd all vaguely heard of it, but not what it did. That it was genetic, degenerative, fatal. And it made you go *crazy*: the hallucinations were caused by dopamine upregulation problems (same thing happened to Parkinson's patients), and the jerky movements, the dancing was all neurological. Huntington's patients could also be very, very violent.

"We're stuck in the house with a crazy person," Marla whispered. "Remember? She told us she had a terminal disease—I thought she was just saying one of her crazy things like, *Life is a terminal disease* or something."

"I'm a little surprised you didn't know," Al said. "But I suppose HIPPA and all that, probably Brown couldn't tell you."

"Do you think she'll kill us?" Sussannah asked, her thoughts turning to Sri.

"I don't think she's homicidal," Al said. "I mean, it's not that Huntington's patients haven't been homicidal, but she doesn't seem like it. I think."

But once he left, the three of them looked at each other.

Sri. He was too nice to her.

"She probably lured him out somewhere," speculated Sussannah.

"Stabbed him and hid the body," added Marla.

They ran up to the cupola, breaking the yellow *Danger No Entry* tape, half-expecting to find Sri's body cut up in little pieces. They did find one of his favorite Pilot pens and a roach clip.

"Um, April's not in the best physical shape, and Sri's like six feet tall," Brent pointed out. "She'd have to kill him without making a mess and then get rid of the body."

"Maybe if they went to India Point Park, and she stabbed him and pushed him off the pier?" This was Marla.

"Unlikely, but . . ." said Brent.

The three of them spent the night dreaming up ways Sri could have been killed by April: poison, carbon monoxide, car accident, railroad tracks. This made them really start hating April. It was unseasonably warm, and in their un-air-conditioned house (of course) their anger heated it up even more.

Sussannah was also mad at herself for not figuring this April thing out earlier—she was so creepy, how could they have missed it? Marla was mad at Sussannah for lying to them about seeing

Sri only at dinner. Brent was mad at her as well, and for not loving him back *in that way.*

Sussannah thought back to the night, because it was the last thing she had of Sri.

Yes, they'd gotten a little drunk. Little bottles of booze *glug, glug, glugged* into those big thirty-two-ounce soda things they had at Metro Mart.

Tipsy but not enough to be detected, they'd sashayed into the SciLi.

"Covered container!" Sri had said, saluting the attendant with his alcohol-laced Big Gulp. The SciLi was where Sri (and most of Brown) procured Ritalin and Concerta so he could stay up all night and write his plays; and he was definitely buying that night, having trouble on his latest, which was due the next day.

"I know what's good for writer's block," she'd said, and given him a smoldering look. They both knew this was going to happen at some point, why not now?

"Fast," he said, because he'd already purchased and consumed a few Ritalin, washed down with the Big Gulp, and he wouldn't want to waste the effects.

Any denizen of the SciLi can tell you there's often no one on the top floor. Especially right after dinner. That night it was the two of them and the twinkling lights of Providence. To preserve the books, the stacks are kept dark, the lights only come on when you press the timer in the one specific row. They sneaked down to the last one, which was "oversized." No one looked for books in the oversized row, it was all thousand-year-old maps and things. It was also dusty. She sneezed. He laughed. Sri was tall, she wasn't so tall. Awkward and fast, but done. Even in the dimmest light, his hair gleamed. She was in love with him. She would have to move out of Environmental House. She was okay with this.

"You go," he whispered in her ear. "I'm going to stay and

write." There was a trace of bitterness in his kiss, from the Ritalin.

"So, Sussannah," said Brent, "you lied and said you saw Sri last at dinner, but in reality you were fucking him in the SciLi stacks."

Sussannah was so shocked, she just looked back at him. His face fell in disappointment. His bluff had worked too well.

"Ah, you were, weren't you?" said Marla, but she seemed a little more amused than Brent. She often said that she thought Sri was "delicious." Sussannah would tepidly agree, carefully concealing her truest heart.

"You can't fuck someone who's in EH," said April, stepping from behind some curtain like Polonius, as usual. "It's against the rules.

"Shut up, April," Sussannah shot back. "Why don't you tell us where you fucking buried Sri's body?"

"Why would I want to kill Sri?" replied April, and then she sniffled. "He was the only one of you who was nice to me."

"God, I can't believe you did it with Sri, you sly little girl," said Marla. There was an edge to her voice. It occurred to Sussannah that maybe Marla liked him too. But had just restrained herself better. Or did so in the name of their friendship, to keep them all together. Or had been too scared and timid. Who knew?

And what kind of friends were they all, Sussannah wondered, if they couldn't show their true selves to each other?

She thought back to that summerlike Saturday in September—they'd gone on a road trip to Newport, spent a day at the beaches, ate seafood, and headed back to Providence in the early evening.

"That was fun, but I think I might be sunburned for the first time in my life—take me home!" Sri had howled. Marla had busted out laughing.

"*What?*" said Sri. "Is my pain that funny to you?"

"You said *home*. When I say *home*, I mean Clayhatchee."

"I dunno. I guess I now think of Brown as home."

"Environmental House is where the heart is . . ." said Brent.

And then they'd started singing "*Country road, take me hoooooome . . .*" in their cheesiest voices. Sussannah could swear she felt the car lifting with their energy. And they'd had that feeling, the one that overcame them sometimes, like they were in the movie of their own lives. A brightly lit comedy. Happiness, the future, all on that road in front of them.

"Holy shit," said Brent. "Holy fucking shit."

"Look what the cat dragged in," said Al, grinning from ear to ear, like he'd just caught the biggest fish at a fishing derby.

"Sri—" said Brent. "Sri?"

It was Sri, but he looked like a middle-aged janitor; Sansa-belt slacks, plastic sandals, a *Stuffies Quahog Chowdah* T-shirt. His beautiful hair was cut short, shorter than the Boston detective's, his face, as if in compensation, a cactus mess of stubble.

"Sri," said Marla.

Sussannah was stunned into silence.

"Yes," he said. "I'm Sri. And you are . . . ?"

"I thought amnesia only happened on soap operas," said Brent. "As a convenient plot point."

"Apparently not," said Sussannah. A little accusingly, she added, "And you *never* noticed him all that time you were at that homeless shelter?"

"I wasn't there for the shelter, I was there for the obesity clinic," he replied tetchily.

"But it was in the same building, Einstein."

Apparently that fateful night, for whatever reason, Sri left the SciLi in a rush, loped down College Hill to the tiny park that overlooked the city. In the dark he tripped, fell into a puddle. Ritalin and alcohol and sugar, not a good combination. A few minutes later, he tripped again, and this time hit his head.

When he was brought in, the ER docs saw a drunk with no ID and, as was typical, booted the inebriated man to the homeless shelter, where he remained, affable but memoryless, looking like any of the dozens of brown-skinned men who inhabited the place. Until the day he saw Al in his Brown University medical student coat, which reconnected a neuron or two, and he said, "Hey, I go to Brown."

Bits of Sri's memory came back, like the *Tetris* game he'd helped his friends with. Sussannah sometimes thought she saw *that look* in his eye. It took all of her will not to ask, *Do you remember us having sex?*

Whether he remembered or not, the damage was already done. The senior year housing lottery had come and gone, and Brent, Sussannah, and Marla had pointedly each pursued their own options. Marla was going to the Young Orchard Apartments, Brent was living off campus with Al, Sussannah was going to be a counselor in a dorm. Sam was graduating (going to film school), April would be moving to hospice. Environmental House would be Sri and whoever the new people were.

Sussannah and Sri were walking down Thayer.

"Are you Sri Patil?"

They turned. A man in a dark suit and sunglasses. Sussannah instinctively stiffened.

"FBI," the man said, showing them a badge.

"Am I under arrest?" This was part of a liturgy Sri had memorized, that he'd been told could keep you from getting busted for pot. "Am I under arrest? Am I free to go? I do not consent to being searched."

"You're not under arrest," the man said, smiling a little. "I just want to talk to you." He motioned that Sussannah should scram. She felt reluctant; she didn't want to leave him.

"It's okay, I'm not under arrest," he said softly.

Sussannah forced herself to turn and walk away. What it was, she realized, was that she was in love with him. For him, she'd lost her best friend—both of them. And you know what? She'd do it again. What an unimaginable gift it had been when he'd reappeared, and she knew right then it would be him. No matter what. Even if he never remembered her, she'd stay by his side. She'd wait.

Sri whipped around, yelling, "I remember! I remember! Sussannah!" And he started to run to her. She turned, her face blasting open with the stupidest smile, her arms opening.

And for reasons that no one seems to know, will probably never know, because those in power don't have to tell anything when they declare that an incident has to do with "terrorism," that's when the FBI agent drew his gun and shot the running Sri right through the heart.

$1,000 NASSAU

BY THOMAS COBB

Triggs Memorial Golf Course

He was on the third tee at Triggs Memorial when he slid his left thumb to the right side of the grip, strengthening it. He swung hard, a little harder than usual, and watched the ball come off the tee, sailing upward and out before it started to draw to the left as he wanted, then turn harder, through the trees and over the chain-link fence and onto College Road. "Shit."

"Your little draw grew up, didn't it?" Victor said. "And looks like it ran away from home."

He shook his head slowly. "It does that sometimes."

"Looks like it wanted to go to college," Don said. "Can't blame it. Lots of pretty girls over there."

Bobby took another Titleist from his pocket, teed it up, regripped the club, sliding his thumb back to the center of the grip, and sent the ball down the right side of the fairway, drawing back to the middle. "Why didn't I do that the first time?" he said, anticipating the likely response. He walked off the tee and watched Don and Victor send shots down the middle, Don's twenty yards short of his, Victor's back another ten or twenty yards. "Good shots," he said. "All of us."

"Except we're lying one and you're lying three."

"That's okay," Bobby said. "I'm all right."

"You all right to increase the bet?" Don asked.

"I don't know if I feel that good."

"You think he's playing, us, Vic?"

"First bad shot he's hit, Don."

Don went to his bag, took out a cigar case, extracted a cigar, already unwrapped, clipped the end, and lit it, expertly toasting it to get an even light.

"That smells good."

"Because it is good. Montecristo No. 2. Straight from Havana, Cuba."

"Nice," Bobby said. "Hard to come by."

"Nothing's hard to come by if you have the right connections. I have the right connections. You want one?"

Bobby hesitated, tempted. "Thanks, but I'll pass."

Don nodded. "On the bet too?"

"What did you have in mind?"

"A thousand."

Bobby paused, waiting to make sure the hook was set. He had been on the practice green for over an hour when Don and Victor showed up. They were older guys, well dressed, good equipment. He figured a grand each for the outfits and shoes, more than that in the bags. He had watched them chip and putt as he did too, for about fifteen minutes, before he went into the clubhouse to see if he could be sent out with them.

He had been through a rough couple of weeks, blocking tee shots for some reason he couldn't quite put a finger on. He had been playing in Connecticut and Massachusetts. A fellow at a course in Massachusetts had told him about Triggs in western Providence, a Donald Ross course, once the Providence Country Club, now a public course with a lot of old money and a lot of old egos.

He was broke and he needed a score, and Triggs Memorial seemed like the place. He had played it three times earlier in the week, his swing gradually straightening out, and figured he knew the course well enough to make a play.

"Don and Victor?" Stan at the desk had asked. "They're good."

"How good?"

"Victor is a ten handicap, maybe. Don's about a seven. Be careful with them."

"That sounds good to me." Bobby was officially a five, though it was a carefully managed five. He could be scratch easily if he didn't keep the handicap up where he wanted it. He gave up the last of his money, except for fourteen dollars for the greens fee and a cart. On the first tee they had exchanged the information. Bobby had suggested a hundred-dollar Nassau—a hundred to the winner of the first side, another hundred for the second side, and a hundred on the total score. Pretty simple, pretty conservative. If they didn't take the bet, he would have to beg off and wait for someone else. He didn't play for free.

"I don't know," Victor had said. "Young kid like yourself. Probably hit the ball a ton. How about you against both of us? We'll play a better ball, our best score against you."

"We're within three strokes of each other. That gives you a huge advantage. Odds are at least one of you is going to play pretty well on every hole. I got to beat that."

"You're young and I'm figuring you're a little bit better than a five. I think it's a good bet."

"I need a lot of incentive to pull this off."

"How much?"

"Five hundred?"

Don and Victor exchanged looks, then Don nodded. "Done. Five hundred–dollar Nassau."

They had played even on the first two holes, birdie, par. Now he was in the fairway of the third in three. He would lose the hole and go one down. It was exactly what he wanted.

"We're up by one," Victor said.

"Maybe Bobby Boy here would like to increase the bet. Say, a thousand."

"A thousand?" he asked.

"That's right. You've made your mistake. Don't figure you're going to make a lot more from here on out."

With no money, he could afford to lose only one of the bets. He had to have at least one very good side and a decent score on the other so that he would take two of the three bets, win a thousand, and be on his way. If he didn't, he was in trouble. He didn't have the thousand, and he hadn't had the hundred, either. Neither did he have an obvious way to get it. He was pretty much tapped. He would need to lose a couple more to make it convincing, which meant he would have to win four or five holes by at least a stroke. That was doable. "Okay. Fuck me for a fool. A thousand."

"Oh yeah," Victor said. "Now we got a game."

Bobby bogeyed the third, Don and Victor each parred it, Don lipping out his birdie putt, then giving Bobby a smile. They played the par-three fourth hole even, Bobby and Don birdieing it, Victor parring. They did the same on the fifth, with Victor getting the birdie to match Bobby's.

At six, he was still one stroke down, feeling pretty good about the way this was going. Don and Victor had the tee, and both put good shots into the middle of the fairway just beyond the beginning of the dogleg. Bobby teed his high and hit a long fade that took the turn and left him little more than an eight iron to the green.

Bobby dropped his eagle putt, Don parred, and Victor bogeyed from the fescue in front of the green. Bobby picked up two strokes and went one up.

On the seventh, Don made the birdie to tie Bobby. On the eighth, Bobby's tee shot ended up in the rocky burnout in the right rough, and he carded his second bogey. Don and Victor both parred. They were even after eight.

On the ninth, Bobby's drive put him just in front of the green, forty-five yards out. Both Don and Victor were behind him some forty yards. Don got his second shot to within fifteen feet, Victor was at the very back of the green thirty-five feet away. Bobby followed with an easy wedge to within six feet. Victor lagged to within five feet, but Don put his in for a birdie. Bobby had an easy six-footer with a little right-to-left break at the end. His ball rolled toward the hole, hopped on an old ball mark, and lipped out.

"Damn. Did you see that?"

"One of the drawbacks to a public course, my friend," Don said. "One of the drawbacks. And there are a few. Lots of people here don't bother to fix a ball mark, replace a divot, nothing. You got to watch your ball like a hawk, or someone will pick it up. Balls just vanish into thin air."

"Into pockets," Victor corrected. "No fucking respect for the game."

They went past the clubhouse to the tenth tee. Bobby was one down on total strokes, and he had lost the front side. He was a thousand dollars down, and could only take the lead by winning the back by at least two strokes, taking that side and the cumulative too. He would have to win at least three holes and not lose any.

"How you feeling, kiddo?" Victor asked on the tenth tee.

"I'm feeling all right," Bobby said. "Thanks for your concern."

"Not just a little bit nervous? A little angry? I'd be pissed off if two old futzers had just taken a thousand bucks out of my pocket."

"You haven't gotten it yet."

"No, but we will. Come over here." Victor motioned toward his bag. "You get nervous, need something to do, help yourself." He unzipped a pouch in the bag. "The cigars are right here. Right here, do you see?" There was the black cigar case, and next to it, Bobby could see the walnut grip of a revolver. "You see?"

"What's that?"

"Cigars. What, you think we're going to shoot you if you win? No. I want you to see where the cigars are. Help yourself. Maybe that's just a lighter, you know? A gag. You got nothing to be worried about."

Don walked over. "You're worried? It's a brand-new nine. You're down a stroke. So what? This is a Nassau. You still win a grand if you beat us by at least two strokes on this side. What are you worried about?"

"You do have enough to cover the bet if you lose, don't you?" Victor asked.

"Of course I do," Bobby lied. "I wouldn't take a bet I couldn't make good on."

"That's good. Because this is a gentleman's game. I would hate to think that we were playing with someone who's only pretending to be a gentleman."

"Yeah," Don added. "We like you. You seem like a nice boy. I would hate to find out different."

"No. I'm good for the money," Bobby said.

"That's great. That's what we want to hear, right, Vic? Let's play some golf."

There was nothing to do but go ahead and play, and play well. But he had been threatened, and if he played his full game, he knew he would be threatened again, or worse. To successfully sandbag someone, you had to keep the illusion going. But he had an adrenaline spike too, and on the tenth tee he unleashed a drive that went past Victor's and Don's on the fly. He stuck a five iron within five feet and carded an eagle to take a one-up lead on the back, and a one-stroke lead in the cumulative when Don and Victor both parred the hole.

"See there? Everything is all right with you now. Right? You're in the lead in the first hole on the back. Being behind didn't last very long, did it?"

Bobby birdied the short par-four eleventh and the par-three

twelfth, as did Don. Still, one up going to the par-five thirteenth.

"Maybe the thirteenth isn't going to be so lucky for him, Victor. What do you think?"

"I don't think luck's got a lot to do with it."

"He is playing pretty well. Eagle, birdie, birdie. Like Tiger Woods, except right now I don't see a flaw in his game. You think he's sandbagging us, Victor?"

"No. I think he's smarter than that."

"He's a pretty smart boy."

"Go on, hit away. Don't mind our gabbing."

There was only one more par five after this one. One more great opportunity to put the match out of reach and make his thousand bucks. He didn't like the sandbagging remark, though. He kept thinking about that gun in Victor's bag.

Bobby held back a little on the drive, but kept it far enough out for the green to be easily reachable in two. Both Don and Victor hit good drives, within twenty yards of Bobby's.

"You know, Victor," Don said as they put their drivers into their bags, "I can't play this hole without thinking of that guy you caught rolling his ball over in the rough."

"You think he still limps?" Victor asked.

They both laughed. "I think he still does, and I think he's grateful that he only limps."

"You're not getting in my head," Bobby said.

"Wouldn't have even considered it," Don said.

Bobby hit a four iron, low and long. It landed just in front of the green and hopped on, rolled at the flag, then past it and into the tall grass at the back of the green. Don and Victor both reached in three. Don was in easy birdie range. Bobby had a long chip that traveled down for about thirty feet, then broke to the right a good two feet. His ball stopped two inches from the hole. He tapped in the par and Don followed with his birdie putt. They were back to even.

"See," Don said, "I told you. Luck. And his is running out. Thirteenth hole got him."

On the short par-three fourteenth, Don and Victor were both on with makeable putts. Bobby's shot sailed over the pin, spun back, hit a ball mark, and veered right. Victor and Bobby both made their putts.

At the fifteenth tee box, Victor came up to Bobby as he got ready to tee his ball up. "The way I see it, this is a big-decision hole for you, my young friend. After this are three par fours. This is the scoring hole. Do you unleash it and show us how good you really are, how that five handicap is bullshit, or do you hold back and keep it at even which gives us the front and cumulative, and leaves you with a bill for a grand, which I'm not positive you have. It's a real interesting decision. Glad it's not mine." He patted Bobby on the back.

Bobby was still unsure how serious these guys were. Were they just bullshitting him, getting into his head by playing tough guy? He knew he couldn't pay the bet if he didn't win the side by at least two. And if he couldn't pay the bet, it was going to go hard on him if these guys were for real. If they weren't for real, they were doing a good job of pretending.

He let it go. He had no real choice. He needed to get up by a point in order to make any kind of decision about what he was going to do. The ball stayed on the right side of the fairway. It was easily three ten or three twenty.

"Jesus Christ," Don said. "You been keeping that in your bag, haven't you?"

"It's a good drive," Bobby agreed.

"And I'm guessing that's not even close to your best," Victor said.

"It's close," Bobby said.

"You're full of shit," Victor said.

"Victor, hit the ball," Don said.

Bobby missed the eagle putt, got his birdie, and watched Don miss a birdie putt and Victor scramble to save par from the right-side bunker. Back up by one.

He was in control now. They had a short par four and two longer par fours to go.

"Boy, you can hear the wheels in his head spinning, can't you, Victor?"

"They better spin the right way. I'm thinking this little monkey is running out of tricks."

With the stroke-shot lead and three holes to go, he didn't really have a decision to make yet. If he needed to, he could even drop a stroke. He took a five iron out of his bag and put it into the turn of the dogleg with less than sixty yards to the pin. He birdied the hole, and Victor parred it. Don got tangled up in the trash on the right side of the fairway and got away with a bogey.

Bobby went to the seventeenth tee ahead by two strokes. Don sidled up to him. "A kid like you cheated us awhile back. Quite awhile. Vic tuned him up in the lower parking lot. But you don't have to worry unless we think you're cheating us. We'll discuss it later."

His drive on the seventeenth didn't draw as much as he wanted it to, and he came close to the water at the right side of the fairway. Still, he chipped on and made an easy par that kept him two strokes up.

"This is it, ducky. This hole decides everything that hasn't already been decided. And things have been decided. Try not to let that influence your play here."

Bobby wasn't going to lose and have to welch on a bet. He stepped up to the tee with that in mind. He let it loose, and his stomach churned when he blocked it right. He watched as the ball cleared the trees on the right and ended up on the ninth fairway. Don and Victor both hit good drives that left a hundred and fifty and less to the hole.

Bobby drove over to the trees, through them onto the ninth fairway. He had seen it clear the trees, but it wasn't on the fairway. He drove across the fairway to the rough on the right of nine, then through another line of trees. Nothing, and there was no one on the first tee.

He headed back to the ninth fairway. There was a threesome just getting on the green. He drove up. "Any of you see my ball? Titleist black three. Two blue dots?"

One guy shook his head, but the other two looked at him.

"You find my ball?" Bobby shouted. "There's a match going on. You find my ball?"

The guy shook his head.

Bobby got out of the cart and walked to the green. "This is serious, man. Did you find my ball? I need that ball. I'm not joking. This is very serious. If you took my ball, there's going to be trouble."

"Stan," one of the guys said.

"I didn't take his ball," Stan said.

"Stan." Victor had come up behind Bobby. "I'm going to ask you one time. Nice. You have his ball? Not going to ask again. Think very seriously about this."

The old guy dug into the pocket of his shorts and pulled out a Titleist black three, two blue dots.

"Now, Stan, you take that ball and put it back where you found it. Exactly where you found it. Come on. I'm going with you. You put it exactly where you found it. Exactly."

Bobby got back in his cart and followed Victor and Stan as they walked back up the ninth fairway.

"You see," Victor said, "golf is a game for gentlemen. It's about honor and courtesy and good sportsmanship. You don't steal in golf, you don't lie, you don't cheat. You understand? 'Cause if you don't, you shouldn't be playing. Now, is this right? This is exactly where you found it? Place it down where it was. Thank you."

Then Victor hit the old guy hard, an openhanded slap that they must have heard in the clubhouse. The man went down hard and stayed there until Victor told him to get up. The old guy was crying now.

"Bobby," Victor said, "take him back to his buddies, would you? Then you can play your shot. I'll watch your ball."

After he had delivered the guy to the ninth green, Bobby stood over his ball, lining up a shot with a sand wedge. His hands were shaking a little. He stepped back, took a practice swing, then another. He moved up to the ball and hit a high arching shot that put it over the trees and four feet from the cup.

"Nice shot," Victor said. "All you got to do is drop it and you've won a thousand. Not bad for a few hours of work. Miss it, and it's going to be ugly."

There was no choice, really. No choice. He lined the putt up and dropped it.

"Victor, it's over," Don said. "He did it. Back side and gross total." Don walked up to Bobby and shook his hand. Victor came up on the other side of him and shook Bobby's hand as well. "Victor," Don continued, "let's get this young man paid."

"Money's in the car," Victor said.

"Then we go to the car." Don took Bobby's left arm and stepped off toward the parking lot. Victor, not actually touching Bobby, marched along at his right.

They got to the bottom parking lot. Bobby considered calling for help, but figured he wouldn't get it, and would only end up making things worse. As they crossed the lot, they veered left toward the dumpster. Bobby tried to bolt, but Victor had him firmly by the right arm.

"Let me ask you something. You didn't have the money, did you?"

Bobby looked at Don, then over at Vic. He shook his head.

The first blow caught him in the solar plexus and he went

down to his knees hard. "That's for the lie. This is for winning the back." Bobby tried to cover up, but Victor's hand came across his body and pushed something under the collar of his shirt. "It's also for being a great player. And this, this is for being a dirty sandbagger." Something exploded behind his right ear and Bobby went all the way to the ground, out cold.

When he came to, and after he brushed the dirt from his mouth, he reached into his shirt and took out the little roll of hundred-dollar bills Victor had left for him. All in all, it was a decent day's work. He was back in business.

PART III

GOD'S MERCIFUL PROVIDENCE

ALL IN THE FAMILY

BY BRUCE DESILVA

Federal Hill

I n the pause between Bruno Mars's "Grenade" and Maroon
5's "Moves Like Jagger," Val caught a few yaps of his barking-
dog ringtone. He plucked out his earbuds, glanced at his cell
phone, and saw an unfamiliar number on the screen.

"Hey, Charles?" he said before thumbing the answer button.
"Would you mind turning your music down, please?" His office
mate's desktop speaker was still belching Bach, which is why Val
had sought refuge in his own tunes.

"History of Art and Architecture. Sciarra speaking."

"Valerio Sciarra?" The voice rumbled like distant thunder.

"That would be me, yes."

"Rudy Sciarra's grandnephew?"

Val hesitated. His grandfather's deceased older brother, an
enforcer for Raymond L.S. Patriarca back in the '60s, was not a
relative he liked to acknowledge. "Well . . . I've been told that
we were related, but I never actually met the man. What is this
about?"

"There's a car waiting for you outside. New Lincoln MKS.
Black with tinted windows."

"There must be some mistake. I didn't call for a car."

"Just come outside and get in it, professor. Don't make me
send the muscle in there for you."

Before Val could protest, the caller was gone.

Six years with the army rangers had left Val confident he
could handle all the muscle that could be stuffed into a luxury

car. But what if they were packing? He considered calling the campus police, but Brown University security officers didn't carry firearms. Instead, he punched in the number for the Providence cops, then hesitated, his thumb hovering over the call button.

Val was more curious than apprehensive. Who the hell was the caller, and what could he possibly want with an Ivy League assistant art history professor? He set the phone down and weighed his options, his hands absently shuffling the papers splayed across his desk—copies of scholarly articles about the dendrochronological properties of the oak panels favored by Rembrandt and many of his contemporaries. He couldn't think of anything he'd done that would make him a target, but if he didn't cooperate, the muscle might come charging inside, and somebody could get hurt. After a moment, he shoved his chair back from the desk, got up, and slipped into his bomber jacket.

"Where are you going?" Charles asked.

"Out."

"The department meeting commences in fifteen, Val."

"Perhaps Higgerson won't notice my absence."

"He will."

"I'll risk it."

"Missing another mandatory meeting is not advisable. Not if you still aspire to a tenured position."

Not advisable? Aspire to a tenured position?

The way Charles—never Chuck nor Charlie—talked always irritated the hell out of Val. But after three years of sharing a cramped and cluttered basement cubicle where they were never more than four feet apart, Val feared he was picking up some of the same fussy affectations.

"They're never going to promote me anyway, Charles."

"You don't know that for a certainty."

For a certainty? Val shrugged and strode out the door.

His days at Brown were numbered, and he knew it. He was

never going to fit in. He didn't even want to. He was Radiohead to their Mozart, Budweiser to their chardonnay, Levi's and T-shirts to their elbow patches and bow ties. He enjoyed teaching undergraduates and despised the obligatory research into the few obscure and dusty corners of art history that remained partially unexplored. They despised students and lived to see their bylines on scholarly articles in impenetrable academic journals that no one ever read. Federal Hill, the Italian working-class neighborhood where he grew up and still lived, was a ten-minute drive from the campus on College Hill, but it was not a distance that could be measured in miles.

What sustained Val, besides the teaching, was the work he did over summer breaks with the Association for Research into Crimes Against Art. Last year, he'd scored a minor triumph, assisting in the recovery of two paintings by Eugene Joseph Verboeckhoven that had been stolen from the undistinguished collection of a small museum in Des Moines.

Unimpressed, Dean Higgerson had decreed that plebian detective work would have no bearing on tenure. And, he'd been quick to add, Val's lively, sometimes hilarious blog on stolen art most emphatically could not be regarded as scholarly publication.

Val pounded up the stairs to the first floor, fleeing the specter of another soul-sucking department meeting. He dashed across the lobby, burst through the outer door, skipped down the marble steps, and saw a navy-blue suit standing beside a black Lincoln parked illegally at the curb. The suit opened the car's rear door. Val silently nodded and climbed in, then slid over as the suit squeezed in beside him.

As the car eased into the flow of light midafternoon traffic, the suit tossed a black cotton hood at Val's chest.

"The boss says you gotta put this on."

Val took it as a good sign. If they didn't want him to know

where they were going, they probably intended to let him go once they were done with him.

They'd been cruising in silence for an hour or so, long enough to reach Boston or New Haven, when Val felt the car roll to a stop. If the drive had been a ruse to confuse him, they might still be in Providence. As he was roughly pulled from the Lincoln, he sucked in a deep breath and detected a faint hometown whiff of spilled fuel oil and sewage. Still, he couldn't be sure. Boston and New Haven often smelled the same way.

He was led down a short walkway, up two steps, and through a door that closed behind him. Inside, he was tugged down a hallway, the tile or stone floor slick under his Converse All Stars, and then left through another door onto a thick carpet. There he was turned and nudged into a chair that felt like leather in a room that smelled of cigars.

The voice from the phone: "Good afternoon, Professor Sci-arra. You can pull off the hood now."

Val did so.

"Take a moment to let your eyes adjust to the light."

What light? Heavy drapes had been pulled across the win-dows, perhaps to prevent Val from guessing their location, and the lamps had been left off. In the gloom, he took a slow look around. Gold brocade wallpaper, Tiffany-style lamps, a Hum-mel collection in a glass-front bookcase, and, across from him on a brown leather sofa, a fat man in tan slacks and a cardigan sweater.

"Better now?"

Val nodded.

"Sorry about the hood. Necessary precaution."

"Who are you, and what do you want?"

"You don't recognize me?"

"No," Val said, although those jowls and hooded eyes seemed

vaguely familiar. He had a feeling he'd seen the face in the newspaper once or twice, but he couldn't put a name to it.

"We met when you were a child. I was a friend of your
uncle's."

"I don't remember."

"Probably for the best. Can I offer you something? Marco has
brought us an excellent bottle of French wine."

Val looked at him then, the suit from the car, standing in
shadow by the room's open pocket doors, hands clasped in front
and a telltale bulge under his left arm. Val felt the urge to rush
him, snap his wrist, and take the gun away, just to show that he
could; but he figured it was best if they underestimated him.

"Fine wine would be wasted on me," Val said. "I'm a Bud-
from-the-can kind of guy."

"Budweiser? I don't have any of that camel piss. How about
a Wychwood?"

Val had never heard of it, but he nodded.

"Marco?" the fat man said.

The suit disappeared into the hallway and returned moments later with an uncorked bottle of wine in one hand and an
open bottle of beer in the other. With his hands full, Val mused,
snatching his piece would be even easier.

A crystal goblet, already holding a quarter-inch of white
wine, stood on a piecrust table beside the fat man. The suit
refilled it and set the bottle down. Then he went to the glass-
front bookcase, bent to open the bottom shelf, and removed an
odd-looking vessel. It was shaped like a distended hourglass and
looked to be about ten inches tall. The suit handed it to Val and
tipped the beer bottle as if to fill it.

"Hold it," Val said, covering the top of the vessel with his
left hand. He twisted in his chair to turn on a lamp on the table
beside him and examined the object under the light. He glanced
up and saw a sly smile cross his host's face.

"It's bronze," the fat man said. "Beer won't do it any harm. Let Marco fill it for you, professor."

Val did as he'd been told, then raised the vessel to his lips and felt a thrill that had nothing to do with the contents.

"Tell me what you know about this object," the fat man said.

"It's a Chinese ku."

"And?"

"I'm not an expert on Chinese antiques, but it resembles ritual vessels that have been excavated from ancient tombs in the Yellow River Valley. If it's genuine, it could be Qin, or perhaps even Shang Dynasty, which would make it exceedingly rare and valuable."

"It's Shang," the fat man said. "You're probably the first person to drink from it in three thousand years."

Val shook his head in amazement. He took another sip and asked, "How did you come to own it?"

"I don't. I'm holding it for some associates. I understand the FBI has been searching for a ku just like this one for quite some time."

"Oh, Jesus," Val said.

"For twenty-three years, to be precise."

"The Isabella Stewart Gardner Museum robbery," Val said.

"What do you know about that?"

"I only know what's been in the newspapers."

"Even so."

Val took a moment to gather his thoughts. "In 1990, the museum's security was a joke. Two poorly trained, unarmed guards. An alarm system that was not connected to the Boston PD. Even back then, a lot of home owners had better security for their Beanie Babies collections. Late one night, two men dressed in Boston Police uniforms knocked on the front door and said they were there to investigate a report of an intruder. The guards let them in and ended up spending the rest of the night handcuffed to pipes in the basement. The thieves spent nearly an hour and a half traipsing about the building, taking what they wanted. They got away with more than half a billion dollars in rare art. It was the largest art heist in history."

"Exactly what did they steal, professor?"

"That was a puzzler," Val said. "Most of the value was in two large oils, Vermeer's *The Concert* and Rembrandt's *The Storm on the Sea of Galilee*, but they also took several lesser pieces including the ku, five drawings by Degas, and a finial that once stood atop a flag carried by Napoleon's army."

"Why a puzzler?"

"Because they passed up dozens of priceless paintings—masterpieces by Raphael, Rubens, Michelangelo, Botticelli—many of them small and easily portable."

"What does that tell you?"

"Either the thieves were rank amateurs or they were working from a shopping list supplied by an interested buyer."

"Your best guess?"

"Amateurs."

"Why?"

"Because they cut several paintings from their frames, damaging the edges. A professional art thief would have known better."

"Let's say they were amateurs," the fat man said. "Let's suppose that until they read about the robbery in the newspapers, they had only a vague idea of what they had. Only then did these two jerkoffs figure out the loot was so famous that it would be next to impossible to find anyone crazy enough to buy it."

"Okay," Val said.

"Let's also suppose they found out from the newspapers that the art was going to fall apart unless it was stored someplace with temperature and humidity controls. What do you think they'd do next?"

"You tell me."

"I'm betting they'd turn to someone they could trust," the fat man said. "Someone who had a way to keep the art safe and hidden until such time as it could be returned."

"Makes sense," Val said. "Are you saying that time is *now*?"

"Let's suppose I am."

"Why?"

"Because the thieves can no longer be charged with the theft. The statute of limitations has run out."

"Why not just give everything back, then?"

"Because anyone holding it can still be charged with possession of stolen goods."

"Ah. Of course."

"There's also the matter of the five million dollars the museum has offered for their return."

Val raised an eyebrow.

"What I propose, Professor Sciarra, is that you serve as a go-between to get the art back where it came from. Do this service for me and 10 percent of the reward money is yours."

Val flashed on what five hundred thousand dollars could buy. A luxury condo on the East Side. A new Ford Mustang to replace his aging Toyota Celica. The freedom to tell Higgerson to fuck off.

"Why me?" Val asked.

"Because you know the art world and the people in it, because you have experience with this kind of thing, and because I have always had the utmost respect for your family. As a Sciarra, you understand why we need to keep the authorities out of it."

"I see. May I examine the rest of merchandise, then?"

"What for?"

"So I can satisfy myself that you have it and that it's still in good condition."

"Well, it's not here," the fat man said. "I suppose I could arrange a viewing . . ." He paused to think it over. "But it would be hard to set up, and I don't see the need for it. Just take my word that I can deliver."

"Okay, then."

"Thanks for coming, professor. I'll get back in touch in two weeks."

The fat man rose and extended his hand. Val pulled himself from his chair and shook it to seal the deal. In the silence, he heard the faint clanging of a bell. It sounded like the one at Grace Episcopal. He glanced at his watch and saw that it had struck three minutes before the hour. Yes, he thought. He was still in Providence.

Moments later, as he was being tugged blindly out the front door, he heard the click of high heels on the sidewalk.

A woman's voice: "Hungry yet?"

A man's voice: "Famished. Let's walk down the block to Andino's."

He wasn't just in Providence, then. He was on Federal Hill.

That evening, after a blind, hour-long ride back to Brown, Val drove home, fired up his laptop, and scrolled through the *Providence Dispatch* archives. Forty minutes later, he stumbled on a three-year-old article about the arrest of Domenic Carrozza, fifty-two, of Providence, on suspicion of conspiracy to extort protection money from the city's strip clubs. The story identified him as a capo in the Patriarca crime family, still called that even though Patriarca himself was long dead and buried. The story was accompanied by a photograph of a man being led away in handcuffs from an impressive Victorian condominium building on Slocum Street in Federal Hill. It was the fat man. A little more research showed that he'd beaten the charge, and that he was still living in the same condo.

Val bookmarked the stories, logged off, and then said, "Shit!"

Too late, he realized he was better off not knowing any of this if he should ever be questioned by the authorities.

Val drove to the Fenway section of Boston three days later for a meeting at the Gardner. The museum's security director, a former Secret Service agent named Percy Twisdale, walked him past the two huge, empty frames where the Rembrandt and the Vermeer once hung and then led him to a spacious meeting room.

"Have you had an opportunity to examine the stolen art?"

"I was shown only the Shang Dynasty ku."

"And you believe it to be genuine?"

"I'm not an expert in that field, but it appeared to be, yes."

"May I ask the circumstances under which you examined it?"

Val ran it down for him: the mysterious phone call, the muscle, the hood pulled over his head, and the long drive to an undisclosed location, leaving out the fact that he had a good idea where he'd been taken.

"I see. And what of the other treasures?"

"I have been assured that they have been properly stored and remain in good condition."

"Do you know where they are?"

"I don't. I've merely been asked to serve as a middleman to negotiate their return."

"And to secure the reward for the people you represent?"

"That is correct."

"And have you been promised a share of the reward?"

"A small one, yes—and the satisfaction of seeing the masterpieces returned."

"Why the cloak-and-dagger? Why haven't these people contacted us themselves?"

"They're worried that they could still be charged with possession of stolen goods."

"I see. You will forgive me if I am skeptical of your story. We have had quite a number of false leads over the last twenty-three years."

"I've read about that, yes."

Twisdale gave him a hard look and drummed his fingers on the table. "If you can indeed procure the works, they will all have to be returned to us and examined by our experts to verify their condition and authenticity before the reward can be paid."

"I understand."

"So how do you suggest we proceed?"

"I've been told that I will be contacted sometime next week. At that time, I'll explain your requirements and do my best to make the appropriate arrangements."

Appropriate arrangements? Jesus. He *was* starting to sound like Charles.

Two mornings later, Val startled awake. Someone was hammering on his door. He rolled over and looked at the alarm clock. It was just after six a.m.

He got up, pulled on a Dustin Pedroia Red Sox T-shirt and a pair of jeans, and padded barefoot to the door. Peering through the peephole, he saw a frowning face topped by a baseball cap. He unlatched the security chain, turned the deadbolt, and opened the door.

"Valerio Sciarra?"

"Yes."

"FBI."

"I gathered that from the letters on your hat."

"We have a warrant to search the premises."

The frowning man shoved a sheet of paper at Val, elbowed him aside, and walked in, followed by three more men wearing the same hat.

"Sit on the floor against the wall, please, and keep out of our way."

Val did as he was told and watched the four agents tear the little studio apartment apart. They pulled books from shelves, dumped bureau drawers onto the floor, dug through his clothes closet, rifled through his kitchen cabinets, rummaged through his Frigidare, and even peered into the grease-caked oven.

When they were done, the agents gathered what they seemed to think was evidence—stacks of articles about art theft, Val's laptop computer, and his properly registered firearms, a .380 Taurus ACP and a .50-caliber AE Desert Eagle. Two of them lugged the stuff out to the car. The other two pulled Val to his feet.

"We need you to come with us," the one who seemed to be in charge said.

"Am I under arrest?"

"No, but our superiors would like you to answer some questions."

Val considered refusing, but that would make it look like he'd done something wrong. Instead, he was driven to the FBI's satellite office on Dorrance Street, taken to a small interrogation room, seated in a straight-backed metal chair, and left alone to stew for two hours.

He was thinking about walking out when the door swung open and two men he hadn't seen before strode in.

"I'm Special Agent Alex Burns of the Boston bureau of the FBI," said the tall one in the pearl-gray suit. "And this," he gestured toward the shorter one in a charcoal suit, "is Special Agent Francis Hanrahan of our Providence office."

Burns took the chair across a metal table from Val and placed a leather briefcase on it. Hanrahan remained standing, his body tense as if ready for trouble. Neither offered to shake hands.

"So then," Agent Burns said, "why don't you begin by telling me why a Brown University art history professor feels the need to be heavily armed?"

"Heavily armed? It's only two handguns."

"True, but the Desert Eagle has enough stopping power to drop an elephant."

"I'm ex-military. I like firearms."

The agent snapped open the briefcase, removed a file folder, and shuffled through the papers inside. "Six years in the army, 75th Ranger Regiment, three tours of duty in Afghanistan."

"That's correct."

"Thank you for your service."

"You're welcome."

"And you like firearms?"

"I just said that."

"Where did you get the Desert Eagle?"

"Proline Firearms in Warwick."

"It would have set you back nearly two grand. Isn't that an extravagant expense for someone living on an assistant professor's salary?"

"Brown pays well enough for me to afford it."

Burns consulted the file again and said, "Huh. Eighty-two thousand a year. So why do you live in a rundown Federal Hill tenement?"

"I'm saving my money in case I don't get tenured."

"Seems odd that you'd splurge on a gun."

"Not to me."

"Okay, then. I see from your blog that you are an expert in stolen art."

"It's an interest of mine, yes."

"In fact, last summer you assisted in the recovery of two stolen paintings, is that right?"

"It is."

"Can you tell me how you were able to do that?"

"The Association for Research into Crimes Against Art, a group that I'm associated with, received a tip that the paintings were hanging in a private home near San Francisco."

"Where did the tip come from?"

"It was anonymous."

"I see. So what happened next?"

"I flew to San Francisco and met with the homeowner, who told me he had acquired the paintings in a private sale and had no idea that they'd been stolen."

"You believed him?"

"They were not particularly important works, so his story was plausible."

"And then?"

"I arranged for him and his lawyer to meet with representatives of the museum to negotiate the return of the paintings."

"Were you compensated for your role in this?"

"I was not."

"I understand that the thieves were never apprehended."

"That's true. The names on the sales agreement proved to be phony, and there were no other leads."

"So now, less than a year later, you are attempting to negotiate the return of the masterpieces stolen from the Gardner Museum."

"Yes, but how did you know?"

"Did you get another anonymous tip?" the agent asked, ignoring Val's question.

So he again described the mysterious phone call, the long drive with a hood over his head, and the meeting with a man he didn't know—although he figured the agent must have already heard all this from the Gardner's security director.

"Did you recognize the man?"

"No."

"Are you aware that lying to an FBI agent is a felony?"

"I am."

"So I'll ask you again: did you recognize the man?"

"I did not." It was not a lie because Val didn't figure out who the fat man was until later.

"And where did this meeting take place?"

"As I already told you, I wasn't allowed to take the hood off until they brought me inside." Another evasion, but still not a lie.

"Did you look out the windows?"

"They were covered."

"Describe the room to me."

Val did so.

"Describe the man."

"I'd rather not."

"Would you be willing to look at some mug shots?"

"No."

"Why not?"

"Because if I identify him, and you pick him up, I won't be able to negotiate the return of the masterpieces. They could be lost to the world forever."

"Did this man you claim you didn't recognize show you the stolen art?"

"Only the Chinese ku. I didn't see any of the paintings or drawings."

"Was the ku genuine?"

"I think so, but I can't say for sure."

"Do you know where the stolen art is being kept?"

"No."

"Have you been promised a share of the reward money?"

"A small one, yes."

"How small?"

"I'd rather not say."

"So you have a financial incentive to obstruct this investigation."

Val didn't respond to that.

The agent shuffled through the file again. "The FBI has reason to believe that New England organized crime figures were involved in the Gardner heist."

"I read that in the newspapers."

"Your family, the Sciarras, have a history of involvement in organized crime."

"Just my late uncle Rudy," Val said.

"And your father."

"My father? That's not true."

"He has a record of multiple bookmaking arrests."

"Oh, right. I heard something about that. It was when he was young, before he had us kids. After that he got out of it."

"Or maybe he just got better at concealing his illegal activities."

"My dad was a bus driver, for godsakes." With that, Val pushed back from the table and got to his feet.

"Where do you think you're going?" Burns said.

"To work, but I'd like my firearms back first."

"Not until we run ballistics tests."

"What for?"

"To assure ourselves that they haven't been fired at any crime scenes. It's routine."

Val headed for the door.

Hanrahan blocked it. "One last question," he said, breaking his long silence. "You claim you didn't recognize the man when you met with him, but do you know who he is now?"

Val didn't answer. He shouldered the agent aside and strode out the door.

The first thing Val noticed when he got to his office was that his desk drawers had been rifled through, the contents scattered on the floor. And his desktop computer was gone.

"The FBI was here, Val," Charles said. "They had a search warrant, and they asked me a lot of questions about you. They talked to Higgerson too. What in heaven's name have you gotten yourself into?"

Val didn't reply at first. Instead he pawed through the debris and saw that his files on stolen art were gone. "What did they ask about?" he finally said.

"They were intensely interested in what you know about the Gardner Museum theft. I told them stolen art was a fascination of yours but that we hadn't discussed it much. They also showed me a dozen mug shots and asked if I had observed you in the company of any of the people in them. I told them that I hadn't."

Val turned to leave.

"Val? Did you have something to do with it?"

"With what?"

"The Gardner robbery."

"It was twenty-three years ago, Charles. I was twelve years old, for godsakes."

"Where are you going?"

"My afternoon class starts in ten minutes."

"Higgerson wants to speak with you."

"He can wait."

Thursday evening, Val was lying on his Salvation Army couch, drinking his third beer and watching the Red Sox–Rays game on his nineteen-inch flat screen, when his cell phone barked. He checked the number, didn't recognize it, and answered it anyway.

"Professor Sciarra?"

"Yes?"

"My name is Mulligan. I'm a reporter for the *Providence Dispatch*. I'm working on a story about stolen art, and I was hoping you could answer a few questions."

"Not right now," Val said. "I've got the Sox on, and Buchholz is about to take a no-hitter into the eighth."

"No shit? Call you back later."

Kelly Johnson, the Rays' first hitter in the eighth, splintered his bat on Buchholz's second pitch but managed to loft a fly that dropped for a cheap hit in shallow right field. Val threw his empty Budweiser can against the wall, and the cell barked again.

"Lucky bastard!" the caller said.

"Yeah."

"So can we talk now?"

"What was your name again?"

"Mulligan."

"Liam Mulligan?"

"Uh-huh. But my friends just call me Mulligan."

Val knew the name. He'd seen the byline on the organized crime stories he'd read in the *Dispatch*'s archives. "What can I do for you, Mr. Mulligan?"

"My editor wants an update on some old art museum robbery in Boston. I don't know a damned thing about art, professor, so I was hoping you could help me out."

The reporter asked about Val's background, his research, and his work with the Association for Research into Crimes Against Art, establishing his credentials, before turning to the matter at hand.

"So what can you tell me about the unsolved heist at the Isabella Stewart Gardner Museum?"

"All I know about that is what I've read in the newspapers, Mr. Mulligan."

"I understand, but a lot of conflicting stuff has been written about it, so it would be a big help if you could summarize the facts for me."

Val did so.

"And that's all you know?"

"It is."

"Well, you've been a big help. Thanks a lot, really. But listen, not that this has anything to do with my story, but I've written a lot of stuff about the mob over the years, and I can't help but wondering. Are you related to Rudy Sciarra?"

Val explained the relationship, but he had a feeling the reporter already knew the facts.

"Must be cool to have such a notorious relative," Mulligan said.

"Actually, it's not."

"Oh. Okay. Just one last question, then. A law-enforcement source tells me you have been questioned in connection with the Gardner case and that the FBI executed a search warrant on your home and office. Can you confirm that for me?"

Aw shit. "I have no comment."

"What is your involvement in the case, professor? Do you know who stole the art? Do you know where it is?"

"Have a pleasant evening, Mr. Mulligan," Val said, and clicked off.

Later, as he watched the Sox postgame show, he wondered, *Was Mulligan really that good, or was the leak an attempt by the FBI to ratchet up the pressure?*

First thing next morning, Val strolled down to Broadway, bought a black coffee and a cinnamon-raisin bagel at the Seven Stars Bakery, and fetched a copy of the *Dispatch* from a sidewalk vending box. Back at his apartment, he sat on the couch, drank his coffee, and skimmed the story on the Sox game before turning to the front page.

In the lower-left corner, below the fold, a two-column headline read: *Brown Prof Questioned in Boston Museum Heist.*

The story under Mulligan's byline said the FBI had identified Val as "an associate of the Patriarca crime family," a relative of a notorious mob hit man, and "a person of interest" in the Gardner Museum robbery.

If the idea was to ratchet up the pressure, it was working.

Val snatched the remote from the end table and flipped to the Fox News affiliate to see if the morning show was carrying the story. Instead, it was running a live feed from in front of the Victorian condominium building on Slocum Street. The first thing Val saw was a tall guy in an FBI hat carrying a clear plastic evidence bag out the front door. Val couldn't be sure, but it looked like the ku was inside. Three minutes later, Agents Burns and Hanrahan led Domenic Carrozza out. The mobster was wearing a terry-cloth bathrobe and bedroom slippers, and his hands were cuffed behind him.

Jesus! How did they know? Then it came to him: they'd found the research about Carrozza on his computer.

Val's ranger training kicked in: if you find yourself in an untenable position, remove yourself as rapidly as possible. He sprang up, threw some clothes into a gym bag, and bolted. It wasn't the FBI that worried him now.

He took the stairs three at a time, burst through the front door, and spotted the black Lincoln at the curb, Marco standing by its open rear door with a semi-automatic in his right hand.

"Get in."

Val dropped the gym bag, shrugged, and shuffled toward the car. When he got within reach, he lashed out with both hands, grabbing the pistol by its slide with his left and cracking Marco's forearm with his right. The maneuver was supposed to end with the gun in Val's left hand, but he was out of practice. The semi-automatic fell and discharged a round as it clattered on the pavement. Val clutched the back of Marco's neck and cracked his head against the roof of the car.

But the Lincoln's front doors were opening now. Two more suits climbed out.

Agent Hanrahan sat behind his desk in the federal building on Dorrance Street, an unlit cigar clamped between his jaws. Burns and Twisdale, the Gardner security chief, sat in leather chairs on the other side of the desk. They all looked glum.

"Carrozza still isn't talking," Hanrahan said. "Claims he bought the ku at a flea market and doesn't know anything about any stinking museum robbery."

"He expects us to believe that?" Twisdale asked.

"Of course not," Hanrahan explained, "but it's his story and he's sticking to it."

"We still got him for possession of stolen goods," Burns said.

"Like I give a shit," Twisdale said. "The rest of the art is still missing. What are you two fuck-ups doing about that?"

The agents didn't say anything.

"What about Sciarra?" Twisdale asked. "Think he might break if you question him again?"

"Maybe," Burns said, "but the asshole's in the wind."

"What? How did you let that happen?"

"Two days ago, when the *Dispatch* story broke, we rolled up to his Federal Hill apartment at six a.m.," Hanrahan explained, "but Sciarra wasn't home. A neighbor told us he liked to walk down to Broadway for coffee and the paper first thing every morning, so we drove over there. We checked three or four coffee places along the street, then headed back to Sciarra's. The same neighbor said he'd come back but that a couple of bruisers forced him into a black car and took off."

"Did he get the plate?" Twisdale asked.

"No."

"Christ! Why in hell did I bring you clowns into this? Should have gone with my first instinct and handled it myself."

The cell on Hanrahan's desk played the theme from *Dragnet*. He answered it, listened for a minute, said, "We'll be there in ten," and clicked off. "Well, gentlemen, Sciarra's not in the wind anymore."

By the time Tisdale and the agents arrived at the construction site behind Rhode Island Hospital, Providence detectives had already cordoned it off with yellow police tape. They ducked under it and looked down at the footing for the basement of a planned suite of doctors' offices.

"A security guard who works for the contractor called it in," a Providence detective told them. "Half an hour later and the body would have been buried under eight feet of wet concrete."

"Medical examiner on the way?" Burns asked.

"Like we need him to tell us the cause of death," the detective said. "I can count the bullet holes from here."

Tisdale held his head in his hands.

Hanrahan gave him a brotherly clap on the shoulder. "Look on the bright side," the agent said. "There's one less mob scumbag running loose on the streets."

ARMORY PARK

BY TAYLOR M. POLITES

Armory District

The squawks of the chickens jerked Cal awake. Red and blue lights flashed off the flat white ceiling. Laura slept, her face toward the wall, Elmo curled at her feet. Cal peered through the narrow blinds. Across the lane, police officers milled around an old Caprice Classic, a decommissioned police cruiser painted a flat black that accentuated scar-like bolt holes where the top lights and flood lamp had been. Parked in a line behind it, their lights sparking like strobes, were two actual police cruisers, Providence PD. There seemed to be others down toward Willow Street. The dead-end lane could not fit more.

Cal moved to the living room for a better view. The chickens squawked and clucked, bobbing and turning in their little enclosure behind hexagonal wire. He could see them from the side window, all six safe but unsettled. Two EMTs rolled a white-sheeted gurney to the black car. There was a man inside. Not moving. The chickens cackled. The police radios cackled back.

His hands tingled like they were asleep. He had been expecting something like this since Laura had insisted they move to the neighborhood. She would never admit she had made a mistake, but how much evidence did you need?

In the morning, Cal told Laura that they had dodged a bullet. What an edgy neighborhood! He could not resist getting in a dig. Laura's eyes turned flat and unresponsive. She had been moody the night before, doubtless judging him for another blunder. Maybe he got the capital of Bullshitistan wrong. She had raved about how the apartments were bigger and cheaper in the Armory. How edgy it was. Well, here was its edge. His dad had suggested they install a gun turret in the living room window.

Cal caught their landlady outside while Laura was in the shower. She gave him the details she had gathered from the police scanner. Hispanic male, twenty-five years of age, five foot eight, 160 pounds. The same age as Cal. Slumped over in the passenger side of the vehicle with a bullet in his head. The car had been left running, which prompted the call to the police, although Mrs. Caracelli made clear that she had not called.

Cal thought she had to be eighty. She was skeletally thin with wiry gray hair and wore a black velour tracksuit with sky-blue piping. She kept a cigarette behind her left ear. From the first showing, she had seemed to favor him. He was handsome, and old women in particular warmed to him quickly. Cal's weak salary as a bank teller hadn't bothered her. She had said, You have to start somewhere. Yeah, he had replied, I've got my share of shit to eat. They were both native Rhode Islanders. He had grown up in an East Bay town with colonial charm and a working-class core. The old lady had been okay with Laura's family kicking in half the rent too, since she was in a grad program at Brown. Italian Early Modern, Laura had said, what they used to call the Renaissance. The old woman had chuckled and looked at her bust of Dante. Laura was from Westchester, but Mrs. Caracelli said New York City with a frown of disapproval. She had even let them keep chickens, another fancy of Laura's. Mrs. Caracelli said it reminded her of her childhood, spent a few blocks south. Cal had been skeptical about the chickens, but Laura went for fads. Like home fermentation and composting. He did like to go outside for warm eggs to scramble, although there was some-thing twisted about it. He enjoyed their game of Farmer Brown. A little *American Gothic* in the city, Laura said.

Laura came down the two wooden steps to the street, her hair wet from the shower, wearing tight jeans, which he liked, and a tight purple V-neck, which he also liked. When he had met Laura just over a year ago during happy hour at McFadden's, his first thought had been that she was just the type of girl he liked to watch get off. The uptight ones were always the best. She proved him right. Before the big move, they were practically porn stars. He knew just where to touch her. Something electric had been working between them. The excitement of the commitment maybe. Another layer of distance removed. He had never felt that electricity before.

"What have you heard?" she asked, coming close to him.

Mrs. Caracelli nodded good morning, smiling brightly, and watched as Cal explained. He stood where the car had been, towed away an hour before. Exhaust hung thick in the air as if the tailpipe still coughed out fumes, filling the lane of tightly packed wood-frame buildings.

"How did we not hear a gunshot?" Laura asked.

Mrs. Caracelli interjected, sitting on the creaky steps to the second floor smoking her cigarette: "They didn't kill him here. They just dumped him. Classic job. I guess they didn't want the car either."

Laura, wide-eyed, turned back to Cal. The look expressed horror either at the violence or at Mrs. Caracelli's indifference. He almost laughed, although none of it was funny. Laura stepped closer to him and whispered, exaggerating the words with her mouth, "We can't live here." She looked back at the old woman and smiled.

"Mrs. Caracelli," Cal called to her, "has this happened before?"

The old woman gave a skull-faced smile and took a drag on her cigarette. She let the smoke pour from her mouth like a dragon. "You should have been here thirty years ago. Needles all in the park. Hookers. Drug dealers right on the street. Jesus."

She took another pull from her cigarette. She reminded Cal of his grandmother.

Laura's eyes grew wider. Her long, thin face had become longer and thinner.

Cal whispered, "We just moved in. We have a lease." Laura didn't seem to care about that, but when you grew up with everything given to you, it never occurred to you that somebody had to pick up the tab.

"Who cares?" she whispered back fiercely. She stood where the car had been, along the picket fence that bordered Liz Westerberg's flower garden. Laura shook her head, short little shakes, as if her processor had hit a snag that caused her to reboot again and again.

"You're the one who wanted to move here," he insisted, still whispering.

Laura shook her head again. Her mouth was open. Total shutdown. She walked quickly and directly into their apartment without looking at him or the old woman. When he went inside, he found her crying on the couch.

Cal took Elmo to the dog run that evening while Laura went to class. She had calmed down after her crying jag and brushed off his feeble efforts to comfort her. He had joked too much, not taken it seriously. He would make it up to her, find a way to explain the dead man. Just twenty-five.

The late afternoon was mild. The park was a short walk down streets lined with trees and Victorians with fancy shingles. Laura liked all that. Sure, what's not to like? Other than the occasional crack house a few blocks west. The park was nice too, with double rows of sycamores. The yellow-brick castle of the Armory loomed over it all, gilded pink and gold in the late-afternoon sun. Their neighbors all knew each other. A plus in Laura's opinion. But how could they not know each other? They were packed in like rats. He'd take the suburbs any day, and a nice, wide yard. Tall fences too.

His friends had warned him that he was marrying Laura by moving in with her. But he and Laura had talked about that. She had agreed: they were serious, committed, but not married. Why not move in together? They weren't rushing into anything, just taking a step. No biggie. It had resolved a common need. Her studio was cramped, and she was fussy about him leaving his things there. His roommates were unreformed frat boys who she could not tolerate. Tell them to grow up, she had said. She and Cal would live like adults. They were getting to that age. He had had plenty of girlfriends, but not like Laura. She was ambitious. She had goals. Get a PhD in art. Travel. Teach. Become an expert.

They had turned the apartment into their home, combined their furniture. His futon had been put out in favor of her couch, but his recliner was there and his big TV and video games. The second bedroom she took as her office, but he could play video games in the living room whenever he wanted as long as he wore headphones. They had settled in. Established routines. The neighborhood was pretty quiet aside from an occasional car window being smashed or the break-in of a first-floor apartment.

They lived on the first floor but were careful with the lights and dead bolts. The last thing they wanted was to put bars on the windows. They felt safe enough. No one had so much as bothered the chickens. One day the birds had escaped. Laura insisted it had been Cal's negligence. Fortunately, Liz Westerberg had seen them. She was collecting borage flowers to candy when a chicken walked by. She told Cal and Laura that she had strutted and flapped her wings at the birds to gently encourage them to return to their roost. He and Laura had laughed imagining small, mannish Liz dancing the Funky Chicken. Cal had told Laura to drop the blame game since nothing bad had happened.

The dog owners stood by the double-gated entrance. He recognized most of them. He did not know their names, but he knew their dogs.

"What happened?" asked the Chinese woman with the bull-dog named Roy.

"That's where you live, isn't it?" The lean, heavily stubbled hipster with the chocolate lab, Keno.

Cal shrugged as if he was a seasoned West Ender. "What are you gonna do?" he replied. His father used to say that. A rhetorical device. A way to end a discussion. There was of course no answer.

He asked about crime in the neighborhood. The black guy with the pit bulls Sophie and Chuck said it was minimal, just kids usually. Another man pulled him aside and told him never to walk in the park at night. Someone mentioned the prior summer when a fourteen-year-old had taken potshots with a Glock on Messer Street. "Just be aware, that's all."

"But this dead man," Cal asked, "what is that about?"

People shrugged.

A thin old man with wild white hair wearing a soiled khaki windbreaker waved his hand as if to speak. He called to his wheezing golden retriever, Goliath, and attached the dog's leash, then said, "The Cambodian drug gangs." He walked away with-out another word, holding up his right fist, index finger in the air. Others in the park rolled their eyes.

Laura was tense when she got home. She didn't like walking by the park or down their lane after dark. Cal poured her a glass of wine, but she refused it.

"I feel sick. I don't want any wine. What are you cooking? It smells awful." She put a hand on her stomach and looked like she was going to throw up.

"Are you okay?" he asked. "I thought you liked this. Chicken and eggplant."

She shook her head.

He changed the subject: "I've been asking people about the murder, but no one seems to know anything. I think it was a drug thing."

Laura narrowed her eyes, her eyebrows pinched together. "Drugs?"

"Yeah. Something to do with gangs and drugs." Saying it didn't make him feel better, but it made perfect sense. He braced himself for her response.

Laura looked out the kitchen window toward where the car had sat. Cal could see the spot over her shoulder. A black Caprice. Old. Patches of rust on the quarter panels. Wheels long missing their shiny hubcaps. The tires almost bald. Black and menacing. The chugging engine the only sound in the darkness, filling the air with poisonous fumes. A young man dead inside.

"Do you feel safe?" she asked. She faced him with crossed arms.

"I haven't talked to the police. I'll call the station tomorrow. We'll figure it out."

"We need to move. My parents agree." She looked exhausted. "Or we can pretend like everything is okay while I expect to find dead bodies every time I open the front door."

"Don't exaggerate, Laura. It's not a zombie apocalypse."

She shook her head and went into her study, shutting the door behind her.

Her fallback position when threatened was condescension, which sometimes made him feel ignorant, which always made him angry. Speed bumps. They had mostly seen each other at night when they were dating—dinners, movies, just hanging out. Now, they were together every day. He liked some of their new routines. They cooked together, which reminded him of his mom's dinner schedule with meals assigned to each night of the week. Laura kept a list on the fridge. Sometimes she called him her sous chef, which made him grit his teeth. She used that tone in front of their friends sometimes. Like he was her pet.

She came out when he called but declined the food. She lay down in the bedroom. He washed the dishes alone, his eyes unwillingly drawn through the window to Liz's yellow picket fence.

He didn't know what was happening. Doubt constricted his chest so that he had difficulty breathing. Laura had changed. She was cold, as if she hated him. He could see the difference in her eyes. He wanted to yell at her and bang his fists on the counter and demand her affection. Was it the dead man or did moving in together change that much? Had she discovered something unforgivable about him? He had plenty to complain about too. Her attitude, number one. She could drop the bullshit superiority any time she chose. He thought of saying that. He thought of pointing his finger in her face and saying it in the ugliest tone he could muster. Then he caught himself, remembering his parents' fights.

Lord, they had had some knock-down, drag-outs. They had always patched it up, pretended as if nothing had happened. Cal and his brother would stay in their room, terrified that their parents' rage would burst through the door—a door with no lock. There was never hitting. His father did not hit, but he tried to make his mother think he would. He had punched a hole in the garage wall once, straight through the sheetrock. His fingers had swollen like hot dogs. He never apologized.

It must have been the pressure release for their relationship. They had to do that or the whole thing would fall apart. Whatever. His parents were still married, but there were fewer fights. Instead, they sat in separate rooms, waiting for the other to die, as if the survivor would win. What was the point of that? Maybe this whole thing with Laura wasn't going to work out. Did he love her? A month ago he would have said yes without hesitation. Now, though, this was not fun. He would go to the police station, get some information, and hope that settled the whole thing.

* * *

The concrete-and-glass police headquarters sat over the interstate like a fortress before a moat. He entered, aware of the surveillance cameras behind mirrored half-globes. An officer waved him through the metal detector.

A crowd milled before the information desk, Latino, Asian, black, some down-and-out whites. Cal braced himself and got in line. Two women with great manes of hair stood behind a green glass wall giving terse instructions over a phone. Their voices were nasal, turning down when they asked a question. Was he really doing this for Laura? When he asked his question, the woman glowered at him. "Let me see if the detective is in. Wait over there." She pointed. Cal obediently hung up the phone and waited in the corner. The line snaked back and forth before him. He had almost walked out three times before the detective confronted him, a red-faced man whose buttons strained against his belly.

"You the kid asking about the murder? What's your interest?" The detective was not friendly.

"The body was right outside my house. My girlfriend is totally freaked out."

"What did you expect living there?" Cal didn't answer. "We got nothing on the case. No suspects, no leads." There must have been something in Cal's face. The officer seemed to soften. He scowled with discomfort. "Between us men, this looks like a gang thing. Some territorial issue, dealing drugs, the rest of it. The dead kid was in and out of the ACI. They aren't after you or your girlfriend, okay? That's all I got."

When Cal came home and told her what the officer had said, Laura locked herself in the bathroom. He heard her crying, but she said she was fine, just taking a bath.

Laura became strident. Her eyes were narrowed and suspicious.

She barked at him for little things—the toilet seat, urinating in the shower, leaving socks on the floor. She refused to take care of the chickens so he had to do it, even though they were her idea, and she refused to walk Elmo after dark.

She avoided him like a bad roommate. She went to class and the library. She stayed in her office with books filled with color plates, frescoes of gaunt faces, and shiny gold haloes. She was mapping the geometry of the Master of Provence, crisscrossing photocopied pages of the *Descent from the Cross* with thick black lines. Christ, bloody and disfigured, lay gruesomely prone across the arms of gray-faced mourners, Mary and Nicodemus and whoever else. Something to do with perspective and arrangement, connecting points located in folds of cloth and faces to create a pattern of diamonds that revealed some hidden structural mystery. She explained it to him, but she was looking toward the kitchen window. She was talking herself through it. She did not want him to respond.

The smell of exhaust seemed to linger in the alley. The plants thrived on it. Liz's garden rose up, green tendrils swallowing the yellow pickets and spilling into the street. When he took Elmo out for his last walk of the night, Cal looked behind him as they rounded the blocks. The streets were usually empty, long stretches of darkness broken by pools of dim light, shadowy and dangerous. Cambodian gangs were a problem, he knew, but there was a Cambodian family down the street. There was a Hmong church across the park. There were black and Latino families along with Italians and Poles who had been in the neighborhood for decades. He and Laura were identified with the new wave of younger people, gentrifiers. In the summer, the park was filled with all sorts of people. Liberian men played soccer in the mornings, screaming over fouls. White urban hipsters played kickball on Saturdays with stereo systems and kegs of Narragansett beer. On summer nights teenagers loitered around the swing sets, lit by intensely bright flood lamps, and they screamed with such intensity that Cal couldn't tell if they were playing or being raped. There were too many trees casting shadows that were too dark. There were too many beat-up cars with rusted wheels and too many people hanging around, like the Latino men who gathered under the trees on hot days, or the bums near the dog run, drunk on cheap hooch from Tropical Liquors.

He turned up Parade Street. The park was on his right. A large elm created a black canopy for two silhouettes that Cal could only discern because of the electric glow of one's cell phone. He thought they looked Hispanic. A third man was straight ahead on the next corner; he looked at Cal, then away. His right hand was shoved deep in his pocket, his other hand on his phone. A man under the tree called to the man on the corner: "What are you doing? Come over here." The man on the corner looked at Cal, then crossed the street. Was that a gun in his pocket?

Elmo sniffed the grass along the curb. Cal's elbows locked. He felt light-headed. He turned stiffly, trying to be casual, to move deliberately. "Come on, Elmo," he whispered, tugging at the leash. He resisted the urge to run. His fear embarrassed him. He was angry with himself, but what were his options? Was he going to ask them for their papers? Comment on the weather? Clearly a drug deal. He rushed home. Security lights clicked on in a flash outside the apartment. It jolted him, and he felt foolish again. A knot of anger stuck in his throat. He had forgotten the old woman had put them in. About fucking time.

Laura was in her office with the door open. She asked how the walk was. His voice rose as he answered, "It was fine, only three dead bodies." She was moody? No problem. He could be moody too.

He left for the bank early the next day, eager to get away from

Laura. The morning was cool, a hint of fall. He looked at where the black car had been and saw a candle and flowers. A tall glass jar with the Virgin of Guadalupe in bright colors on a sticker and a white candle burning inside. Red carnations lay beside it. He knelt and sniffed the candle. The odor was of chemicals. He had expected vanilla or citrus. Behind it was a piece of lined notebook paper, the edges ruffled from where it had been torn from a coiled wire binding. It read in Spanish, *We love you and miss you. We will see you in a better place.* He folded it and placed it behind the candle, just as it had been. The chickens clucked behind him. Without fail, every time they saw him they groused and scratched, expecting feed.

The sunlight cast crossways through the trees, hitting him dead in the eyes. The light was intensely yellow, not like the transparent light of midday, but a color that washed everything in a golden haze. The chickens slipped in and out of the shadows, clucking and bobbing their heads. Three Rhode Island Reds and three Plymouth Rocks. When the Plymouth hens stepped into the sunlight, their feathers, checkered bands of black and white, shimmered like silver. The Reds flashed like brass.

"Beautiful morning." The gravel voice was unmistakably Liz, but he jumped anyway. She wore lime-green Crocs and a nurse's shirt covered in red and green jalapeños. Her gray-striped hair was pulled back in a ponytail.

"Hey, Liz. How was the hospital?"

"Bloody as always, but we all survived." She noticed the flowers and the candle. "What's this?"

"Someone left it overnight. For the dead man."

She picked up the note and read it, then folded it up and put it back in its place as he had. "Terrible for the family. We see these kids—mostly kids, sometimes adults—coming in with gunshot wounds or knife wounds. Gang fights. Bad drug deals. Fighting everyone. How are you two holding up?"

Cal flexed his hand around the shoulder strap of his brief-case. "Doing okay. Laura's pretty freaked. It's made things a little rough."

She nodded and watched the flame in the votive. "Don't let it eat away at you. You're young. Talk to each other. It's all about communication."

"I guess we both want to make sense of it." He looked at Liz as if she knew the answer.

She considered him for a second. "What's to understand? No schooling, no jobs, no opportunities equals violence." She spoke to him like a teacher. "These kids are so young when they get caught up in the gangs, they don't realize they have options. Maybe they don't. The cycle feeds itself. And the rest of us just stand around and watch. Pretend like it doesn't have anything to do with us."

She laughed, showing her teeth, which seemed jagged and carnivorous. Wrinkles folded around her eyes and the corners of her mouth. The breeze moved the gray hair that was loose from her ponytail. The pink sunlight lit it like a red halo. He didn't like her comment about people standing around and watching. He wasn't one of those people. She was. Like a witch, glorying in the blood and death.

"Yeah," he said. "Crazy place."

Liz nodded. "You know you can make a left turn from the right lane in Rhode Island?"

He told her to have a good one and headed to work in a black mood.

He did not want to do it, but Liz's words echoed in his head. He had a choice: ask Laura what was going on, or wait for her to do it. The anxiety made him sick. If not for the constant worry, he would probably not do anything. But he had to end the agony. They would discuss this. Anger kept bubbling up in his throat with accusations of what she had done to him. He was preemptively attacking her, he knew. He wanted to be ready if she blamed him for something.

They sat on the couch facing each other. Her hands were flat on her knees. She did not seem surprised by his request to talk.

"I know this dead man has shaken you up. It's upset me a lot too," he began.

She looked puzzled.

"Look," he continued, "I wasn't a huge fan of moving to this neighborhood, but we're here now. Let's make the best of it. When the lease ends, we'll move. Wherever you want. The East Side, maybe. Or Barrington."

Her hands curled into little balls against her jeans. She looked at them. "That sounds great," she said.

Cal was amazed. No accusations or recriminations. No blame game. He smiled. "Great," he said. He put a hand on one of her balled fists. She relaxed her grip, flattened her hand so that it was rigid against her leg. "I love you, Laura. We can work through this." He had not meant to use the word *love*, but it came out. It seemed like the right thing to say. He did mean it. Maybe not right now, but he would mean it if she said it back.

He put his other hand on her shoulder and leaned in to kiss her. She tilted her head, making herself available to him. Her kiss was tentative. He moved closer, putting an arm around her.

They had not had sex since the body was discovered. Sex had always been the easy part. The dead man had soured that. But Cal sprang to attention. He led her to the bedroom, removed his shirt and pants. Laura sat at the end of the bed. He took off her top and kissed her breasts, cupping them in his hands.

"Too hard," she said. "That hurts."

"Sorry." He moved his hands down her sides to her pants and looked in her eyes. The need galloped inside him. She nodded yes but her eyes were dead. Reluctant. They disturbed him. They said there was something wrong. She did not feel the attraction she used to. She could say everything was okay, but it was not okay.

He became self-conscious. He lost focus and his erection faded. She gave a light laugh, then fell back on the bed and covered her eyes with her hands. He pulled on his pants and left the room.

He went to the kitchen and drank cranberry juice out of the bottle. He sat at the television wearing headphones and playing a video game. He was a Marine shooting at bad guys on the other side of the globe. He fired his weapon while the music played, a monotonous organ at a carnival booth. Blood poured from his victims. He continued playing well after he figured Laura would be asleep.

Cal thought he was dreaming. He had fallen asleep on the couch with the headphones on. The eerie carnival music played on a loop that repeated every ninety seconds. But then, mixed in, there was screaming. At least it sounded like screaming. The kids in the park or something. But close. Right outside. He lurched from sleep and tore the headphones off. It was the chickens who were screaming. Squawking, but with a high-pitched, blood-curdling intensity that extended for long seconds. He leapt from the couch and burst out of the house without thinking.

The security lights snapped on and flooded the street, but the corner of the house kept the side yard in deep shadow. The screeching birds beat their wings against the wire barrier so that it shuddered. Feathers floated in the air, pulled up and twisted into the treetops by the wind. He banged on the fence with both fists. Something else was in the cage. The birds screamed louder. A light came on in the house. Laura was calling his name. He heard a snarling hiss, like a cat or wild animal. The chicken wire shook with the weight of some creature, but Cal could not make it out.

The animal seemed large, too large for a cat but too dark to be a fox. He jumped back involuntarily, his skin wormy. The creature clambered to the top of the fencing, eight feet up, and leapt to a nearby tree branch that bounced with its weight. Leaves and branches crashed to the ground as the animal bounded away. Then everything was silent. Even the chickens stopped their commotion.

Cal looked down. Something wet shone in the half-light. One of the birds was dead. A Plymouth Rock. Black and white feathers danced across the yard. Laura came outside with a flashlight, wearing a T-shirt and his boxers.

"What the fuck was that?" She was shouting.

"Something killed a chicken!" He was yelling too.

She trained the flashlight on the floor of the coop. The bird lay twisted on her side, her entrails spilling from her belly, her throat a red mass of feathers. Nothing more than a carcass now.

"Susie," Laura said. They could tell from her wattle.

Laura moved the flashlight across the pen. The remaining five chickens clucked in a group, huddled together in the corner, jerking their heads left and right, their eyes shiny. Cal thought they must all be in shock.

"What are you going to do?" she asked.

He looked at her looking at him and something went off in his head. "What am I going to do? What the fuck are you talking about, Laura? What in the fuck are *you* going to do?" This was her fault. Fuck her. "What is going on with you?" His eyes strained to bursting in their sockets. He balled his hands into fists, ready to use them.

She covered her mouth and closed her eyes. She mumbled something that Cal couldn't understand.

"Answer me!" he shouted at her.

The old woman's light went on. The shades in Liz Westerberg's house rustled.

"I'm pregnant," Laura said. She began coughing, a convulsive, sobbing cough.

Cal stared, frozen, his fists clenched.

The old woman came out on her porch. "Everything all right down there?" she called.

He and Laura looked at each other. Her hand was clamped over her mouth. Someone had to answer.

"Fine, Mrs. Caracelli," he called back. "Fine. We just lost a chicken."

"A cat get it? I should have told you to put wire over the top."

"I'll do that tomorrow," he replied. "I'll definitely do that."

Laura turned and went inside. He stayed to clean up the mess.

They talked it through. This was why Laura had been so moody. He could understand that. She thought he had figured it out and was angry. How could he have figured it out? Telepathy? Now, they were in it together. And they would stay together. She wanted the child. And he did too, after he had given it some thought. He did want it. It was a surprise, but they were living together. They were everything but married. So why not? They had agreed. They were together for the child, and they would stay together.

The day was like a dream. He called in late to work so he could layer more chicken wire over the coop. He double-layered the sides, ensuring nothing living, not even a mouse, could squeeze in. He walked through work like a zombie. He got dinner together. Something simple that wouldn't upset Laura's stomach. Rice. Grilled chicken. Virtually no flavor.

He walked Elmo down the dark streets. They rounded the corner where he had seen the drug deal. What he had thought was a drug deal. It probably wasn't a drug deal. He stopped and looked where the two men had stood under the tree. What a crazy world, he thought. Left turn from the right lane.

Only in the dark could he see what he was feeling. He was terrified. And angry too. The anger was hard to explain. He was so angry; not like last night with the chickens when she told him, but something more durable. Things seemed to be spinning out of control. It was this neighborhood. The people. The dark streets. This was someone's fault. Like them moving in together. Or those fucking chickens. Her idea. Her fault. He felt like he had been tricked. She had been a different person before. Was the new Laura who she truly was? Too late now. Lucky for her, he was a stand-up guy. He was going to do the right thing. He would grit his teeth and do the honorable thing. But goddamn it. Fuck fuck fuck fuck fuck. Goddamn fuck.

He loved her. He loved her before and he loved her now. That stuff in between was just confusion. They would communicate. He loved her last month and he loved her now. This was the natural next step. They would have gotten here anyway. She was for life. This was for real. They would not become his parents.

He stood on the corner with Elmo. He could let the dog loose right here and maybe he would run away. Probably he would. Elmo would go half-wild if not on his leash. Laura had never trained him, and Cal believed that if there was no structure, at a certain point the dog became untrainable. Elmo might get hit by a car, running in circles on Broadway or caught up on Route 10. He might be picked up by someone, a family who would keep him and care for him, or a thug who arranged dogfights with pit bulls. After a week or two, he might come whining at their back door, weak and exhausted, forever changed by his ordeal.

Cal's hand touched the clip for the leash. He pushed the metal stud back and held it. The base of the clip hurt as it pressed into the tender part of his palm. The pain felt good. Elmo panted beside him, looking up at him expectantly. What are you gonna do? Put off answering, that was an answer. Trust that things will take care of themselves. That was an answer too. He let go of the latch and felt the lock click into place. The metal no longer pressed into his palm. He rubbed the spot against his pants to wipe the feeling away.

He was going to do the right thing. He wouldn't let Elmo run off. He wouldn't let the chickens be killed. He and Laura would have a child and he would take care of it too. And he would lose the anger. It couldn't last, this desire to hit something. To hit it hard. His father must have felt this way. He clenched his fists and relaxed them. Clenched and relaxed. He jerked at Elmo's leash, and the dog stumbled forward with a yelp. Cal ignored him and pulled harder. They needed to get back. Laura would be waiting.

TRAINING

BY DAWN RAFFEL

Providence Station

1.

The Mouth Is Saturated with the Taste of Something New

Wind is what wakes her, wind and rain, against the hotel window: he, in a slant across the king-size bed, as if to fill the whole of it; she curled tightly, knees to chest. Nausea rolls up in her. Feet to the floor. Nose to the glass. The rain, she sees, in the light from the street, falls thick like slush, not entirely liquid. Across the street a flag is madly flapping.

She enters the bathroom and splashes her face. Reflected back: pale, slim, her eyes slightly puffy—younger, she thinks, than hours before, dressed up, made up: the luminary's girl-friend. Young as the daughter he does not have. The light has a flicker. The hotel he'd researched, meticulously. He likes to live in advance.

She tosses a washcloth. Walks back out and watches him breathe.

In the glow from the street, the spit of light from the bath-room, she tries out a password. Second pass. Easy.

Asleep, he is almost as young as she.

2.

The Point of Departure

"Do you want to hear my idea?" he asked.

She didn't, not really, not then. She was tired, having been up in the night. But it wasn't a question, anyway. His mind was his wealth (and her youth was hers). That's why she was with him, wasn't it? She hungered for his fame, however middling it was, his place at the table—and hers as muse. He wasn't one to fool himself (he told himself that; in fact, he prided himself).

They had hours to kill. They had coffee and some kind of sticky tart. Café La France, the place was called.

"It's funny," he said. "I'm setting it here." His story, he meant, the work he'd been absorbed in, grouchy and distant, snappish to her, but now on a high. A triumph: the reading the night before, his old alma mater, the theater packed. A triumph indeed—that woman had said so, clutching his books, brushing her hair back, at the reception (cheese, wine, and something wasabi), again and again, and feting him, late, at the quaint café that the faculty favored.

"Here? Where?" She—the young and increasingly inappropriate girlfriend—opened a packet of sugar.

"Here in the train station. It's perfect for this."

He was ever so slightly hungover, she thought, a check in his pocket, wind in his lungs.

"Obviously, there are nuances and subtexts," he said. "The point of departure . . . and matters will arise in the course of the composition, but this is the gist . . ."

The rain had turned to snow by the time he awoke several hours earlier—wet, sloppy flakes that would soon begin to stick (the forecast was certain) and blanket the city and bring it to a halt. He'd worried aloud—delays, cancellations—he *had* to get back to New York, he said. This wasn't, he said, optional (meetings, et cetera), and so they had packed their bags in haste: he, the ironic jacket and tie, thick books unread; she, the tiny cobalt dress, crushed now and dirty, spiked heels—all wrong, she'd understood, arriving on campus (the way the gaze fell, the moneyed tone of voice)—toothpaste, Advil, mints, gum, her birth control not recently opened, soaps she had swiped from hotels over the years. He was in jeans now and she in dark leggings, a shirt that was his and was huge on her. "Swimming," she'd said, with satisfaction in her voice.

Down to the lobby, past Aspire, the restaurant, the front desk—"We'd better move quickly," he'd said to her. "Let's try to get seats on an earlier train. It's worth a shot, at least."

Business, pleasure, wool, down: checkout was crowded. A mother and daughter (not much older, in fact, than the girlfriend) who'd crisscrossed states for a visit to RISD were heading home, a quarrel in gestation in the cool air between them. Their tour had been canceled: every campus everywhere, it seemed, was set to close. No school for you!

The airport was dicey.

"Taxi," he said.

"Amtrak," he said.

"Crap," he said. "This is exactly, precisely, just what I didn't need to have happen."

"So here's the idea," he said to her. Their train was running late, of course, coming from Boston, and no, there was not a seat, not one, on the earlier Acela. Sold out. Completely. He'd asked more than once, as the line to buy tickets stretched out behind them, heaving in impatience.

"It's snowing," he said.

"I know," she said. "Oh, you mean in the story?"

"Obviously. It's snowing hard, the light is strange, and this young fellow—college student, goes to Brown, he's maybe a senior, handsome, lucky, you know the type—he is waiting at the station to pick up this girl."

"Girl?"

"Okay, woman. This woman, I should call her that. Louise is her name. I am naming her that, Louise, I think. I think I like the sound of that. The liquidy *L*. She is returning to him on the train from New York. But due to the weather . . ."

"Right," she said. Café La France was crowded, a thicket of elbows. Girls eating yogurt. A toddler—God save them, the girlfriend thought. At least they had seats.

"I already had the idea," he said. "Before this trip. That's what's strange. The train, the snow. The guy, I haven't named him yet, but you know, a Chip or what have you, but not quite that, drives a nice sports car."

"Mercedes?" she asked.

"Maybe," he replied. "He'd driven Louise here a few days before, to the station—outbound, her train to New York. But this is the thing: she really hadn't told him exactly, precisely, where she was going or why she was going, details and reasons, this girlfriend of his. He hadn't really asked. She did this sometimes, anyway, the years they'd been together—three, I think. Yes, three it is. But this last time she'd looked so sad, so slumped, he thought, so thin, her long curls spilling into her face, her eyes sad and desolate . . . She'd worn a blue coat. A color like cobalt. Going away . . . and of course he had a car; he had driven her here, to the station. He knew he hadn't wanted to look at her sadness. It angered him slightly. And he, too, was sad—yes, he was, because he knew he had to end it."

He waited for the question, begging for it.

"Why?"

"Why?" he said, as if surprised she had asked. "Because for all that he loved her, for all that she knew him—you know, knew that he wanted, for instance, to act, to be an actor, and not to be the, let's see, the lawyer his father expected—for all they had shared and done and dreamed, he knew it couldn't last. His parents would insist, of course, subtly, but still . . . His father, his mother, the family name . . . Louise was inappropriate . . . smart and ambitious, but still, there was a matter—let's say religion, and, well, ilk."

"Ilk?"

"Don't sulk," he said. "You know what I mean. And this is in the past, I said. Didn't I say? Late '70s. I had to have mentioned that, no?"

"No, you didn't."

"It wasn't so easy for him," he said, becoming defensive.

"Really? In the '70s?"

"Little you know. You know, hippies—post-hippies, whatever they were, free love and all that, the way the world was changing, all of it changing—sure, of course. But not for him. Louise had to go. Louise could not last. He knows that, accepts that, the way it has to be, and he knows that it ought to end sooner than later, and also he knows that she knows that too. Of course she does. She's smart, Louise. And now at the station, he is waiting for her, and he is filled with trepidation and lost in his thoughts; he is waiting and waiting, and so upset—the train is delayed, the station looks strange, looks wrong, transformed, not the way he remembered it, not how he thought of the place at all. Nothing's as it used to be. He's shaking. And also, despite that it's terribly crowded—the station is not that big to begin with, round, domed, and now it is packed full of families and students, the art kids with sketchpads, women in pairs, the men in suits, you know—everyone gives him a sort of berth, as if maybe they don't want to brush up against him. As if he smells. As if, he thinks, it's the sadness he feels, the strangeness he feels. He is tired too. He goes to get coffee but doesn't remember the coffee being expensive like this, fancy like this, and he doesn't have cash, or not enough. He doesn't have it on him. The girl behind the register is looking at him, as if he doesn't belong there. He doesn't much like that. And so he walks away again. He sits on the floor, against a wall, that wall, that one over there—the seats, every one of them, taken, you see. The board keeps rolling, more delays. Coming in increments. Later, later. Snow keeps falling, thicker now, according to the chatter of the people around him, muffled as it is. He, from where he is, cannot see the snow fall. He starts to sleep. He falls asleep. He starts to dream in his sleep. He is possibly even snoring a little, there on the floor. And this is the dream: The dream is the future. His future self. And he is entering a house like the house he grew up in, similar in stateliness, silver and oak, the predictable children—a girl and a boy. He has a briefcase in hand. There is a weight in his heart, and from another room he can hear a woman speaking, maybe on the telephone—yes, on the telephone—and then he sees the woman, the one who is his wife. And she is not, of course, Louise, of course she's not, and he is suddenly flooded, there in the dream, with a bone-chilling sadness, a wave of emotion that makes him ache. He wakes up on the floor."

"Are you sure you don't want a bite of this?"

"No," he says, peevish. "Listen. As I was saying . . . Well, maybe. A taste."

"What happens next?"

"Not bad," he says, brushing a crumb off. "A little too sweet. So there he is, sitting, waiting, filled with this sadness, and that's when it hits him: she might have been pregnant! That must have been it . . . she went to New York, Louise—why else, what for? And of course it was his, his child, and how could he not have known before? He vows on the spot to propose to Louise, to marry Louise, throw it all to the wind, take heed of the dream, the sadness, if only it's not too late . . . you know . . ."

"I get it," she says. "But why New York? It wasn't illegal in Rhode Island then, was it?"

He makes a motion with his hand as if to swat away the question. Logistics, for all of his forethought, annoy him; she knows that well.

"I'll figure it out," he says to her. "That isn't the point. So anyway, the train at last is coming, it's coming at last, and filled with resolve, he waits by the tracks. He goes down to the tracks. Track 2. A mass of people. Confusing. The looks he gets, as if he is dirty—why, he can't fathom. The train comes in, the one heading for Boston, and people pile off. Rush off. Parents and children, their coats and their bundles, their baggage, their breath . . . It's cold down there and snow falls hard, he can see it from the platform. And then . . . there at the end of the platform, the girl at the edge of his vision must be her, Louise, a little bit ghostly, but only for a moment, a moment and then: she is gone. He simply can't find her. He looks and he looks. The train is pulling out again . . ."

She swallows her latte. Glances at her watch.

"And then he reconsiders. He must have been mistaken. He must have been confused. It must have been the next train. She must have told him something. She must have missed her train—they didn't have cell phones, not back then."

"I know that," she says.

"He simply has to wait. He sits on the bench now, a seat newly vacant. He's tired, so tired. The room seems strange. And then he falls asleep again. I think he falls asleep again, waiting, and feels her, Louise, her arm around his shoulder, her presence, there as if to comfort him, as if to forgive him, and then . . ."

"Then?"

"The trains come and go, come and go. The light dies. At last it is the last scheduled train of the day that's arriving. Announced on the speaker. Track 2."

Around them are people holding their coffees, their yogurts, their muffins, waiting to sit. She does not interrupt him.

"He gets off the bench now and goes down the stairs, descends, so cold, so tired, track 2, and snow is still falling, falling . . . There she is! Yes, there she is! But dressed wrong, somehow, there amid the passengers coming off the train, and the lines of her body, and then her face, her eyes . . . Not her. He heaves an awful, crushing sigh and breath fills the air. And he looks in the windows, looks in a door, but the train is on the move again, onward to Boston. Onward to Boston."

She hears how his voice is filled with emotion.

"Back in the station, he looks and he looks, by the news-stand, distraught, and out by the cab stand . . . and then . . ."

"Then?"

"The ladies' room! The ladies' room! He thinks that must be it. She must have gone in there. He ought to have known. He goes and he opens the ladies' room door, and a woman yells, *Hey! Hey, mister! What do you think you're doing in here?* And here come the cops."

"Police?" says the girlfriend. "There in the station?"

"Well, station personnel," he says. "Really. Whatever. The point is, they take him by the arm, they've come to take him away, but just for a second he catches a glimpse of a ravaged old man in the ladies' room mirror. *Come, you have to leave now,* the cop or the guard or whoever he is says, shooing him out. *You know you can't be here.*

"*Louise!* he cries. *Louise! Louise!* And he is out on the street."

People are listening in on them, the girlfriend thinks.

His voice is raised: "*The poor soul, he's harmless,* the second guard—he's worked there longer—says to the first. *Whenever it storms like this, he's here. The poor old guy.* He shakes his head, the guard does. *Somebody told me he once was a lawyer. Crazy now. That girl died thirty years ago,* the guard says. *Before the new station—back when the train stopped south of here. They say the girl jumped—to the tracks. Track 2.*"

"She jumped?" said the girlfriend.

He looked at her expectantly.

"That's it, the story?"

"What do you think? The point is he's guilty. He killed her. Okay, he didn't push her, at least, I don't think so; it's still his fault. He is crazy from guilt, regret that was dormant for much of his life."

"*You* killed her," she said.

"Oh, please."

"You wrote it," she said. "You got rid of the girl."

"Come on, don't be like that. You really don't get it."

"What should I get? Do you want me to like him? Is that it? Forgive him? Feel sorry for him? And anyway, this story," she said (she simply couldn't help herself—she knew she shouldn't say it, she ought to let it go, she always did, but the woman last night at the reading, the way she was carrying on and on, the way he'd lapped it up . . .),"it doesn't make sense. I mean, the timing is wrong."

"I know the timing is wrong. He—"

"No," she said. "The story. If this, this business with Louise, was in the '70s, he's . . . your age. Not so old. Not yet. Not old enough yet to have dementia like that, to be ravaged like that."

"But he's crazy." He crumpled his napkin. "I guess you have a point, maybe literally speaking. But listen. Maybe the framing is different. The '50s or something. Or, I know. Maybe—he might have had a stroke."

"Now, why would he have a stroke?"

"An addiction," he said. "Gone mad. I said that."

"We ought to give up our table," she said. "All of these people are waiting to sit."

"So who was she, really? Louise?" she asked. "You based her on someone."

"No one," he said.

She turned away.

"Don't do this," he said.

"She had to be someone. Everyone you write about is someone you know. And why would you tell me a story like that?" The snow was a cliché, she thought, and she was no writer. He ought to know better and probably did. So what was his point?

They stood by the time board—every seat taken under the dome—as new delays clicked into view.

"For God's sake, let it go," he said.

The air hung between them. The damage was done.

She could see the future; she didn't need to dream it: Sooner or later the train would come. The law of things. The two of them: grasping their bags, boarding the train, claiming their places. Each would read, or fake it. Back in New York, they would stop for a drink. They would laugh over nothing. Make up, brush it off. Neither of them would speak of the story ever again, though later he would publish it. Nevertheless, for the rest of the time they were lovers (which wouldn't, of course, be very much longer), she'd cease to adore him; for him, she was a phase. And the woman—Louise—whoever she'd been, whatever she'd done, whatever her significance, for them, she was real and could not be un-invented.

He knew what he was doing.

"People you've known for a very short while will stay with you always," he'd said to her once. "Regret. Impossibility. That's something you don't understand yet . . ."

3.

Soon, She'll Be a Master

She turns off his laptop, there in the dark. His name is his password. First. Last. Crackable. Practical precautions—he isn't very good at them (she tells herself that), for all of his planning, for all of his critically acclaimed self-awareness. She'd read the thing twice—"The Point of Departure."

The action she's taken cannot be reversed.

He murmurs in his sleep as she lies down beside him, nose to nape.

Soon he'll awaken. Soon he will worry (delays, cancellations). Soon they will go to the station and quibble. This, that. Café La France. The ladies' room. Unswallowable breakfast.

The future he can't completely imagine, for all that he tries.

Listen, he'll say.

Do you want to hear my idea? he'll say, before he pays cash, before he finds fault, before the train comes, before he opens his case, before he answers a text, before he knows what he knows, before he clicks on a file, before she swallows a pill, before he pleads an excuse, before he changes a lock, before he apprehends that it is she, Louise, who has deleted the body.

WATERFIRE'S SMELL TONIGHT

BY PABLO RODRIGUEZ

WaterFire

T he smoke was different tonight.

Maybe the onlookers attributed that to the humidity, or the wet wood. But not Jose Cadalzo. Jose had finally landed a volunteer job on the boat that went around the floating fire pits, feeding the pyres with crisp, specially chosen wood, giving him the best seat in the house for the now world famous Providence tradition. Who would have ever thought that setting up a bunch of floating fireplaces accompanied by piped-in music on a not-so-clean river would become the main attraction in the renaissance of a former industrial city?

The color and the acrid smell of the smoke reminded Jose of his youth in the Dominican Republic. When cows or horses died by the roadside, their owners would douse them with gasoline and set them on fire. That was it! Jose realized. The fires tonight smelled like burnt flesh. And why not? Human flesh and animal flesh are not that different, are they?

Just three days earlier, Jose and his best friend Luis were playing dominoes at Club Juan Pablo Duarte, discussing the typical Dominican topics of politics, making money, and the meaning of life, when the issue of US and Dominican citizenship came to the fore. In all Dominican gatherings the pitch of the discussion increased when talk turned to politics, and that night was no exception. In spite of being best friends and originating from the same town in the DR, Jose and Luis were political enemies, therefore their arguments were especially loud. Not that they were the I'm-going-to-kill-you kind of enemies, but their differ-ence of opinion regarding the two political parties, the PLD and PRD, was legendary.

When he was twelve years old, Jose had come to the US illegally from the DR with his mother. Luis was second genera-tion, born here from a Dominican couple whose skin color was a reminder of the omnipresence of Haitians on the island of Hispaniola, the shared landmass comprising the two countries. Their discussion three days ago concerned the change in the Dominican constitution revoking citizenship for descendants of Haitians living in La Republica, retroactively to 1929. Almost two hundred thousand people found themselves stateless over-night as a result of the ruling by the constitutional court in Sep-tember of 2013. Even though Luis was born in the United States he had always maintained pride in his native country, and no one flew more Dominican flags from his or her car during the annual Dominican festival at Roger Williams Park.

"How could they do this, *coño*? Don't they know that the DR is a black country? *Todos somos negros*," Luis argued. He rubbed the top of his forearm with so much vigor that it seemed like he wanted to rub off his skin. "Everyone has a little bit of this."

"Speak for yourself, *cocolo*," Jose replied. "My family are de-scendants from Galicia in Spain, and we can trace our arrival on the island to the second trip by *el Almirante* Cristóbal Colón, and to the founding of Santo Domingo, the first city in the New World."

"*Mierda*," said Luis, raising his middle finger in disgust as he prepared to overturn the table, which was customary during dis-cussions of the constitution. "You have *pelo malo* just like me and your lips are most definitely African. You just won't admit to your own race."

This was true. Jose Cadalzo was white. He had blue eyes and the bridge of his nose was like the bow of the *Titanic*. But his lips were not typical for *gallegos* and he had never yet met a comb that would slide through his hair, or a breeze strong enough to disrupt his hairdo. He never knew his father, but his mother, Doña Carmen Maria Cadalzo Frias, was the spitting image of *la Virgen de la Altagracia*, the venerated Madonna of the Dominican Republic whose porcelain skin and Roman nose were the ultimate expression of beauty and love. But Jose's incongruent features did not dissuade him from his guttural certainty that he was white, and as a white person he felt threatened by the increasing numbers of Haitians crossing the border, having babies, and changing the complexion of the Dominican people.

"They are different," Jose said matter-of-factly. "They're not like us and never will be. They're just good for hard labor and they like it that way. You don't know this because you were born here, you're American."

Those were fighting words for Luis, the number one Dominican in Providence.

The dominoes started to fly, and cries of racism and ignorance filled the room. Pedro Jose, the president of the club, came down from his office to see what the ruckus was all about, and found himself in the middle of a fistfight, with both men landing punches on him. More than one chair passed by his head as he dodged from side to side.

"*Paren esto, CARAJO!*" Pedro Jose screamed as he slammed his Louisville Slugger on the only table still standing. "You better take this outside, otherwise I'm going to crack both your heads open."

Pedro Jose was a small man with a small-man complex, but his baseball bat had broken up plenty of fights and more than a few skulls. Both fighters knew better, and just like the response to the bell in a prizefight, they stopped. But this particular argument changed something in their relationship. Luis was angry at the world because the motherland he so cherished had rejected him. Jose was angry because in the depth of his soul there was always a doubt as to his father's race, especially since any mention of him during family gatherings was met with the same universal sign of silence reserved for churches and libraries: index finger to the lips.

As Mozart's "Requiem" played through the speakers on the banks of the urban river, the first round of stoking the fires ended. The skipper guided the vessel to the pile of wood near the end of the river, just before the hurricane barrier, to reload it with fresh red cedar. The full moon illuminated the pile, which appeared redder than usual, and the sweet smell of the cedar carried a slight tinge of decomposing matter.

"Dead mice," the skipper announced as the logs were loaded onto the cargo area.

Some of the volunteers waved at the air as if shooing flies. When the cute blonde from Brown University picked up a broken piece of cedar, something dangled from one of its shards.

"Check this out!" she called with the enthusiasm of someone winning the lottery. "I think it's a necklace."

Sure enough, hanging from the wood was a gold chain with a pendant for *la Virgen de la Altagracia* on one side and a Dominican flag on the other. The virgin glistened under the light of the moon like a magic talisman with its own internal light.

"That's mine!" Jose yelled with such conviction that the young woman immediately handed him the chain. "I was loading this pile on the truck this morning when I noticed I no longer had my chain," he explained as he took it from her.

This much was true. He had worked with the wood crew for the last two days, cutting and loading the cedar for tonight's event. What his boat mates did not know was that the chain belonged to his friend Luis, whose family had reported him missing two days ago when he did not return home after his fracas with Jose.

At that moment, "El Niágara en bicicleta," a song by Juan Luis Guerra, burst from Jose's pocket. As Jose answered his phone, the loading of the boat resumed. At the other end of the line, he heard the familiar sound of his mother's voice. With a deep exasperated sigh, he said, "*Qué pasa?*"

His mother was worried. She had received a call from the police asking about her son. Apparently, witnesses of the fight at Club Juan Pablo Duarte had spoken to the agents investigating Luis's disappearance and therefore Jose had become a person of interest.

Luis's words, "*Todos somos negros,*" repeated in Jose's brain like a broken record.

"Jose," his mother was asking, "did you have anything to do with Luis's disappearance?"

"*Por favor, mamá*, don't believe the worst," Jose replied. "Luis is probably partying in New York or Boston and has not bothered to call."

Any other time he would have been mortified at the prospect of lying to his mother. But now he felt completely justified: she had lied to him all his life about his father. He knew. He had been there when Luis uttered his last words, nearly drowned by the sound of the wood chipper: "*Jodio negro.*" You damned negro.

"When are you coming home?" his mother asked him.

"As soon as the fires are out," he said. Then he bade her farewell, "Okay, okay, okay!" When he hurriedly pressed the red bar of the iPhone, he noticed the cuticle of his index finger was stained red.

The skipper whistled with two fingers in his mouth to signal that it was time to return to the fires. The boat was loaded and the pyres were hungry for fresh wood. Barnaby Evans, the artist and director of WaterFire, stood on the other bank of the river forming a giant V with his arms to convey his impatience with the volunteers. When the skipper noticed the boss, he waved and nodded, signaling that he understood and was on the case. It was Jose's turn to be in the front of the boat leading the effort of rekindling the fires. As the boat slowly approached the floating cauldron, the line of volunteers on the side loaded the wood onto the fire with a solemnity very much in tune with the piped-in music.

Jose was distracted by his thoughts, so there was a slight delay in loading the logs onto the next bonfire.

"Wake up, Jose!" the skipper screamed.

But his mind had drifted back to forty-eight hours earlier when Luis came to visit the lumberyard where Jose was preparing the cedar. Long, slender red logs had to be cut into cylindrical pieces and then split, ready for lighting. As he cut his last log he heard the familiar greeting from his friend. Luis had a somber face and his shoulders were rolled forward with the weight of a truth he had been carrying for a long while.

The fight the day before was the final straw for Luis, and he could no longer hold his peace. He had come upon the truth of Jose's father during his last trip to the DR when he was inquiring about his citizenship status. Luis was in the final steps of obtaining his dual citizenship, something he cherished enormously, dreaming of a day when he could return to the land of his ancestors full of money and respect. Born a US citizen from Dominican parents would have been a slam dunk the year before, but now, after the constitutional court had revoked his parents' citizenship, he had to reapply under a different class: a Haitian. As he was researching his grandparents' entry into the country, he met his Uncle Frantz, still living in the house where his ancestors first set foot in the country to work in the sugarcane fields. Luis was delighted by the stories his uncle shared, until the conversation turned to people they both knew.

Uncle Frantz gazed toward the sky searching for memories in the clouds above.

Many of the folks from their hometown, the border town of Dajabón, had found work in Rhode Island and were eventually able to bring their families to the States. But when the topic turned to family and children, Uncle Frantz became quiet and told Luis not to ask any more questions about such a touchy subject. Index finger to the lips. After much prodding, Uncle Frantz revealed the identity of a lover he'd had many years before when interracial sex was very much taboo. He knew she had become pregnant right before she left for the capital, Santo Domingo, in order to escape the poverty and misery of the border town. He also knew she could never reveal the nature of their relationship and had decided to leave in part to hide the truth of a child who would have been born black to a family whose proud Galician traditions permeated every celebration, and whose ancestry could be traced to the Spaniards' arrival in 1492. As a devout Catholic, there had been no other options. Frantz was aware she had lived in Santo Domingo for twelve years and then left for Puerto Rico in a rickety *yola* with her young son. Last he'd heard she was in Providence.

"You're still in Providence, right?" Uncle Frantz asked.

Luis nodded.

"What family was she from?"

"She was a Cadalzo," Uncle Frantz whispered.

No other words were spoken. The pain of not knowing his son overwhelmed the old man and the gravity of the revelation overwhelmed the young one.

"What the hell are you doing here?" Jose demanded when Luis showed up at the lumberyard. He stuck his chest out like a gorilla defending his turf, and he held a splitting axe tight in his hand.

"I'm sorry that things between us have become so strained,"

Luis said carefully. "But I just came from meeting with your mother and she confirmed something for me that she would never tell you. As a matter of fact, she made me promise not to share it with you. And here I am violating my oath to her." He looked down at the ground as if apologizing for what he was about to say.

"What are you talking about, man? What can my mother tell you that she wouldn't tell me?" As he barked the questions, Jose moved closer to Luis, almost bumping chests.

Luis began to narrate the tragic story of Frantz and Carmen Maria, their illegitimate child, and their lack of contact after all these years. Jose's shoulders rose higher and the muscles around his jaw tightened.

"Who the hell are you talking about and why are you telling me this?" Jose growled through clenched teeth.

"My Uncle Frantz is your father. And just like me, you are a black Haitian. And just like me, you can no longer call yourself a Dominican citizen," replied Luis with both an air of certainty and a sense of relief at sharing the weight of the truth with his newfound cousin.

"*Mentiras*, you lie to make yourself feel better about losing your citizenship. My mother would never sleep with a negro like you. How dare you insult my mother this way!" Jose grabbed a big branch and began chasing Luis through the lumberyard, howling and spitting insults half in English and half in Spanish.

Luis frantically tried to stay ahead of the swinging lunatic. He climbed onto a platform above the moving Morbark 950 Tub Grinder, which was used to turn big branches into toothpicks, hoping that the machinery would somehow slow down the attack.

But Jose kept in pursuit, screaming obscenities and swinging the branch wildly. Was he trying to hurt Luis? Or was he just swinging at the truth, hoping that with one blow everything would return to normal and he could become white once again?

Luis grabbed the railing for balance, hoping he could jump

off and over the tub of the grinder. Unfortunately, his sweaty right hand slipped and he fell swiftly to his death, but not before cursing Jose with his last breath: *"Jodio negro."*

In the commotion, the grinder's exhaust chute got knocked around from the pile of wood chips to the pile of split wood, and a wide spray of red covered the tree guts, just as the sky broke open in one of those New England thunderstorms that seem to come out of nowhere. Jose was taken aback, not by the scene of his cousin being pulverized in a few seconds, but at his lack of feeling for what had just taken place. With a mixture of righteousness and relief, Jose thought, *All is good in the world again.*

As the final bonfire faded, the crowd slowly left downtown. The crew on the boat high-fived another successful WaterFire, and once the boat was tied to the dock everyone headed to the Brewhouse for a well-deserved drink.

When Jose lifted his beer to toast to his first night on the job, the bartender pointed to his index finger. Under the dim light of the bar, Jose's finger was red with what was obviously blood. Maybe from the night before, or maybe from the logs he'd solemnly placed on the fires tonight.

Jose lifted his finger to his lips and placed it to his mouth. "Don't worry," he said, "this is my own blood."

THE SATURDAY NIGHT BEFORE EASTER SUNDAY

BY PETER FARRELLY

Elmhurst

After graduating from Rollins in '74, Roger Tenpenny returned to Rhode Island with the understanding that he would never have to work or worry a day in his life. At twenty-one, he'd kicked off a trust that the men at Industrial National Bank quipped could support the lives of one hundred ne'er-do-wells. Owing, however, to an astonishing four divorces in fifteen years, and several business misfires, all the money was back in circulation before Reagan was steered out of office. Although Tenpenny considered himself a private person, the divorces were the one thing he wore on his sleeve. Most were stunned to meet a four-time loser still in his thirties, but Tenpenny had discovered that a certain set found this odd fact charming, and naturally that was the crowd he played to. When asked why he would possibly marry a *fourth* time, he always responded with the joke: "I missed the cheating." This could be counted on for a laugh, but stung him in a place that most were unaware, for the truth was *he* had been the fucked-over one at least twice.

Like many multiple divorcées, Tenpenny had bouts of unbridled optimism, and he was in such a frame of mind in March of '92 when he met his neighbor Ellie. Although he was still doing time in the Elmhurst section of town—a triple-decker neighborhood filled mostly with Providence College students—the tide had turned in his favor. Almost free of his marital debts—for the blessed fact that there were no children in the mix—he felt chipper enough to write a couple long letters to old girlfriends, shots in the dark. He'd even begun to outline a business plan for a chain of sporting goods stores that catered to women only. (No one had ever done that before, as far as he could tell.) Even this blue-collar street gave him comfort, as it protected him from running into anyone of importance. Once he'd righted his ship, he'd make a triumphant return to Newport and the people that mattered.

Tenpenny was parking in front of his apartment when he spotted his neighbor walking back from class with a friend. Ellie had moved in beneath him just after Christmas, and, from the lack of visitors, he'd assumed her to be a transfer student. Though clearly attractive, the silver light of winter had disguised just how so. He'd watched her come and go for two full months with nothing more than businesslike nods. Then a bright yellow spring arrived and as layers of wool and down were shed, her breasts seemed to thaw and expand, and—well, that was enough for him.

"See you on the Saturday night before Easter Sunday!" Ellie called to her friend heading away down the hill.

"What did you say?" Tenpenny asked as they were converging in step toward the house. "Did you say *the Saturday night before Easter Sunday?*"

She looked at him oddly.

"I'm sorry, did you just say those words—*the Saturday night before Easter Sunday?*"

"Um . . . yeah."

"That's the name of my book! How weird is that?!"

It was a crazy lie, a stupid lie, the kind of lie that good liars rely on. She gave him a hesitant, uncertain smile. "You're a writer?"

"I mean, it's weirder than you even know. I've been having second thoughts about that title ever since I started getting offers from the houses, and I've been struggling with maybe changing the name. You know, is it too oblique? Too confusing? Maybe it doesn't say enough? But this is like a definite sign! I'm not changing it—that *is* the title, that *should be* the title, I think it's a great title."

Her flickering smile had ignited into a glow by the time he was done with this rant. No big surprise. Published writers are Spanish fly to coeds, oldest story in the book. And she'd just played a part in *naming* the thing. This could easily become a big part of her identity in the coming months—certainly if she did coke.

At twenty-two, one can tell the difference between a nineteen- and a twenty-one-year-old, but Tenpenny was at an age where he could only break it down to decades. Eighteen to twenty-eight, he guessed. Twenty-three, it turned out—he'd been right on the nose. They hung out for a few days—a couple coffees in her apartment, a few wines in his—as she filled him in on her life. For financial reasons, she'd been forced to drop out after freshman year to work, and was just now, four years later, returning. Though pleased to be back, she was having a hard time relating to the younger students. He liked her burlap voice and she his patience and authoritative air. They'd flirt and he'd cut it off. As a young man Roger had been swayed by beauty, but experience had left him cold toward it. He could take it or leave it, and that was his advantage. Quickly, she let down her guard. One morning a card game got her down to her bra and panties while they watched cartoons. Not so he could make a run at her, but to show that he wouldn't. This flipped the tables, clarified who was calling the shots, made it all inevitable.

One Saturday Tenpenny packed crustless cucumber-and-pimento-cheese sandwiches and drove them to Newport in his orange Saab. He showed her the church where JFK had wed, and Purgatory Chasm, then took her along the Cliff Walk, past the gilded-age mansions, a neighborhood Tenpenny knew well. He slid them through a row of privet and helped her over a fence and they set up a picnic on the expanse of lawn behind the Breakers. He poured them each a Dark 'n' Stormy—the correct way—Barritt's ginger beer, short glass, stiff, the Gosling's floating *on top*. This had been his drink of choice back in his St. Croix days and the whiff of ginger beer and sweet rum brought back memories of making money in the sun.

He'd moved to the islands in '81 with Wife #2, running from Wife #1, and he'd fled four years later with #3, running from #2. Despite the drama, those had been mostly good years for him, and the one time in his life that he'd managed to come out ahead financially. This had not come without hurt feelings from some associates he'd entered into a land deal with, but that's the way business worked. There were winners and losers and this time his name had ended up on the correct legal documents and he'd been the winner. When one of his ex-partners (a former prep school pal and sometime cokehead named Wellsy) eight-balled out of control and died, Tenpenny was called all kinds of libelous names in the Caribbean press. He chalked this up to small-town pettiness and, rather than suing their asses, returned to Newport with Wife #3, where, as destiny would have it, he was soon to meet #4.

Of course, Tenpenny had been divorced-four-times long enough to read a crowd, so he kept most of these details from Ellie.

"How old are you?" she asked as he was mixing the second round. It was low tide and he could smell the rocks that had risen from the water.

"Thirty-eight," he said, though he was thirty-nine. He made a mental note to stop lying like that. One fucking year—what was the point? He should've said thirty-four. Or twenty-nine. Thirty-eight was like breaking into Fort Knox and stealing a hundred bucks.

Tenpenny feared he'd just messed things up, but before they'd finished a fifth of the fifth, they were screwing.

Sort of.

She might've overreacted to sinking her fingers into relatively old ass-cheeks for the first time, or maybe it was his disappointment at finding large, depleted breasts on a college kid, but it was unmemorable for both.

This cooled their friendship and they didn't see much of each other after that, except in passing, where, to his annoyance, Tenpenny had to maintain the book lie. "How's your book?" "Who's publishing your book?" "When's your book coming out?" "Next fall," he would say, or, "Leaning toward St. Martin's," or he'd mumble something about "publishing seasons." Doubly annoying was that he detected a trace of skepticism in her tone. A good part of him wanted to just tell her the truth: She'd fucked a guy because she thought he was a writer. Deal with it.

But Tenpenny wasn't raised that way. Ellie was a sophomore and would be doing her junior year abroad—certainly he'd be long gone before she returned—so he resolved to be the bigger man and play out the lie for a couple months, rather than throw her shallowness in her face. Thankfully, time kept to its schedule and when school ended Ellie went back to whatever part of Connecticut or Virginia she'd come from. Though they'd ended on less than stellar terms, Roger recognized the growth in being able to have a relationship with a beginning, middle, and an end that didn't involve lawyers, and he took heart in this.

So we come to the day that young Beresford came banging unannounced on his door. It was the following October and the leaves were just starting to lose their green. A few yellow ones were stamped to the wet pavement, returned to sender.

"You're a writer?!" the smiling Brit blurted out as Tenpenny opened up. Beresford was tall with short, reddish dreadlocks. He reeked of sweat and pot and some cologne that was doing a bad job of drowning out the sweat and the pot.

"Excuse me?"

"I'm told that you're a writer. I'm a writer too!"

"Who the hell said I'm a writer?"

"Eleanor who used to live downstairs, she told me that . . . ? Are you Roger?"

Good lord, Tenpenny thought. It had been a mistake to protect her. No good deed goes unpunished.

"Yes. I write. What's your point?"

It should be noted again that Tenpenny had been high on the day he met Ellie six months earlier—high on life—as he was inclined to be every four years or so, for the better part of a season. His shrink would describe his mood in more clinical terms, but it was happening to *him*, not to Dr. Samuels, and Tenpenny had a clearer insight into his own emotional ecosystem. He believed that every person had many people inside them: the angry guy, the happy guy, the loudmouth, and the quiet guy; the guy who always wanted to make him late for everything, and so on. When he'd met Ellie, the *fun guy* had been present and Tenpenny had taken advantage of him, but now that guy was gone and on the day that Beresford arrived someone else answered the door.

"Um, no point," Beresford said, reeling a bit. "I just never met another real writer before, so . . . just wanted to say hello."

"Yes. Well . . . nice to know I'm not alone."

This was the realist Tenpenny, the one who recognized that women don't give a pig's ass about sporting goods stores, and his bank account was still shrinking, and the old girlfriend letters could officially be deemed *unanswered*, and he was still living on Admiral Street in a part of Providence he considered beneath himself—and now this Simply Red–looking idiot was standing there.

"So . . . anyway . . ." The kid leaned timidly toward the stairwell. "Eleanor told me to send her love."

"*Really*," Tenpenny said, not as a question but in that declarative, upbeat way. He was surprised but pleased that she'd chosen to remember him fondly, and this softened him enough to step from behind the door. "How's she doing?"

"Okay, I suppose—she seemed fine." Then: "To be honest, I don't really know her all that well. I met her on a tram in France this summer, and when I told her I was a writer and was moving to Providence, she said, *You've got to look up my friend Roger—he's a writer too.* I wouldn't normally just pop in like this, but . . . she made kind of a big to-do about it, so . . ."

Ah, now it made sense. Ellie wasn't helping the Brit, she was busting Tenpenny's chops. Then Beresford opened his backpack, revealing something wrapped in brown paper.

"Here," he said, "this is for you."

Tenpenny lifted the package and opened it, revealing a half-gallon of rum.

"Ellie told me that's what you drink. It's Cuban."

This took Roger aback. "What? No. What? You're shitting me . . . ?"

Beresford held out the backpack and said, "You can stuff that paper right back in here—I'll reuse it."

Roger Tenpenny had been raised to always ring a doorbell with his elbow, and the fact that this poor, smelly Englishman lived by that same tenet gave him hope for all humanity.

"Well, come in, come in!"

Tenpennys had lots of tenets—like those about drinking too early or too late—but the fact that Beresford had gifted him with a bottle of Havana Club threw those rules out the window. This was an *occasion*, as opposed to a habit, which freed him up to enjoy a rare Monday-afternoon cocktail while the kid spilled his life story.

Charlie Beresford looked like any other British tramp running amok in America, but was in fact nothing like one. He was an Americanophile who had huge aspirations—a long-term plan, in fact—and, though still a few months shy of twenty, he had the confidence of a much older man. Two years earlier he'd been admitted to King's College before deciding, to everyone's chagrin, to stay home and kick out a novel. Now that he was finally in the States, his life was just beginning. His book had been sent off to one publishing company—Knopf—and he'd applied to one college—Brown University. While waiting to be admitted as a January transfer student, he was living a shit-stained version of the Kerouac life at the Providence YMCA. He wrote at night and bussed tables at the Rusty Scupper (Scuzzy Rubber, he called it) by day, trying to save up enough cash to put a first-and-last down on an apartment, preferably one not on the south side of town.

"So what's the title of your novel?" Beresford asked. "I want to get it."

"Sorry, you can't."

"Why not?"

"Not out yet."

"Oh? When's it coming out?"

"Not for a long time, I hope." Tenpenny smiled as he handed Beresford his drink.

"But Eleanor said it was getting published this fall."

"No, no, I told her they *offered* to publish it. But I politely declined."

Beresford made a sour face. "Why?"

"I take it you don't know much about the publishing world, Charlie?"

"No. Well . . . no, not really."

Tenpenny lit a cigarette. "Publishers *ruin* writers. Yeah, it seems like a good deal—a little dough, your work's finally getting out there, and so on—but ultimately, being published is the kiss of death."

"So you said *no?*"

"I did indeed." He held up the Viceroys but Beresford waved him off.

"Then why'd you submit the manuscript in the first place?"

Which, Tenpenny realized, was an excellent question. He took Beresford's drink back to the counter and sullied the rum with tonic water. "You like lime?" he asked, as he worked out this riddle.

"No, I'm good. So . . . I don't get it—why'd you send it to them if you didn't want to be published?"

"Send it to who?"

"The publishing houses."

Tenpenny slowly stirred Beresford's drink as he deliberated. "See, I have a writer friend and I gave it to him—you know, I needed fresh eyes, typos and whatnot—and *he* took it upon himself to pass it on to a few editors without my knowledge. Prick. Well, he was just trying to be nice. Next thing I know, I'm in the middle of a very modest bidding war, which was kind of flattering, I guess—no, I *admit*. But then I started having nightmares about it, so I pulled the plug and told them I didn't want it out there until after I die."

Beresford blinked. "Wow. That's . . . wow. May I inquire why?"

Tenpenny finally returned his drink. "Well . . . for the same reasons the *Catcher in the Rye* guy refuses to publish *his* new stuff." (Despite his Rollins education, Tenpenny had always gotten Caulfield and Salinger confused, as far as who was the writer and who the whiner.)

"Because making money off it is a form of prostitution?"

This remark chafed at Tenpenny's genes and, though being agreeable would've tied a nice bow on the discussion, he snapped, "There's nothing wrong with making money! Nothing! *Not ever!*"

The channeling of Tenpenny's objectivist grandfather had

shrunk Beresford, so Roger throttled it back a bit. "It's just . . . I choose not to publish my work for the simple reason that once it's out there, you're no longer pure. You start writing for the public, or worse, the critics, and once that happens—when you start caring what other people think—you're tainted." Then he added, "That's true in life too."

"I suppose. But even Salinger published four or five books."

"No he didn't. *He did?*"

"*Catcher, Franny and Zooey, Nine Stories*, a couple others."

"Oh." Then: "Well, I don't intend to make the same mistake."

It was three days later that the package addressed to Beresford arrived. Tenpenny wasn't the least bit curious of its contents and spent the afternoon writing a new business plan—this time for a life-settlement start-up. This was a new AIDS-inspired industry that allowed people to cash out their life insurance policies early, but at a steep discount, and then the new beneficiaries would claim their fruits "at the time of harvest," as stated in his presentation.

Beresford phoned that evening. "You're going to be receiving my novel *Danke, Dolores* in the mail," he said.

"Believe I already have."

"Brilliant."

"Can't promise I'll get to it for a while, though, kiddo. Kind of busy these days."

"No, no, you don't have to read it. I just had to mail it to someone for copyright purposes because I still haven't found a permanent flat yet."

"Oh." Then: "How's that?"

"See, I don't have enough money to be ladling it out to the Library of Congress when I can get an official copyright simply by mailing it to myself. Long as it's not opened, the postmark is a valid copyright, so I saved myself ten bucks."

"You shrewd bastard."

Beresford chuckled. "One other thing. When I sent the book out I had to give the publishing house a phone number, and the Y said I'm not allowed to receive calls here, so I gave them yours. Hope you don't mind, sir?"

Tenpenny smirked at Beresford's youthful optimism. "Oh, that's okay. I'll man the fort when the calls start streaming in."

There's an old saying in non-WASP circles (radioactively leaked to Tenpenny by his outgoing third wife) that the reason trust funders are so cheap is because if they ever did lose their money, they wouldn't have a clue how to get it back. Of all the mean things #3 said to him, this one hurt the most, because it was the truest, and every broke day that Roger suffered through was a victory for the cheating bitch and a defeat for him. Roger had had a few interesting business ideas over the years—a combination toilet paper/baby wipe dispenser for adults who liked extra cleanliness; a nonalcoholic tequila; a fake bumble bee on a stick that you could scare your friends with, etc.—but what he had in creativity he lacked in follow-through. After the initial excitement over the concept, his only avenue was to find a successful CEO who could do the heavy lifting and split everything 50/50 with him, which of course is not how commerce works.

As the fall progressed and money grew scarce, time seemed to speed up for Tenpenny. This was an illusion, of course, caused by sleeping fourteen hours a day and being foggy-brained for most of the waking ones. Suddenly the Christmas season was at Tenpenny's throat—seemingly leapfrogging over a couple other holidays—and with it came the vestigial pain that Jesus's birthday brings to the downtrodden.

Roger sat picking at a tin of sardines with crispless crackers at four o'clock on a darkening afternoon. It was his first meal of the day. His adrenals, shot from stress and worry, had not permitted three cups of yesterday's coffee to register, so when his phone rang all he could do was stare. The machine picked up, informing the caller that everyone at the "Providence branch" of Guardian Angel Associates was either on another line or out to lunch.

"Hello," a man said, tentatively. "This is Paul Scholl calling from Alfred A. Knopf in New York. Could you please ask Charles Beresford to call me regarding his novel *Danke, Dolores*—"

Tenpenny grabbed for the phone. "G-A-A," he trilled in a high, officious voice, "How can I direct your call?"

"Yes, um, I'm not certain I have the right place. Is there a Charles Beresford at this number? I'm calling about a manuscript he sent us."

"You must be looking for Mr. Tenpenny. He's our resident scribe." Tenpenny tried to sound jovial. "I'll connect you."

He tapped a couple numbers on the phone and then in his own voice said, "Roger here, what's shakin'?"

"Hello," the man said. "I'm calling from Knopf Publishing in New York and I'm looking for a Mr. Charles Beresford."

"That's me. Well, I'm him. That is, Charles Beresford is my nom de . . . whichimicallit. Is this about my book?"

"Well, yes it is, Mr. . . ."

"Tenpenny."

"My name is Paul Scholl and I have rather quite good news for you. We loved your novel and want very much to publish it."

Rather quite seemed rather quite wordy for an editor, and for a millisecond Tenpenny wondered if this was the right publishing house for him, but then he glanced at the sardine can and said, "Fantastic! That's wonderful news!"

After a little more back-patting and some small talk, the editor asked if Tenpenny could find a gap in his schedule to come to the city for a few days. Roger beamed. "How does tomorrow sound?"

* * *

A puffy-eyed Tenpenny was leaving his apartment early the next morning when he heard a shout and saw Beresford bounding up his front steps.

"Monsieur Ro-jay!"

"Hey. How's it going?" Tenpenny bustled past him toward the sidewalk. The city had sustained an overnight dumping and the trees were shaking off the snow, their limbs animate and noisy.

"Great," Beresford said. "I've been meaning to stop by and pick up my novel."

Which was inside the briefcase Tenpenny was toting to New York.

"Really shitty timing, buddy-boy. Gotta catch a flight and running late—mind grabbing it some other time?"

Tenpenny trudged briskly to his car. Beresford had to hop every third step to keep up.

"Really? Can't you just run inside? It'll take a sec."

"Problem is, if I open my apartment I'll have to reset the burglar alarm and the little fucker's as fickle as my third wife." Tenpenny chuckled. "What a twat she was!"

"Oh. Okay. No big deal. So . . . where are you off to?"

"New York. Business." Tenpenny brushed snow off the windshield with his coat sleeve. "By the way, have you thought about what we talked about?"

"What'd we talk about?"

"You know, about publishing houses being the kiss of death for writers, and you going home to England?"

"When did you say anything about me going back to Britain?"

"Okay, what about the other thing?"

"You mean about not being published? I thought you were just talking about *you*."

"Not *just*."

"But you said you were having nightmares about it, right?"

"All the time. It was eating me alive—you know, I didn't want to be a sell-out."

Beresford spit out a laugh. "You crack me up, Roger. Yeah, I don't get that—I'm fine with being published."

Tenpenny forced a smile. "Good. Then you should. Be published."

As Roger climbed into his car, Beresford blurted out, "Hey, I don't suppose . . . ? Ah, never mind."

"What?"

"Not important. Bad idea."

"Come on, what is it?"

"Well, it's just, I was going to say, being that you're going to be in New York . . . But you've already done way too much for me."

"For Christ's sake, spit it out. I have a plane to catch."

"Would it be possible for you to pop your head into Knopf and see how my book's doing?"

"Consider it done."

"Really? You don't mind? You could do it?"

"Charlie horse, you have my word."

Manhattan is a gracious town when one is there by invitation. The Knopf people treated Tenpenny like a king. His editor, Paul Scholl, called him a once-in-a-lifetime find. He said his characters breathed, his plotting was seamless, and his style harkened to a more literate era. His was a new voice with an old sound, and they were anxious to get it out there. Incredibly, Tenpenny discovered, there *are* publishing seasons, and in a highly unusual move, and assuming they could quickly reach an agreement, his book was being fast-tracked to the summer season. What's more, they were going to make *Danke, Dolores* their tentpole release. Roger Tenpenny was about to become a household name.

"Whoa, whoa," Roger said. "Household name? Uh, no, that

would be the kiss of death for someone like me. I need to fade into the shrubbery to do what I do. That's why I wrote it under a pen name."

"I didn't *literally* mean a household name," Scholl said. "I just meant, you'll be well known in literary circles."

"But I don't want to be famous in *any* circle, I just want to be able to do what I do in privacy . . . but be well-compensated."

Scholl's droopy-faced assistant Phyllis laughed, though it hadn't been meant as a joke. (Bell's palsy, it had been explained—tick bite.) "I do like what he's saying, though," she slurred. "I shink people will be drawn to that kind of humility."

"Okay," Scholl agreed. "We'll go by your pseudonym."

"Right. Good. Excellent. But I'd prefer something different than Charles Beresford—it has such a stuffy ring to it."

"Really?" Scholl said. "I kind of like it. Beresford's a solid name."

"But a little pretentious, no? I was thinking of something like . . . Thames Bannister?"

Scholl couldn't tell if he was kidding. Phyllis chuckled uneasily.

"What?" said Tenpenny. "It's kind of strong-sounding and memorable and it's—"

"Weird," said Scholl. "It sounds like a soap opera villain."

Eventually they agreed on the name Charlie Pettygrove.

Tenpenny was put up at the Hotel Elysee, and that evening Scholl and a flashy editor named Gary took him to dinner at Nell's, then to the Limelight where Tenpenny charmed them with ex-wife stories until four a.m. A happy, comedic light suddenly shimmered on all the bad things that had happened in Roger's life, because everything had led him to this moment. He told them about Wife #1 buying her father a seaplane without telling him; how he knew the second one was over when his brand-new wife air-kissed him on the altar to protect her makeup; the time he came home to find #1 and #2 rifling through his financial records while the soon-to-be ex-#3 served them wine spritzers. Though often showcasing his own character weaknesses, his detached, it-is-what-it-is delivery charmed the editors. Even when he came across in the worst light—as when he drunkenly lit his Telluride property on fire with Wife #3 inside pounding her lesbian lover (it went out on its own)—his honesty was his redemption. Scholl and Gary recognized that Roger Tenpenny had had his ass kicked in a big way, and those were the dues one paid to become, if not a great man, well, certainly a great writer.

When the topic turned to his novel and what had inspired it, Tenpenny pleaded the artist's Fifth: his motivation didn't matter, it was how *they* were inspired by it that counted. He had speed-read through the 450-page manuscript the night before, but the prose was dense and not much had stuck. He knew that it had something to do with an old man named Fritz and a young ghost named Dolores, so he satisfied them by recounting the time he and a friend had reached out to the other side.

It happened in St. Croix soon after his prep school friend Wellsy's death. "He had died just a couple weeks earlier under less than ideal circumstances," Tenpenny said, without elaborating about the contentious land deal. "Poor guy's pump blew doing blow. So we figured if anyone would be hanging around it would be Wellsy. He was kind of clueless and wouldn't even know he was dead. We lit candles and meditated on him for a while, asking him to give us some kind of sign—a flicker of light, a cool breeze. When nothing happened, we turned on a tape recorder and asked again, this time out loud, and we also opened up the floor to any random spirits that were floating around, just so long as they were good-natured. Anyway, it didn't seem like anything was happening but we decided to play the tape back anyway."

"And . . . ?" Gary asked.

"Nothin'. It was a big waste of time and we felt more than a little stupid for spending the last couple hours talking to the air. Then, just as my friend was about to leave, he said, *Hey, I wonder what would happen if we rolled the tape backward.* So we did."

The editors leaned in anxiously and Tenpenny milked the moment. Then . . .

"Still nothin'."

As the men laughed, Tenpenny wished that Beresford could be witnessing this from some detached, egoless parallel universe where the benefits of Tenpenny taking the reigns would be as evident to him as it was to the rest of the world. Certainly Beresford deserved props for writing the songs, but Tenpenny was Roger Daltrey to his Pete Townshend—an infinitely better front man—and the main reason the book would ever reach a wide audience. Even in this happy state, though—perhaps *because* of it—Tenpenny recognized that humans are tragically tethered to their egos and thus he was forced to plan accordingly.

The next afternoon Tenpenny stopped by Scholl's office and dropped a couple bombshells.

"I don't want the book released in Europe," he announced.

"What are you talking about? Why not?"

"I just don't think they'll get it."

"Of course they'll get it—it takes place in London."

"Right," Tenpenny said, "but it has a particularly American POV."

"Shat's silly," the palsied Phyllis added, unnecessarily.

Scholl offered, "Roger, you're being too hard on yourself. I don't think you know what you have here. This is a book for the world. The entire world."

This was true, Roger knew, and for a brief moment he hated Beresford for making him keep it from the French and Germans and those newly freed Russians. But what could he do? If he allowed it to be read everywhere, it was only a matter of time before it seeped into England, which is where he planned for Beresford to be residing again soon.

"And I want the title changed."

"A new title too?" said Scholl, exasperated.

"Yes. I want to call it *The Saturday Night Before Easter Sunday*."

"Why?"

"Because that's what I want to call it."

"*The Saturday Night Before* . . . ?"

"*Easter Sunday*."

Scholl looked at Phyllis, who was wearing a kind of half poker face.

"But that doesn't *mean* anything," said Scholl. "What does it even mean?"

"Well, um . . . it means, uh . . . it means, uh . . . well, it means *nothing*. The Saturday night before Easter Sunday doesn't stand for anything, it's a nothing date. It's not like New Year's Eve or Christmas Eve—it's just . . . the Saturday night before Easter Sunday. It sounds good, but it really means zilch. And that's . . . that's really . . . The point is, it's the emptiness of these people, and their world . . . and the disappointment, and, you know . . ."

"No, I don't know," Scholl said. "It's a terrible title, and the original title was great."

"Look, that's my title. Sometimes titles are terrible."

"Sometimes titles are terrible?"

"I mean, not every title has to mean something. Look at *Blood Simple*, that was, uh . . . or *Dog Day Afternoon*—there were no dogs in that, but it gave you a feeling, and the Saturday night before Easter Sunday is the feeling I want people to get when they pick up my book."

"You just said the Saturday night before Easter Sunday means nothing, so what's the feeling?"

Tenpenny thought about this. "I want them to come in neutral."

* * *

Before leaving, Roger requested two pieces of Knopf stationery, ostensibly on which to inform his mother of the wonderful news. On his way back to the hotel, he stopped and made copies of the manuscript he'd brought with him. That evening a typewriter was delivered to his suite and, on the Knopf stationery, he tapped out a letter to young Beresford.

Tenpenny awoke early the next morning and enjoyed a breakfast of caviar, soft-boiled eggs, and garlic potatoes with a split of Moët. At nine o'clock he rode to the post office and mailed a copy of the book to the Library of Congress, in his name, not scrimping on the ten-dollar fee. Another copy he mailed to his apartment, addressed to Beresford. That envelope also contained the letter he'd composed the night before:

> *Dear Mr. Berisford:*
>
> *What I'm about to say may offend you, but I'm hoping that my candor will save you much time, energy, and disappointment later in life. You are not a writer. While I give you kudos for completing an entire novel—quite an accomplishment, no matter the result!—your work fails on myriad levels and is not something that any publishing house in existence would deem printable. Your style is hackneyed, your characters are all too familiar, and your plotting is, well, not good.*
>
> *You seem like an intelligent man—i.e., your grasp of the language is serviceable—but not every intelligent person can write. For instance, the ghost in your story is about as scary as "boo," which is what I did after finally getting to the end. Again, I say this not to denigrate you, but to propel you into a vocation that you are more suited to. Simply put, being a writer is a gift. You either are one or you're not, and like 99.9 percent of the world, you are not. At least you're in good company!*

Sorry that I couldn't bring you more cheerful news but I trust that one day, when you're off conquering a different sort of industry, you'll see the wisdom in my words and think fondly of me.

Happy New Year!

Yours,
Paul Scholl
Editor in Chief

A week later, Beresford finally stopped by Tenpenny's apartment. It was nearing midnight on a Saturday night.

"Sorry to pop in this late, Roger, but I had to work until eleven."

"Think nothing of it, kid—you're welcome anytime. You still at the Scuzzy Rubber?"

"No, they said I needed a Social Security number, so now I'm working at a pizza place on the East Side." He shrugged. "It's a job."

"And jobs build character."

Roger offered Beresford a small snifter of Hennessey's, and after much beating around the bush, the Brit inquired if he'd had a chance to stop by Knopf.

"Did I say I would?" Tenpenny asked innocently.

"Well, you said if you had any extra time."

"Then I did. Charlie, I *make* extra time for my friends. I can't say they were too hospitable, though. In fact, the guy I spoke with was a complete ass. I was tempted to tell the jerk to get off his high horse, but I didn't want to jeopardize your career so I kept my trap shut." Tenpenny downed his drink. "Oh, incidentally, when I returned home I found this for you."

Roger retrieved the package with the manuscript and rejection letter inside, then excused himself to take a shower. When he came out forty-five minutes later, Beresford had left. Tenpenny poured himself another brandy, then sat back and listened to the loud, happy drunks stumbling back to campus.

Tenpenny was buying smokes at a Cumberland Farms convenience store a few nights later when in walked Beresford. He hadn't shaved since Tenpenny had last seen him and it appeared he hadn't slept much either.

"Charlie Horse!"

Beresford lifted his sickly gaze to him and grunted. The fluorescent lighting danced on the bags beneath his eyes.

"Jeez, it's good to see you, rascal. What's going on?"

"Nothing much," he sighed. "I didn't get into Brown."

Tenpenny stepped back, stunned and relieved. Two horribly blemished coeds walked past them.

"What? But . . . that's crazy. You're nineteen and you wrote an entire book—that alone should've gotten you in."

"Not if the book is a piece of shit."

"Hey, hey—I don't want to hear you talk that way. You wrote a book—that's a huge accomplishment. *Huge*."

Beresford looked up with a glimmer of hope.

"On the other hand, I admire you for being honest with yourself. That's the only way you're going to grow as a human being."

The young Brit looked away. "I'm quitting writing and returning home."

Tenpenny didn't speak or move, for fear of betraying the jig that was happening inside of him. Then: "*What?* No. You can't be serious, Charlie. Of course you're serious. Oh, man. Wow. Well, I'm sorry to hear that, but I can't say I blame you. It's a tough road to hoe, writing is. Very, very, very few people make it, and those who do can hardly earn a decent living at it. So when are you getting out of here?"

"I have no idea."

This took some of the cha-cha from Tenpenny's step. "What do you mean? What's keeping you here? Why not go now?"

"Money. Soon as I have enough to buy a plane ticket, I'm out of this hole forever."

Tenpenny delivered him to the airport the next day.

They hugged out front, Charlie thanking him over and over for purchasing the coach ticket.

"Stop it," Tenpenny said, "you sound like a low-class bum. I know you'd do the same for me."

When Charlie entered the terminal, Tenpenny emitted a short, involuntary gasp and welled up, for he knew that now he could finally go home.

Writing success has a way of shining a rosy light on life's failures. If you run for public office and lose, or get drunk on national TV and make an ass of yourself, or stab your wife with a penknife, you're considered a failure. But if you do all those things and you write well, you're Norman Mailer.

The Newport establishment welcomed Tenpenny home with open arms at a publishing fete high atop the Clarke Cooke House. Oysters, little necks, and lobster rolls were washed down with buckets of champagne, and though Tenpenny's name and likeness were noticeably absent from the oversized book jackets hanging everywhere, the Knopf people made it very clear who the star of the evening was. He was the shiny-jawed fellow whose arrival was preceded by the sound of the Red Hot Chili Peppers singing over the clippety-clop of horse hooves on cobblestones. A nineteenth-century carriage pulled up to the entrance and out piled Tenpenny and several long-lost friends, an invisible pot mist swirling about them. Photographers from the Boston and Providence papers captured the happy moment when Five-Oh, the Cooke House's iconic bartender, greeted Tenpenny at the door with his first of the evening's many Dark 'n' Stormies.

Roger bowed to Five-Oh, then paid his respects to bar-keeps Dennis and Kenny, before making his way up top to the blue blazer–dotted Sky Bar. All the regulars were waiting with cheek-taps and handshakes, as well as some of the New York society crowd who had come north for the event. They laughed and drank and talked and shared one-hitters on the back deck. Late in the evening, a pack of local writers Tenpenny had never heard of arrived and made themselves quickly known. When introduced to the most obvious of the group, a poet, Roger had a difficult time concealing his disdain. Tenpenny viewed poets as overly-doted-upon children who'd never gotten the dressing down they deserved. There was a reason no poet had ever died rich—because nobody gave a shit! The guy who invented the toilet plunger, he died rich. "Melancholy ruled the trees" and "a bouquet of swan necks"—how was that going to make the world a better place?

As if being a poet and drinking sherry wasn't disgusting enough, the fucker was actually wearing a beret. Tenpenny noticed the man's poor wife standing off to the side, drinking a Perrier and looking unsure of herself. The woman had long legs, but not the good kind. They were *too* long and she was slightly off-kilter and ass-less, like Gumby. His heart immediately took pity and he decided he would fuck her. This was the kind of self-destructive behavior that defined Tenpenny. Though any number of attractive and available women would have happily serviced him that evening, he wanted the morose, crooked one whose husband stood eight feet away.

"Would you like some champagne?" Tenpenny asked.

Her perfume was sweet and childish, something like Pez candies. "I wasn't going to drink tonight, but now I'm thinking maybe I should," she said.

"Go for it! It's the first few brain cells you kill that feel the best."

She smiled and he popped open a bottle of Cristal and they passed it back and forth. Like he, she was a novelist and was just beginning a new book.

"Sometimes the toughest part for me is deciding on a good name for my protagonist," she said. "I like Lily, but . . . it's kind of common now."

"How about Governor?" said Tenpenny.

"Governor Jones," she said, giggling. Then: "I love the name Mabel."

"Very old-fashioned."

The poet's wife was surprised that the man of the hour would waste his precious time talking to the lanky married woman, and she liked him for this, despite what she'd heard. "What do you think of Summer?" she asked.

"Cute."

"I think so, but my husband says it's a stripper name. He should talk—he likes Lu-Lu."

Tenpenny tapped his tongue against the inside of his cheek.

"What?"

"Cocksucker name," he said.

She started to laugh, but caught herself. "What do you mean?"

"Lu-Lus—they like to suck the cock."

The line had been crossed and she was still smiling. "That's his sister's name," she said.

"Well, am I right?" He held the woman's gaze until her face flushed.

"Sort of."

"Wanna get out of here?" he said.

"Out of where?"

"Here. You and me. Let's boogaloo. Now."

"But you're the man of the hour."

"So?" He had a good buzz going and his smile didn't break.

"And go where?"

"Wherever. We can go to my room at the Viking. I have a horse and carriage waiting outside."

She looked around. "I don't think so."

"Why not?"

When she looked back into his eyes, he saw the lights flick off. "Are you for real?"

"Do you want me to be?" he said, his grin losing air on one side.

Thankfully, someone grabbed him and told him he had a phone call at the hostess station.

Tenpenny got a pit in his stomach the moment he heard his editor on the line. Scholl sounded different. Roger could have sworn he felt the presence of the Beresford brat beside him.

"New York. First thing in the morning. Be here," Scholl said curtly.

"Tomorrow morning? Jeez, Paul, I've already had more drinks than the Pacific Northwest has serial killers—how about the day after?"

"I want you on the seven a.m. shuttle, do you hear me?"

"Um, okay, will there be a ticket waiting for me at the—"

"Buy your own ticket." With that, his editor hung up.

Tenpenny walked straight out and up the hill to the Viking Hotel without saying goodbye to anyone. He lay in bed with a drink on his chest. He watched the vodka pulse, confirming that he was alive. He tried to convince himself he was overreacting to the phone call. Maybe Scholl meant he'd reimburse him for the plane ticket later. If stellar reviews were pouring in, perhaps his editor just wanted to read them to him in person.

There was a knock on his door. He opened it to find the poet's wife tilting there like a human Tower of Pisa.

"Hi," she said.

He glanced down the hall, then back at her. "What?"

"Uh, you invited me here."

"Yeah, but . . . maybe that wasn't such a good idea."

"I'll let you do anything you want to me."

Tenpenny looked her over. "Yeah, okay, come in."

When he flew to the city the next morning, Roger Tenpenny knew exactly what he was going to say. He'd stick to his guns, laugh at the accusations, work his way to outrage later. It was his word against the kid's. He would not vacillate. He even popped an Inderal in case a lie detector was requested. They would not steal this from him.

He arrived at Knopf just after nine thirty. The lobby was decorated with poinsettias, the fruitcake of plants. His editor led him into his office where they were joined by another very businesslike-looking man. Beresford was not present. The man introduced himself as Jack Sheehan, FBI, shook Tenpenny's hand, offered him a seat. Stick to your guns, Roger thought. When the fed switched on a small tape recorder, Tenpenny looked to the grim Scholl for an explanation, but his glance was averted.

"Mr. Tenpenny," Sheehan began, "you have the right to remain silent. Anything you say—"

"Yes, yes, yes," Tenpenny said. "Enough."

"Would you like to consult a lawyer, sir?" the man asked, enunciating as if he was teaching at a school for the deaf.

"What are you talking about? For what reason? What is this all about?"

Sheehan and Scholl looked at one another.

"Mr. Tenpenny—"

"Please, call me Roger."

"Mr. Tenpenny," Agent Sheehan repeated, "did you write the book that you have titled *The Saturday Night Before Easter Sunday?*"

This is where Tenpenny had planned to bark out a laugh, but, perhaps because of the Inderal, nothing came out. "Can you please say that again?"

"I repeat: Did you write *The Saturday Night Before Easter Sunday?*"

"Of course I did and I resent the implication."

A curious smirk spread across Sheehan's face. "Mr. Tenpenny, you are stating here that you and you alone are the author of the book that you call *The Saturday Night Before Easter Sunday?*"

"I cannot wait to find out what this is all about. Yes, I and I alone wrote the book—now, what's going on here?"

Scholl ran his fingers through his hair and, standing abruptly, shouted, "Tenpenny, you fuck!"

Roger made a mental note that however this thing resolved itself, Scholl was out.

Sheehan opened a briefcase and took out a book with a German title. "Does this look familiar?"

"No. What is it?"

"It's the German version of your book."

Tenpenny glared at Scholl. "*What?!* I specifically told you I did *not* want it released in Europe!"

"Though the words are the same," continued Sheehan, "the German title is *The Flawed God.*"

"Nice," Tenpenny said bitterly. "No one ran that one by me either."

Sheehan folded his arms and appraised Tenpenny. "You still claim to have written it?"

Tenpenny sucked up every ounce of push-back he had left. "Mr. FBI man, let me explain something to you. Writing is about one thing and one thing only: telling the truth. That's what a good writer does. *He tells the truth.* So for you to stand there and question whether I am the author of my own work is about as insulting as it gets."

"This book was published in 1952."

"Yeah, I had help."

Roger Tenpenny knew enough to end the conversation and immediately ask for a lawyer. That afternoon he was arraigned in US District Court for the Southern District of New York and was unable to post bail.

Over the course of several days, Tenpenny told his version of events to his attorney, who relayed bits and pieces to the authorities in the hope that his bail would be reduced. When this didn't happen, Tenpenny requested another face-to-face with Sheehan and Scholl. Because the evidence against him was so overwhelming, and because his lawyer *believed* his story, Tenpenny was advised to tell them everything, show humility, and plead for mercy.

They met again in a small room at FBI headquarters in lower Manhattan. On a chalkboard someone had jotted down a crude outline of the story Tenpenny had told his lawyer. At the bottom, Roger could see that B.S. had been written and then erased. Despite the media beating he'd taken over the past week —and it had been harsh—Tenpenny was still mostly convinced of his innocence, and was comforted by the fact that he truly hadn't known the work was plagiarized.

"What I'm going to tell you is the truth, so help me God," he began.

"Okay," Sheehan said. "That's a good start."

"This was not my idea. The English kid came to me about nine months ago with the book and asked if I would pretend it was mine—you know, to help him out."

"Help him out?" Scholl sneered.

"Right," said Tenpenny.

Sheehan said, "So this would be around . . . September?"

"September/October, somewhere in there. I remember because PC had just started back up. But he wasn't a student, he was just hanging around."

"And you're sure this was *last* fall?"

"Positive. Could I please have some coffee?"

"They're out," Scholl said, rather childishly.

"Look," Tenpenny said, addressing Sheehan, "I did not steal this book—the Beresford kid did. If you just follow the numbers, it'll all make sense."

"Excellent," Sheehan said. "That's going to make my life a lot easier. So tell me how does *you* pretending the book was *yours* make sense?"

"Well . . . I liked the kid. You would too. He was fun, he was sweet, he said he needed my help. So I was like, *Sure, I'll put my name on the damn thing*—with the understanding that once it took off we were going to make a big announcement."

"And what would this big announcement be?" asked Scholl.

"That *he* was the writer, not me."

"And why would anyone care?" Again from Scholl.

"Well . . . he's young, and I'm not. So . . . so it would be fascinating that a guy that young could write something that good."

"I'm sorry," Sheehan interjected, "explain that again. It's not like you were Updike and people bought the book thinking it was from a master, only to find out later that it was written by some brilliant unknown kid. *You* were unknown too, correct?"

"That's what *I* said. It seemed silly. But he thought that if he went to New York and everyone saw what a hick he was, it'd queer the deal."

"A British hick?" said Scholl.

"I mean, in the sense that he was rough around the edges, like one of those Johnny Rotten guys, only with dreadlocks. How do you send someone like that out on a book tour? The kid wasn't exactly Tom Snyder material, you know?"

"You mean like you?" Scholl said, chuckling. "Let me tell you something: that would've made it *way* more interesting. Having a middle-age man write it—that's not interesting. A twenty-year-old punk-rocker Bret Easton Ellis—*that's* interesting."

"Look," Tenpenny replied softly, "I was just trying to help the kid out."

"By getting paid for the work that *he* did?"

"Yeah, well . . . that was going to be worked out later."

"And again, this was this past fall?" said Sheehan.

"Yes."

"I only ask because your old neighbor," Sheehan checked his notes, "a Miss Eleanor Morehouse, she told us that you were talking about this book the previous spring when she lived in your building."

"That's a lie."

"She swore to it."

"No, I mean it was *a lie*. I told her a lie." Tenpenny leaned forward. "Look, I was just trying to get . . . *in there*, you know? And she was a little . . . precious. So I told her I wrote a book." He squinted sheepishly.

Sheehan raised his chin. "And then a few months later, a boy you'd never met shows up at your door with an actual book that you took on as your own?"

"Yes."

"Wow, what a nice coincidence. For you."

"It wasn't a coincidence. They'd met in Europe, on a gondola or something, and she told him I was a writer and that's why he came. Trust me, guys, if you just follow the numbers, it'll all make sense."

"Actually," Sheehan said, "we *have* been following the numbers. Like the number of times Eleanor Morehouse has been to Europe. Zero."

"That's im— Well . . . who said . . . ? Well . . . maybe she met him somewhere else?"

"She never met a Charlie Beresford, or anyone fitting his description."

Tenpenny shifted in his seat. "Well . . . did you check with the Y—they'll know him, that's where he stayed."

"No one fitting that description has been there since . . . well, *ever*."

Tenpenny's lawyer finally offered up a couple questions: "What about the Rusty Scupper—he worked there . . . ?"

"Nope."

The lawyer sighed. "Did you check with Brown admissions?"

"He never applied."

Roger started feeling a darkness rise up inside him. "His airline ticket?" he asked.

"Unused."

Even in this state, Tenpenny couldn't help but wonder if the ticket was refundable. Then: "Look, maybe he gave Ellie a fake . . . or maybe she just has a shitty memory. I'm telling you, they met. Otherwise, he couldn't have known that I'd told her I was a writer."

"We checked her passport—she's never been to Europe."

Dizzy now, Tenpenny rifled through his notes, searching for something they'd overlooked. Then he saw it. "What about the envelope?"

"What envelope?"

"The envelope that the original manuscript was mailed to Knopf in—I never touched it. Check that envelope for fingerprints and that's how you'll find the kid!"

"Oh, we did," said Sheehan.

"And?"

"We found quite a few fingerprints on it. Most of them yours."

"That's bullshit."

"Not according to Quantico, it isn't."

"Now *you* are lying," Tenpenny said, moving toward full

panic. "That's not possible, I never touched that thing. *You* are the liar!" He turned to his suddenly bored-looking lawyer. "They're trying to frame me. I made mistakes, but I wasn't the one who sent that book in!"

Scholl stood. "Cry me a fucking river, Roger. Even if you were set up—which you weren't—why would we care? You can't unmake a cake."

"Can't unmake a . . . ? What the hell are you talking about?"

"It doesn't matter how it came to be—you're the one who came to my office, you're the one who insisted the book not be published in Europe, you're the one whose name was on the contracts, and you're the one who cashed the paychecks."

"Right, and I admit that. But don't you care about the truth?"

"Truth? You're talking to me about *truth?*" Scholl slapped his thigh theatrically. "Oh, that is rich."

"Fuck you!" Tenpenny screamed. "You do realize that this wouldn't have happened if you just did your damn job—it's called vetting, dummy."

"You motherless cunt!" Scholl sprung toward Tenpenny, but Sheehan quickly wrapped him up.

"How was I supposed to know about some old German book?" Tenpenny said from where he'd retreated to across the room. "I'm not an editor, I'm a . . ."

"You're a what?" When Tenpenny didn't respond, Scholl said, "You're an arrogant piece of shit." He grabbed his briefcase and headed to the door. "And by the way, the Saturday night before Easter Sunday is not a *nothing* date. It's the day that Jesus descended into hell before His resurrection." Scholl pushed out a smile. "And now that day is here for you."

After the door slammed and the echo had died, Tenpenny turned to Sheehan. "Did he just call me Jesus?"

There's a reason that convicts find religion, besides the obvious winning-over-the-parole-board motive. After the scathing news stories, the daily lashings by judge and prosecutors, and an aggressive abandonment by everyone close to him, Tenpenny was finally humbled, and this humility brought him closer to what he imagined could only be "God." This, however, did not happen overnight. His first weeks in prison were angry and bitter, as he loudly proclaimed his innocence over a hellish playground of smirks and angry stares. This was an American tragedy, he said. He'd been set up and the authorities didn't care. The real villain was running happily free somewhere and no one—absolutely no one—was trying to right this wrong.

Alone in his cell, Tenpenny wracked his brain to the point of nausea trying to figure out what had happened. Who would target him? Why would anyone *want* to target him? Or maybe he hadn't been targeted at all. Maybe it was random—somebody saw an opportunity and took it. This made no sense either. What did the Brit stand to get out of all this? And who the hell *was* he?

One night he sprung out of bed, suddenly remembering the bottle of rum the kid had given him. Tenpenny had taken it out of a brown paper bag, and Beresford had returned the bag to his backpack. That's how he'd done it! He must have used the bag to wrap the manuscript, which is how Tenpenny's fingerprints had ended up on it. But again, why? What was Beresford's endgame? In what way could he have possibly prospered from Roger's nightmare? Unfortunately, Tenpenny had never had the patience or mind-set to complete even a crossword puzzle, and if this were one, he would have needed giant thematic clues such as *WELLSY* and *KARMA* and *FAMILY* and *REVENGE* to come even close. Eventually he just accepted it, and learned to live with the eerie feeling that he'd been framed by some invisible force, a ghost as such, which was as close to the truth as he'd ever come.

ABOUT THE CONTRIBUTORS

ellen foto

LaShonda Katrice Barnett is the author of the novel *Jam on the Vine* and a story collection, and is the editor of two volumes on music and the creative process: *I Got Thunder* and *Off the Record*. Her short fiction has appeared in the *Chicago Tribune, Guernica Magazine, New Orleans Review, Juked,* and elsewhere. She lives in New York City. For more information visit www.LaShondaBarnett.com.

Eugene St. Pierre

Thomas Cobb is the author of *Crazy Heart,* which was made into an Academy Award–winning film, along with *Shavetail* and *With Blood in Their Eyes,* both of which won Spur Awards, and the forthcoming novel *Darkness the Color of Snow.* He lives in the woods beyond Providence.

Patricia Smith

Bruce DeSilva's hard-boiled crime novels featuring investigative reporter Liam Mulligan are set in Providence. He has won the Edgar and Macavity awards and has been a finalist for the Anthony, Barry, and Shamus awards. Previously he worked as a journalist for forty years, editing investigative stories that won virtually every major journalism prize including the Pulitzer. He has reviewed books for numerous publications including the *New York Times* and *Publishers Weekly.*

Hopper Stone

Peter Farrelly grew up in Cumberland, Rhode Island, and is a graduate of Providence College and Columbia University. He has written and directed several movies and is the author of the novels *Outside Providence* and *The Comedy Writer,* as well as the children's book *Abigail the Happy Whale.* He and his brother Bobby were inducted into the Rhode Island Heritage Hall of Fame in 2002.

Anita Licis-Ribak

Amity Gaige is the author of three novels, *O My Darling, The Folded World,* and *Schroder.* A *New York Times* Notable Book, *Schroder* has been translated into eighteen languages, and in 2014 it was short-listed for the Folio Prize. Her short stories, reviews, and essays have appeared in numerous publications. A graduate of Brown University, she lived in Providence and Cranston for a combined ten years. She currently lives in Hartford, Connecticut, and is a visiting writer at Amherst College.

Catherine Sebastian

ANN HOOD is the author of the best-selling novels *The Obituary Writer, The Knitting Circle, An Italian Wife,* and *Somewhere Off the Coast of Maine.* Her memoir *Comfort: A Journey Through Grief* was a *New York Times* Editors' Choice and chosen as one of the top ten nonfiction books of 2008 by *Entertainment Weekly.*

HESTER KAPLAN'S books include the story collections *Unravished* and *The Edge of Marriage,* winner of the Flannery O'Connor Award for Short Fiction, and the novels *The Tell* and *Kinship Theory.* Her work has appeared in literary journals and anthologies, including *The Best American Short Stories* series. Recent awards include a fellowship from the National Endowment for the Arts and the McGinnis-Ritchie Award. She lives in Providence, the noirest city of them all.

Deborah Lopez

MARIE MYUNG-OK LEE is a graduate of Brown University, where she taught for fifteen years. She is the author of the novel *Somebody's Daughter* (Beacon Press). Her next book is forthcoming from Simon & Schuster. Her essays have appeared in the *New York Times, Slate,* the *Guardian,* the *Nation,* the *Atlantic,* and *Salon.* She teaches creative writing at Columbia University and is a founder and former board president of the Asian American Writers' Workshop.

Santina Leuci

ROBERT LEUCI worked for twenty years as an NYPD detective assigned to narcotics and organized crime. Since retirement, he has published six novels and one memoir, and has written various TV scripts, book reviews in the *Providence Journal,* and magazine pieces. Leuci is currently an adjunct professor in the English department of the University of Rhode Island, and in 1998 won a Rhode Island State Council on the Arts award.

Jamie Casertano

TAYLOR M. POLITES lives in Providence with his Chihuahua Clovis. His first novel, *The Rebel Wife,* was published by Simon & Schuster. His work has appeared in *Knitting Yarns: Writers on Knitting,* as well as *Provincetown Arts* and the *New York Times* Disunion blog. He received his MFA from Wilkes University, where he was awarded the Norris Church Mailer Fellowship. He teaches at the Wilkes University MFA program, Roger Williams University, and the Rhode Island School of Design.

Claire Holt

DAWN RAFFEL is the author of four books, most recently *The Secret Life of Objects*. Her next book, *The Strange Case of Dr. Couney*, will be published by Blue Rider Press. She has a degree in semiotics from Brown University.

Adrian Kinloch

LUANNE RICE is the *New York Times* best-selling author of thirty-one novels that have been translated into twenty-four languages. The author of *The Lemon Orchard, Dream Country, Cloud Nine,* and *Beach Girls,* Rice often writes about love, family, nature, and the sea. She is an avid environmentalist and advocate for families affected by domestic violence. Rice lived in Fox Point in Providence, and now divides her time between New York City and Old Lyme, Connecticut.

Women & Infants Hospital

PABLO RODRIGUEZ is chair of the Women & Infants Health Care Alliance and a clinical associate professor at the Warren Alpert Medical School at Brown University. He is a past chairman of the Rhode Island Foundation, the Dorcas International Institute of Rhode Island, and the Latino Political Action Committee. He currently hosts a daily call-in radio show on Latino Public Radio.

Thomas Caruso

JOHN SEARLES is the author of the best-selling novels *Help for the Haunted, Strange but True,* and *Boy Still Missing.* His essays have been published in the *New York Times,* the *Washington Post,* and other publications. *Help for the Haunted* won the American Library Association's Alex Award and was named a Best Crime Novel of 2013 by the *Boston Globe* and a Top 10 Must Read by *Entertainment Weekly.* Searles appears frequently on NBC's *Today* show to discuss his favorite book selections.

Dario Lasagni

ELIZABETH STROUT is the Pulitzer Prize–winning author of *Olive Kitteridge,* as well as *The Burgess Boys,* a *New York Times* best seller, *Abide with Me,* and *Amy and Isabelle,* which won the *Los Angeles Times* Art Seidenbaum Award for First Fiction and the *Chicago Tribune* Heartland Prize. Her short stories have appeared in various publications, including the *New Yorker* and *O, The Oprah Magazine.* She lives in New York City.